The Courtship of Eboni Law

The Courtship of Eboni Law

M.J. Grayson

Redbaby Publishing, Inc.

Publisher: Redbaby Publishing, Inc., Clinton, MD 20735

ISBN 978-1-952163-07-4 eBook
ISBN 978-1-952163-08-1 Paperback

First Printing, 2021

CONTENTS

Dedications

**For Marvin whose philosophy of
self-determination and take no prisoners
outlook helped shape me....**

One

Chapter 1

Eboni secured the top and bottom locks of the glass doors to her restaurant. She stretched to pull down the black overhead steel door, and a smile touched her lips as a light drizzle fell on Manhattan.

"Your money or your life! Drop the purse and keep your hands where I can see them!"

Eboni turned her head to the left with her hands held up. Her eyes stared into the barrel of a nickel-plated revolver. Through blurred vision forcing her eyes to cross, she could see the pale hand gripping the gun. Without hesitating, she dropped her purse. She shivered as she felt the five bottled waters she'd drank over an hour ago draining over her right leg.

She peeked at the man, reaching down for her purse, then shut her eyes tight. Eboni wanted to run, but her feet froze to the ground. Her body shook as rain blended in with the nervous tears streaming down her face.

"A measly sixty dollars?" the robber snarled, going through her purse. "Really?! That's all you got?!"

Eboni's head nodded quickly in response. She tried to calm herself.

"Yes, that's all I have in my purse," she stammered. His angry blue eyes bore into her from behind a black ski mask.

"Unlock these doors and take me to the register now!" he ordered.

"After we close every night, we take the cash out of the registers and put it into a safe in my office," she explained to him.

"Take me to the safe then!" he commanded, growing more impatient.

Eboni's hand trembled as she put one key into the bottom lock and turned it. She grabbed another key and placed it inside the top lock of the glass doors. She unlocked the door and pushed it open.

"Huhht!" a screaming voice said from behind her.

Eboni turned around in time to see a foot connect to the robber's chin. The criminal stumbled sideways and fell to the wet pavement. As he struggled to get up, he lifted his gun, but another foot kicked it from his grip, and the firearm went flying toward the street and ricocheted off the windshield of a vehicle speeding down Mott Street. When she realized what was actually happening, Eboni saw a tall black man with a milk chocolate skin tone standing in front of the robber in some sort of martial arts stance. A smile touched his calm countenance. She detected a gentle friendliness in his eyes.

The robber got up and charged him. But the trained combatant stopped him by connecting a roundhouse kick with the man's jaw, and the gunman reeled. The black man, apparently well-schooled in some discipline of self-defense, stood over the crook and snatched the mask from his face. Thunder clapped as the sky opened to a full barrage of torrential rain. Eboni blinked and wiped away the rain to see a white man, possibly in his mid to late thirties, with a bald head and a full blonde beard.

"You like pulling guns out on helpless women?" the martial artist asked Eboni's culprit.

"I just needed some cash to pay my bills with," the culprit cried.

"But you would've hurt her badly if she didn't give you what you wanted," the martial artist spat back, eyeing the lawbreaker who had his eyes half-closed now.

The ruffian rested on his knees for a moment as Eboni watched him through pouring rain. She snuck a glance at the talented self-defense practitioner as the crook stood to his feet. Breathing hard, the lawbreaker suddenly snatched a switchblade from his back pocket and a creepy smile played on his face. The well-dressed man remained still and simply reached out a hand, motioning the miscreant towards him.

"Take your best shot," Eboni heard him say to the criminal as he smiled joyously.

The transgressor took a swipe at him. The martial artist dodged in the opposite direction. As the skilled warrior eyed him with intentional focus, the hollowed villain took another stab and another and another. All the culprit's thrusts missed. The martial artist delivered a hard jab to the man's nose and kicked him in the side of his knee. Eboni thought she heard a bone snap as the switchblade dropped from the crook's hand. The robber fell to his side, but the karate expert, or whoever he was, lifted him up by his collar, drove a series of left knees to his solar plexus, and dropped him with a final roundhouse kick to the chin.

For a moment it appeared the perpetrator had trouble breathing as he lay on the concrete, gasping and groaning. The offender shot a glance at her before turning his head to the sharply dressed man again. She saw her hero looking at the wrongdoer intensely as if daring him to attack either of them again. But the disorderly man turned his head and shut his eyes tight as he took shallow breaths.

Eboni saw the robber crawling on his hands and knees. He examined his modish opponent as he struggled to get up.

"I never want to see you around here a second time!" the black guy pointed at the troublemaker. "Now get the hell out of here!"

Lightning shot through the sky as thunder rattled through the air. The crook scrambled to his feet and limped away, hunching and holding his abdomen with both hands. Her protector continued to stare in the bearded man's direction, watching him disappear from view. He turned towards her and Eboni saw his blazing hazel eyes gazing at her.

"Are you alright?" he asked her, looking her up and down. He had shoulder-length brown braided hair and a neatly trimmed goatee. The guy was wearing a flashy black suit, a black dress shirt underneath with a white necktie, and a pair of glistening matching Gucci's.

Relief had replaced her fear at the masterful skill he had just displayed. The only time she'd seen something similar was while she was watching a martial arts movie.

"I'm fine, thanks to you," Eboni said, smiling as she eyed him. "I hope that awful man doesn't come back."

"Doubtful," he noted, with a hint of intolerance in his voice. "That fool isn't coming back."

The martial artist knelt to pick up the fallen contents from her purse. She saw her three twenty-dollar bills resting on the moistened pavement by her purse. The man picked up her purse and money and walked toward her.

Eboni hastily wrapped her arms around him through falling raindrops. She felt his strong right arm fasten itself around her. Her soft lips found the side of his cheek. It was a tender kiss she wanted to make sweeter than all the sugarcane in Brazil.

"Thank you, kind sir," Eboni said to him, eyeing the switchblade on the pavement with a sideways glance.

"I'm happy I was here," he said with a smile.

"Where did you come from?" Eboni asked as her rescuer gave the items to her.

"I had just closed the dojo fifteen minutes ago," he said to her, "and was on my way to a bar in Union Square to talk business with a guy who wants me to train him for a tough man competition in three months. I was walking up Mott Street when I saw asshole pull his gun on you."

"I'm so relieved," she said to him.

He dropped his arm at his side while she still held onto him. She gazed up at him, seeing him smiling at her with a boyish grin.

"I can't be late for my appointment," he said with a cheerful smile.

As Eboni removed her arms from around him, she saw a kind fondness in his eyes. "Thank you again," she said, wanting to kiss him on the cheek one more time.

The martial artist respectfully bowed to her and walked off. She watched him until he disappeared into the night.

****

Jocelyn checked on Joy and Lori. She stood quietly, peeping through a crack in the opened bedroom door to make sure they were both asleep in their beds. Jocelyn watched as both girls instinctively scratched their Afros as they slept. Quietly she closed the door, hurried down the hall, and quickly entered the bedroom she and her husband shared. She removed the housekeeping uniform she had on and quickly grabbed her royal blue bathrobe. She made her way past her daughters' bedroom and entered the bathroom.

Jocelyn eyed herself in the mirror. Despite being pudgy, her face was lovelier than six dozen purple roses. Her eyes were the color of grass before dawn, complemented by long lashes her husband loved. And her magnificent smile was far more than dazzling.

Freeing herself from the loose bathrobe, she stepped into the shower. She let the cold shower water hit her as she bathed, rubbing a raspberry scented bar of soap all over her body. She thought about Lorenzo, and how much it would mean to make love to him once he got home.

After stepping out of the shower, Jocelyn dried herself off and comfortably wrapped her towel around her. She picked up her robe before heading back to the bedroom. Jocelyn combed and brushed her long wooly hair that extended down to her shoulders, and glanced inside her closet at her wardrobe. She retrieved a beautiful white maxi dress with a long skirt split on the left side for the entire leg to be visible. A grin appeared on her lovely face. She put on a matching pearl necklace, slid on the splendid fragrance of a cheerful vanilla Giorgio Armani perfume on her neck and arms, and propped the pillows on the made-up bed.

Jocelyn retrieved four barely used lanterns from the basement and placed them on the floor on each side of the bed. She walked over to the stereo and cued up the CD in the player. A few seconds later, the sound of opera music played.

Jocelyn smiled brightly as she turned the ceiling light off, climbed into the bed, propped herself up on her elbows, leaned back on the pillows, and waited for Lorenzo to come through the door. About twenty minutes later, her husband came through the doors with his eyes half-closed. He quickly took off his stylish suit, the pants, shirt, and blazer, tossing them on the other side of the bed.

He studied Jocelyn for a moment and looked around the room. Lorenzo frowned confusingly at her and climbed into the bed. She peered at him as his head hit the pillow.

"What the hell, Lorenzo?" Jocelyn roared.

"What is it, Jocelyn?" Lorenzo asked, closing his eyes as he placed a hand on his chest.

"Are you serious?" she asked him with a frown.

Lorenzo's eyes opened as he sat up. She saw him looking at her stupidly. Jocelyn glimpsed at him for a second. She was sitting here all dolled up in this romantic scene, and he didn't have a clue.

"Lorenzo, did you notice something?" Jocelyn asked him.

"Soft music and glowing lanterns in the dark," he said.

"I'm trying to set the mood so you can make love to me!" Jocelyn told him irritably.

"Not this again," Lorenzo said as he flopped down on the bed. "You do not know what I've been through today. I had to teach and be a hero."

"Why can't you make love to me, Lorenzo?" she asked him.

"Jocelyn, I just worked all day. I'll make love to you in the morning. I'm totally exhausted."

Jocelyn shook her head in disgust. She slapped him on his back. Lorenzo eyed her and sat up again. Jocelyn folded her arms and kicked her heels on the bed. "You make me sick!" she exclaimed.

Jocelyn got up out of the bed. She watched Lorenzo for three heartbeats before exiting the bedroom. She closed the bedroom door, put her back to it, and took a deep breath. Jocelyn stumped her foot on the floor before marching downstairs. She quickly made her way to the basement, turned the light on, and sat on the long, black leather sofa.

Lorenzo, I really hate you sometimes, she said to herself.

Jocelyn sat with her legs crossed and clenched her fists, frowned, and stumped her feet repeatedly on the floor.

Lorenzo, I'm really hating you!

<h1 style="text-align:center">Two</h1>

✼

Chapter 2

"Damn," Jocelyn said as Lorenzo looked away from her. "That's it? That was quick."

Lorenzo saw his wife's disappointing frown staring back at him. He closed his eyes. For a long silent moment, all he could hear was his own heavy breathing within their quiescent bedroom. She turned her back to him and laid her head on her pillow.

"You call forty minutes too quick?" he asked her with a smile, looking across the room at the clock on the dresser. It was 2:04 in the morning and he had to be up by 5:00 in order to get ready for work.

"You know I enjoy doing it for long periods of time," Jocelyn complained from beside him, running her fingers through her frizzled hair.

"Forty minutes is more than enough," he disputed. "You make it sound like it was two minutes or something."

"I like for our coitus to be all night!" she expressed, her eyebrows bumping together in a scowl. "You know I hate it when you finish too soon. How soon can we do it again?"

Lorenzo's eyes rolled skyward. "Again?" he asked her.

Lorenzo had always hoped marriage would calm Jocelyn's insatiable sex drive, but no such luck. He enjoyed her steamy, sizzling sex. But she always craved more from him, and although he felt satisfied, Jocelyn wasn't.

"Yes, again," Jocelyn answered with an unrelenting stare. "What, you're not up to it?"

Lorenzo stared across the bedroom and closed his eyes. "No," he answered her. "I've got to get some sleep and get to work first thing in the morning. There is a big day tomorrow."

"I have to be up early too," Jocelyn said to him, reaching for his arm. "Why don't you open the dojo late tomorrow?"

Lorenzo thought about his clients- students who were learning Judo, Jiujitsu, Aikido, Karate, Wing Chun, variants of Shaolin kung fu, and Taekwondo from him daily. It was how he made his living. It was what he enjoyed doing. The martial arts were his life.

"I have an obligation to my pupils," Lorenzo said. "You know that. There will be time for us later."

"Let's make another baby," she said.

"Jocelyn, please!" Lorenzo exclaimed, closing his eyes as he laid his head on his pillow. "I want to go to sleep now."

How did it come to this? Lorenzo wondered. He started reminiscing about his life before Jocelyn, missing his days at the Shaolin Temple under Master Kimlau Li's tutelage when he was celibate years before opening his own martial arts school, focusing on combat readiness and personal tranquility. But when Jocelyn came along, he couldn't resist her.

God, she was sexy; he remembered. *If only things were easier, like back then.*

Lorenzo enjoyed kissing Jocelyn's luscious lips. A day never went by when he didn't admire her sexiness. But making love to her had produced a set of beautiful twin girls, Joy, and Lori. Being married to her wasn't easy. Being a peaceful man, was the most challenging thing he ever had to face. As Lorenzo reached for the lamp on his side of the bed, he could feel her cool breath on the back of his neck.

What's wrong with her these days? Lorenzo thought. *I hope she's not up to something.*

He turned his head towards her. Jocelyn sobbed as her eyes closed. Lorenzo turned away from her and turned the lamp off.

****

"I need you, please," Jocelyn said, blowing him a kiss as Lorenzo got dressed.

"Jocelyn, no!" Lorenzo said to her with a frown. "I'm exhausted. I didn't get hardly any sleep last night, just like the night before that and the night before that. And I have an endless day today."

"What about when you come back home?" she asked, looking at him with raised eyebrows.

Lorenzo shook his head. "Chances are I'll be ready to crash when I get back," he declared calmly.

"You don't find me sexy, Papi?" she asked, standing up straight, her mouth forming into a pout.

"Gosh!" he shouted, eyeing her with his eyes half-open. "That's not it. I just don't feel like making love all the time."

Jocelyn rolled her eyes and looked away from him. She could see the fatigue building on his face. To her, he appeared completely worn out. And to think she kept him awake last night longer than she should have. But he was her husband! He should find it in his heart to take care of her needs whenever she required him to.

Whenever they made love, Jocelyn could tell when Lorenzo wasn't giving her his all. He gave a fainthearted effort whenever they had intercourse. It was as if she didn't turn him on. But she had always known Lorenzo truly didn't enjoy it as much as she did. Rarely was he into it to the level she was.

"Lorenzo, I'm sorry for depriving you of your rest yet again," Jocelyn said to him.

"I'll drink a lot of ginseng and an energy drink or two to get me through the day," Lorenzo said cheerfully. "It's okay."

"Have a nice day," she said to him as he walked out of the door of their bedroom.

"You too," he said to her.

Lorenzo walked over to her and placed his hand on the back of her neck. He leaned forward and kissed Jocelyn's lips tenderly.

"Te Amo," Jocelyn told him softly when their lips parted.

Lorenzo gazed into her emerald eyes. "I love you too," he said back to her.

He gave her a smile and hurried out of the house. As she opened the door to their bedroom, she reached down and closed her eyes. Jocelyn frowned.

Damn you, Lorenzo! She said to herself.

****

Joy and Lori were both still sleeping. They wouldn't be up for a few more hours. Jocelyn closed the door to their room and walked downstairs. She went to the front door and opened it, only to see a relentless downpour.

She closed the front door and thoughts of Lorenzo came back to her mind. Biting her lip, she thought maybe she should be more patient with him.

What in the hell is wrong with me? Jocelyn thought.

There had always been passion lacking in the life she and Lorenzo shared. At least by him. Lorenzo never pursued her. She was always the aggressive one. She sensed it intimidated him. Lorenzo had felt a wife should be chaste, have more self-control and be more ladylike. But Jocelyn wasn't that way. And this was the root of the problem in their love life. Sometimes she would attempt to do things his way. She would allow him to come on to her. But he never did. And it was why she kept being the forceful one in their marriage.

Jocelyn hurried to the basement. As she walked past the sofa, she peered across the room to a cabinet by a bookshelf full of encyclopedias where she and Lorenzo both kept their high school yearbooks. She hurried to the cabinet and opened it, seeing a pile of magazines stacked high in the corner in front of a prescription bottle of Prozac she had emptied over two years ago. She moved the prescription bottle to the side and grabbed the stack of magazines. *Time, Life, Ebony, The New Republic, National Geographic, Essence, Don Diva, Sports Illustrated*, and many others. At the bottom of the slush pile of magazines, she spotted an issue called *Wild Lesbians of Croatia.*

Jocelyn frowned. *What the hell?* she asked herself. *Lorenzo, this couldn't be yours?*

She opened the magazine and flipped through the pages, seeing nude plus-sized women far prettier than her. Jocelyn's eyes widened as she continued to turn the pages, her mouth dropping to the floor.

Jocelyn placed the magazines back in the cabinet's corner before spraying the basement with a pleasant scent. Looking at the prescription bottle one last time, she closed the cabinet door. Jocelyn rushed back upstairs and eyed ahead.

Spotting the telephone on the floor by yesterday's mail, Jocelyn walked over to it. She dialed a ten-digit number and waited.

"Hello?" the dispatcher at her job said on the other end.

"Good morning," Jocelyn greeted cheerfully. "I'm running a little late."

"Jocelyn Cortez?"

"Yes. I'll punch my time clock, probably twenty minutes late. But I'll be there."

"Okay. I'll let Crystal know."

Jocelyn heard the faint click before she hung up. She took a deep breath as she thought of her children. She knew she had to hurry and get them ready for school now if she didn't want to be tardy for work more than she already knew she would be.

****

When Lorenzo got back home at sunset, he found Joy and Lori playing in the living room when he opened the front door. As Lorenzo dragged his feet in their direction, both of his girls ran up to him. Lorenzo smiled as he scooped them both into his arms and picked them up, smelling the delightful scent of food coming from the kitchen.

"Welcome home!" Jocelyn's voice said from the kitchen.

Lorenzo turned and saw his wife in the entryway. She walked up to him with a pleasant smile on her face and kissed his lips. As he put his children down, Lorenzo studied Jocelyn.

Ding Dong.

"Someone is at the door," Jocelyn said with a beautiful smile.

"Oh, it's just one of my students," Lorenzo said. "I invited him over for dinner."

Jocelyn hurried to the front door. When she opened it, a short red-head stood there with a smile on his face. He was wearing beige karate attire with a black belt tied at his waist. She gazed back at Lorenzo and he motioned for her to let the young man in.

"Jocelyn, this is Kurt," Lorenzo said proudly, folding his arms. "Kurt here is my best student."

"Pleased to meet you," Kurt said, shaking Jocelyn's hand.

Jocelyn analyzed him for a moment. His essence seemed somewhat soft, and his handshake felt gentle. Her eyes studied his pointy nose, crimson-colored beard, and trim mustache. Kurt's smile was extravagantly bright.

Kurt walked to where Lorenzo stood in the living room as Jocelyn disappeared into the kitchen. Lorenzo watched Kurt and gestured towards the bright dining room. While Kurt walked in that direction, Lorenzo took both of his daughters by the hand and followed Kurt. The four of them sat down at the table and waited for dinner.

****

Jocelyn dimmed the light in the dining room and brought large plates of chicken, mixed vegetables, mashed potatoes, gravy, beef Alfredo with stringy noodles, and coleslaw. Jocelyn happily piled food on their plates. They said grace, and everyone started eating.

"So, Kurt, how long have you been into the martial arts?" Jocelyn said, looking across the table at the young man.

"Four years," he said. "Do you know martial arts?"

Jocelyn smiled. "No," she answered. "It's not my cup of tea."

"I've been trying to teach her Krav Maga for years, but she's not interested in learning," Lorenzo said from Jocelyn's left as he looked at her sternly. "And I have to teach my daughters in secret because Jocelyn doesn't want them to learn any of it."

"Learning the arts of Aikido or Judo would give your children discipline and confidence," Kurt said to Jocelyn as he nodded his head.

"Martial arts are dangerous," Jocelyn argued, her smile vanishing as she protested to Kurt. "I don't want my daughters to hurt anyone. I don't mind them learning it once they're older, but they don't need to learn it now."

"That's where you're wrong," Lorenzo disputed, looking in her direction with his eyes half-open. "The sooner they learn the martial arts, the better. By the time they're in their mid-teens, they might not want to do it."

"Then that will be good."

"Not knowing how to defend yourself effectively is never good," Lorenzo said shaking his head.

Jocelyn shook her head. "I don't want to talk about this anymore, Lorenzo," she muttered.

"Well, I do," Lorenzo retorted as his eyes fully opened when he peered at her.

"I want to learn Jiujitsu, Mommy," Joy broke in from beside Kurt.

"Mommy, I want Daddy to teach me Taekwondo," Lori said from the other side of Kurt, taking an imaginary aim with her toy slingshot towards the television in the living room.

The two little girls were clearly identical. They both had the same birthmark below their right cheek, and they each wore their hair plaited with colorful barrettes. The only noticeable difference between them was Lori was a half-inch taller than Joy.

Kurt smiled. "So, how old are your children?" he asked Jocelyn. "Master Royal never talks about them."

"They're both four years old soon to be five," Jocelyn said, her beautiful smile returning. "So, Kurt, tell me something about yourself. Are you in school?"

Kurt shook his head. "I was," he said, shrugging his shoulders. "I left Villanova University after my sophomore year. But I had to take care of some things in my life before I returned to school. I took care of those things. Now, I'm just looking to transfer to a university here in New York."

"What needed taking care of so much that you had to stop going to school?" Jocelyn asked Kurt.

Kurt was silent for a moment. "Well, I'm in and out of New York a lot," the young man said. "I compete nationwide in Judo, Wing Chun, and Taekwondo tournaments. I have won none yet."

Lorenzo glanced over at him. "You will one day," he told Kurt. "Intensify your training."

"I train hard," Kurt said. "I just haven't won yet."

"I wish you well," Jocelyn offered nonchalantly, dipping a fork into her Beef Alfredo.

Kurt stared down at his plate. "There're so many great Wing Chun, Judo, and Taekwondo practitioners out there," he said with a bright smile, looking up. "The closest I've come in Judo competition in fourth place. I came in fifth place in a Taekwondo tournament in Boston a year ago. I came in sixth place at a Wing Chun tournament in Beijing once."

"Four years is adequate time," Lorenzo said, looking down at his plate and scratching his chin. "But you have to push yourself. That's what I'm here for. I'm trying to push you to beat me one day."

Kurt played in his mashed potatoes with his fork and looked away from Jocelyn to Lorenzo as his eyes circled the room.

"You have a black belt in all three disciplines," Lorenzo said, looking at his student intensely. "There's no reason you can't win these tournaments."

"I know, Sensei," Kurt said. "I know I can do it because you did it when you trained under Master Kimlau Li."

It almost appeared Kurt had no confidence. But Lorenzo knew that wasn't the case. Kurt's feverish training and dedication had set him apart from almost all the other students who attended the martial arts school. Perhaps he just hadn't been fortunate to win a tournament yet. But Lorenzo knew Kurt would be successful.

"I'll be a grand champion in Taekwondo and Judo one day," Kurt stated. "And in Wing Chun also."

"Of course, you will," Lorenzo told him.

"Do you have a girlfriend?" Jocelyn asked, changing the topic. "Just curious."

"I'm actually married to the prettiest woman in the world," Kurt said to Jocelyn, showing her his bronze wedding ring on his ring finger.

"You should bring your wife to the dojo one day, Kurt," Lorenzo suggested. "Or maybe we can all hang out in Chinatown after teaching the students. I would love to meet her."

"I would love to meet her too," said Jocelyn as she watched Kurt.

Kurt smiled and eyed both Lorenzo and Jocelyn as he scratched his nose. "I'm sure she'd like that, Sensai," he said to Lorenzo.

The room fell silent as everyone continued to eat.

Three

Chapter 3

As the cab raced down 42nd Street, Jocelyn sat comfortably in the backseat as her legs rubbed together. The text message she'd received from the gigolo with who she had once been in a physical relationship many years ago in college showed where she would find him. She expected his touch, his kiss, and his.... and now, she was on her way to him.

For the past few weeks, intimacy with Lorenzo had been continuously nonexistent. And whenever Lorenzo managed something, she really didn't enjoy it the way she thought she should. Either he didn't do it for the long periods of time she needed it done, or when he did it, he just didn't do it effectively enough.

"Times Square Hilton," the cab driver said, snapping Jocelyn to the present.

Jocelyn reached into her faux-Chanel purse and handed the cab driver a twenty-dollar bill.

"Keep the change," she said with a straight face.

As she stepped out of the cab, her heart skipped a beat. She walked into the lobby thinking; Do *I really need to do this? What am I doing?*

Inside she found a bright bar with countless colorful people drinking, laughing, and talking. *There he is*!

Jocelyn unbuttoned her blouse, exposing her deep caramel cleavage. She could feel her heart race as she expected the occasion. Jocelyn strutted towards Buck, who was sitting in a turquoise velvet armchair, drinking a margarita. Light-skinned with broad shoulders, a neat brown mullet, and a handsome face with a trim beard, he was even more attractive than he was years back. He was wearing a sky-blue-colored shirt, a deep blue necktie, and brown suspenders that held up a pair of loose-fitting black slacks that matched the pair of tar-colored boots he had on.

I can't resist him, she thought.

Jocelyn walked over to him and tapped Buck on the shoulder. "Hello," she said when Buck gazed up.

"Jocelyn, you found me," Buck said to her with a bright smile.

"How far is your room from here?" Jocelyn asked him as a woman with long dark brown hair wearing a black bodysuit with corresponding opened-toe high heel shoes walked up behind Buck and placed her hands on his shoulders.

"It's on the twenty-fourth floor," he said to her, his eyes looking her up and down.

"Who is this?" Jocelyn questioned as she stared at the mysterious woman.

"Let me finish my drink," Buck said, reaching for his glass in front of him. "This here is Sophie."

"Buck, I have kids and a husband!" Jocelyn shouted. "Let's get this over with so I can get back to the Bronx."

"Okay," Buck said. "Sophie here is going to join us."

"Excuse me?" Jocelyn voiced loudly, looking at the sultry woman standing behind Buck as she massaged his shoulders.

Sophie was about 5'4 and couldn't have weighed over 130 pounds. Looking at her facial features, she could tell the woman's nationality was Dominican.

Jocelyn watched as the other woman gazed at her softly with a narrow and inviting gaze yet curious smile.

"I'm Sophie," the woman answered before Buck could. "You can call me Sophie. I've heard a lot about you from our mutual friend."

Jocelyn smiled. "Have you now?" she asked Sophie. "Buck, I don't like this."

"Jocelyn, do it for me," Buck said to her. "It'll be enjoyable."

Jocelyn had done many things with men during her life, but none of which involved multiple partners at the same time.

"If you're not comfortable with me there, I can understand," Sophie said in a light, yet sweet voice.

"Sweetheart," Buck said to Jocelyn in a smooth-sounding voice. "Let's go find the elevator so we can go upstairs."

Jocelyn closed her eyes. The idea of being with this man was intriguing. After all, it was the reason she was here. Her body quivered as she pressed her lips together. She felt an instant drop of sweat pour down her face. She thought of Lorenzo and opened her eyes.

"Buck, I can't!" she told him.

"I can leave, and it will be just the two of you," Sophie said to Jocelyn.

Jocelyn frowned as she shook her head. "It's not you," she said to Sophie.

"Jocelyn, what are you saying?" Buck asked her.

Jocelyn forced herself to look at him as she became watery-eyed. "I know I called you here, but I can't be unfaithful to my husband," she conveyed as her bottom lip trembled. "I'm sorry I wasted your time."

Jocelyn turned away and hurried out of the hotel.

****

When Jocelyn got home, she found her Bronx neighborhood quiet. Both Lori and Joy were with their father at the dojo. So, for the time being, she had the house all to herself. There had been an avowed spirit driving her to cheat on her husband- a voice inside her head telling her she could easily get another man to satisfy the needs her husband had been neglecting. But her unwavering love for Lorenzo didn't allow her to go through with it.

Jocelyn took off the jean dress she had worn and walked into the bathroom. There she turned the water to the shower on. As she felt the soothing warm water hit her head and body, she thought about her marriage. It wasn't farfetched to think Lorenzo could ever satisfy her. For the past couple of months, the requisite for sex grew more and more. Her hormones had raged like an angry child that couldn't get its way. She tried to get Lorenzo to take care of her needs, but he had been unwilling or unable to. He spent so much of his time in the martial arts world instructing adults, children, senior citizens, and even members of the NYPD occasionally. Since she had known Lorenzo, martial arts had taken up so much of his time. By the time he was through with his day, Lorenzo was just burnt out. He didn't have it in him to make love to her after being on his feet for fourteen, fifteen, and sometimes sixteen hours a day.

Soldiers went off to war, leaving wives behind who remained faithful while they were away. If those women could remain faithful, she could too.

Cleaning the house spic and span only exhausted her. Jocelyn took a nap on the sofa in the living room when she finished. She dreamed of her native Puerto Rico. Her parents, sisters, brothers, aunts, uncles, and cousins had moved back to San Juan and Farjardo after being in New York for most of their lives. She often had sweet dreams of them. And she would have gone back with them if not for meeting Lorenzo, marrying him, and having two children with him.

She saw an image of her father holding her hand, and she woke up. As Jocelyn stretched, the front door opened. Joy was sleeping in Lorenzo's arms as Lori walked in front of them. Jocelyn smiled as she sat up. As her husband closed the door, she got off of the sofa and walked over to them. She bent down and kissed Lori and reached for Joy.

"Hi, honey," she said to her husband, fixing her hair into a ponytail as she smiled.

"Hey," Lorenzo greeted back, placing Joy in Jocelyn's arms.

Jocelyn carried Joy to the sofa and laid her down gently as the child slept. She peeked towards Lori, following Lorenzo to the kitchen. Jocelyn gave Joy one last look before she walked into the kitchen. When she got there, she noticed an angry look on Lorenzo's face. The angry look found her quickly.

"Why didn't you prepare dinner?" he asked, opening the refrigerator.

"I worked hard today," Jocelyn replied in her defense. "I took a shower and a nap when I got home."

Lorenzo took a deep breath and chuckled. "I'll fix dinner," he said, his mood swiftly delightful.

Retrieving a frying pan from underneath the sink, he pulled three frozen T-Bone steaks out of the freezer along with packages of broccoli and corn a moment later. In addition, he boiled noodles to go along with it. As the steaks fried on the stove, he seasoned them with garlic and other seasonings. Next, he diced green pepper to fry along with the steaks.

Cooking the steaks well done, Lorenzo fixed everyone's plate. He and Jocelyn each got a steak while they intended the third for Joy and Lori to share. Jocelyn woke up Joy, and the little girl joined everyone else at the dining room table. The little girl sat on Jocelyn's lap as Lori sat on Lorenzo's lap at the head of the table.

"So, you were so tired that you didn't make dinner?" Lorenzo asked Jocelyn as he bit into his juicy steak.

"Yes, I was," Jocelyn said to him, her eyes narrow in his direction. "They exhausted me after work, so I took a very long nap. I woke up just as you and the kids were coming through the door."

"Jocelyn, you slept by my side for eight hours last night. You only worked six hours at the hotel. Did you go to the gym? Or watch a long movie? Did you take any sleeping pills? How could you be so tired?"

"Because I was!" Jocelyn snapped. "Why are you interrogating me?"

"Because not coming home to a home-cooked meal is very disappointing," Lorenzo said, looking at her with a frown. "I see now I have to do the cooking too!"

"Excuse me?" she said, returning his frown back at him. "It is not my duty to cook for you, Lorenzo. I do it because I like to do it. If you don't like the fact that there wasn't any food ready to eat, go out and buy some Kentucky Fried Chicken or McDonald's."

"Are you serious?" Lorenzo argued, his piercing gaze dark. "There are two children involved here. They should come home to a home-cooked meal. You're their mother, Jocelyn. And you have a husband as well. Your children and your husband are your top priorities."

"You enjoy telling me what to do, don't you?" Jocelyn asked, slapping a hand on the table as she scowled at him.

"What?" he questioned, standing to his feet as he held Lori.

Her foot stomped on the floor, a shaking finger pointing to him in emphasis as her scowl darkened. Her foot stomped the floor a second time before she lifted her voice and spoke fearlessly at her husband.

"Kiss my ass, Lorenzo, you stupid *pendejo!* Never talk to me like that! I work just like you. I don't feel like cooking every single day. It gets tiring. I do it out of love, not out of obligation! If I so choose, I could go to the supermarket and pay the goddamn grocery bill just like you! I'm not your fucking maid! Cook your own goddamn meals from now on. Fucking *pendejo!*"

Their eyes locked on each other for a long moment, Jocelyn's mean-mugging facial expression still present. He retook his seat and placed Lori back on his lap. Jocelyn turned away from him as she held Joy closer to her. Jocelyn took a deep breath and focused on the food on her plate. She gazed at Lorenzo, who still frowned upon her.

When they finished eating, Jocelyn took the girls up to their rooms to put them to bed. As she told them a bedtime story, they both fell asleep. She closed the door quietly to their room and walked down the hall to her and Lorenzo's bedroom. When she opened the door, she saw him standing in front of his dresser in nothing but his underwear.

A part of her wanted to curse at him some more, but she noticed he had an MP3 player in his hand, listening to music with small headphones on. She walked to the closet and picked out a white nightgown. Dressing, she ogled into Lorenzo's direction, seeing him turn around. When he locked eyes with her, he left from out of the room and closed the door behind him.

She left from out of the room and followed him, seeing him rushing downstairs. Jocelyn followed him halfway down the stairs and saw him lay down on the sofa. As Jocelyn continued to look at him with fire in her eyes, she saw him fall asleep.

You dumb asshole! she said to him under her breath.

Jocelyn quietly went back upstairs to their bedroom.

****

The next morning Jocelyn sat comfortably on a brown leather sofa in the employee lounge, sipping a glass of ice coffee through a straw, wondering how much more she could take from her husband. The physical neglect and the pointless bickering had drained her energy. How was she able to cope with his nonsense? She was doing what her mother and both of her grandmothers would do. That was the only thing that prevented her from crossing the line.

The door to the lounge opened. A woman wearing a housekeeping uniform walked by her, giving off a wonderful fragrance of the rosy perfume. The woman made her way to the refrigerator on the other side of the room. She opened its door and retrieved a blue thermos and unscrewed the cap as she walked towards Jocelyn. Jocelyn could see the woman looking at her from out of the corner of her eye.

When Jocelyn looked up into the woman's face, she saw wrinkles amid a long scar that traveled from the left side of the woman's forehead to the bridge of her nose. Her eyes were a deep blue ocean color. The woman wore her black hair shoulder length. Her lips were a little less than full. Her Diane Sawyer-like face was a sign she was much older than Jocelyn.

"Taking a break?" the woman asked, sitting down next to her.

The woman was a supervisor Jocelyn knew worked on the evening shift. But lately, she had been covering both the mornings and evenings since the morning supervisor left recently.

"A small one," Jocelyn answered.

"Why are you looking like that?"

"And you are?" Jocelyn asked.

"I'm Pearl," the woman answered, showing a toothy smile. "Pearl Bianchi, to be exact. And you look pissed off about something."

"Do I?" Jocelyn asked the woman.

"It involves a man, doesn't it?" Pearl questioned with raised eyebrows. "Why else would a woman who comes to work every day, earns a very good hourly wage, and likes her job look so uptight?"

Jocelyn didn't know this woman. She didn't need to know any of her personal business. But Jocelyn knew the woman was right. Jocelyn was going crazy, and she was unhappy because of her husband. But this battle-ax who was obviously much older than Jocelyn was trying to pry. Rather than be defensive, Jocelyn engaged the lady in conversation. Perhaps she could provide her with some kind of guidance to help her navigate through her tribulation with Lorenzo.

"Ms. Bianchi, do you really want to know?" Jocelyn asked as she smirked.

"What is it, dear?" Pearl asked the smile vanishing. "Cheating husband, stupid boyfriend, or maybe nothing is really wrong with you?"

Jocelyn shook her head. "None of those," she told Pearl.

"Just tell me," Pearl said to her. "I want to see you smile. I don't want to see you upset. A frown on your face makes you less pretty."

Jocelyn's eyebrows rose as she laughed. A muscle inside her jaw tweaked. Oddly, when she saw Pearl laughing along with her, she appeared ravishing herself.

"My husband works a lot," Jocelyn explained. "Because of this, we have little of a love life. It's driving me absolutely crazy. I don't know how much more of this I can take."

"I knew it had to be something major," Pearl said, positioning herself on the sofa closer to Jocelyn.

"I was about to cheat on him recently. But when I met the other man, I just couldn't do it. I lost my nerve."

"Infidelity is never the answer," Pearl said to Jocelyn. "You did the right thing to call it off. You showed maturity and wisdom."

"I'm very frustrated," Jocelyn said, bringing her legs together.

"How frustrated?" Pearl asked, putting the thermos to her head and drinking whatever beverage it contained.

"I need my husband to love me!" Jocelyn exclaimed.

"Mind over matter," Pearl said. "You are stronger than you think."

Jocelyn's eyes glistened as she watched Pearl. "I suppose," she responded.

"You know that a good wife remains faithful, right?" Pearl asked, offering a smile as she crossed her legs.

Jocelyn nodded. "I know," she said. "I know you are right."

"Yes, I am," Pearl answered as she nodded and laughed.

Jocelyn's eyes arose as she stood up. She regarded Pearl as she put a hand to her mouth. "What should I do?" she questioned.

"Remain strong," Pearl said with a quiet giggle.

Jocelyn's eyes widened. "I doubt if I can," she said.

"I will not steer you off course, girl," Pearl said. "You need love, devotion, and attention. A man can't give you all of those all the time."

"Ms. Bianchi, don't I know it?" Jocelyn said with a smile.

Pearl stood up and stared into Jocelyn's eyes. For a reason unknown to Jocelyn, Pearl's eyes focused down at her lips briefly. Jocelyn eyed her curiously for a moment. Jocelyn smiled.

"Do you have children with him?" Pearl asked.

"Two twin daughters," Jocelyn told Pearl. "He refuses to give me one more---"

Pearl cut Jocelyn off. "It would be foolish to jeopardize the family you've made anyhow," the older woman said most seriously.

Jocelyn eyed away from Pearl and shook her head. "I know," she said to Pearl.

"Continue to hold out," Pearl said and left the employee lounge.

Two minutes later Pearl came back with a large mahogany purse. She handed it to Jocelyn.

"I want you to have this," Pearl said, leaving Jocelyn alone.

Jocelyn looked down at the brown handbag. It smelled like perfume and leather. She instantly smiled.

****

Jocelyn sat on Joy's bed, reading *Jack and The Beanstalk* to her kids as they both fought with heavy eyes. She didn't read them a bedtime story every night before bedtime, but she did sometimes. As Jocelyn closed the book, she heard the sounds of Lori and Joy snoring as they both sat on her lap.

She picked them both up and lay Joy down on her bed first. Jocelyn carried Lori to the other side of the room and lay the lad down on the other bed. She placed the book gently on the shelf facing the bedroom door and watched both of them for five minutes before turning off the light switch and leaving the room.

Thinking of Lorenzo, Jocelyn went downstairs and opened the front door to peak down the block just in case he was walking towards the house. But she didn't see him. More than likely her husband was still at the dojo teaching. Jocelyn closed the door and walked quietly by the closet door, right by the basement doorway. She searched the back of the closet behind a broken vacuum cleaner and thought of the mahogany handbag Pearl had gifted her when she was at work earlier.

She left the closet door ajar and walked down into the basement. As she beheld herself in the mirror next to the small cactus tree given to them years ago by Lorenzo's oldest brother Silas, Jocelyn took a deep breath. She undressed. She took off the grey sweatpants she was wearing along with her red tank top.

Jocelyn thought of Pearl and reminisced about the delightful handbag that was given to her earlier.

Damn you, Lorenzo! the words screamed in her thoughts as she backslid into her most recent emotions.

Jocelyn's eyes watered. Her bottom lip quivered. Abrupt tears fell. She reached for a fluffy suede pillow on the arm of the sofa. She embraced the pillow, buried her face in it, her back and shoulders trembling as she continued to skirmish against the torment.

Four

Chapter 4

"He was like a superhero," Eboni told Stuart as she sat behind the desk in her office, thinking of the ninja- or the samurai- or whoever the guy saved her from peril precisely three weeks ago.

Stuart smiled, put a hand on his hip, and wiggled his foot on the floor. His eyes widened as his smile became brighter. Eboni's eyes gazed at him while he walked sweetly across the room before he stopped at the head of her desk. She stared him up and down, seeing his blazer fit him loosely and his uniform pants hugged him tightly like he barely stuffed his legs and ass in them. She had told Stuart the constricted pants were inappropriate many times. But she knew why he did it. He wanted to attract queer male customers while he was working. No customers or staff ever complained, so she let him wear his tight pants at work as he saw fit.

"Girl, I can't believe this guy saved you from a robbery attempt," he said to Eboni as he flexed his toned muscles. "I'm just glad you weren't hurt. He's certainly a nice guy."

"It's not every day a man comes to my defense like that," Eboni retorted with a beautiful smile. "Did I tell you I kissed him?"

Stuart smiled. "Really?" he said, looking directly at her. "You kissed him?"

Eboni shook her head. "I did, Stuart," she whispered. "It was something out of a dream. Except on television, I've seen no one use martial arts on another person before. He looked sexy doing it too."

"Girl, stop," Stuart said, putting his hands on his hips.

Eboni closed her eyes and thought back to that night again as if she was rewinding her DVR.

"You could very well see him again," Stuart suggested. "What if he comes by for a drink or two? You should give him anything he wants on the house."

"He's not coming here," Eboni said to him.

Stuart folded his arms and regarded her. "He might," he said.

Stuart scratched the short wavy hair on his head as she eyed away from him. From out of the corner of her eyes, she could see him looking at her.

Eboni smiled and stood up. She put her hands into the pockets of the stylish mahogany dress she was wearing.

Eboni sat back down, a smile playing around her lips. Her thoughts drifted to work, and what lay ahead for the evening.

Eboni peeked into Stuart's stare. Through his contagiously sunny smile, she saw a look of concern.

"I'll never understand women," Stuart said to her.

"You're not supposed to," Eboni told him.

Stuart sat at Eboni's desk and smiled at her. "I think it's wonderful that you're finally talking about a man," he said to her. "You never talk about men at all."

Eboni laughed, reflecting on her track record. "Because men flow out of my life quick," she told him. "So, I hardly ever talk about them."

"Okay, Eboni," he said to her.

"Can we change the subject?" Eboni asked him. "Let's talk about work."

"Okay."

She'd known Stuart for over fifteen years. He was her best friend.

She had met him about a year before they both moved from Connecticut to New York City.

"Get back to work," Eboni said, and the smile disappeared from her face.

Stuart playfully blew her a kiss and quietly left her office. When the door closed quietly behind him, Eboni walked towards the window to her office and ogled down at pedestrians walking down Mott Street. Her thoughts shifted back to her hero for a moment and she decided she needed a drink.

Changing into a simple navy-blue pantsuit, Eboni came downstairs to the restaurant floor. Much to her delight, the patronage was in abundance. She walked behind the bar and fixed herself a cranberry and vodka. As she sipped it slowly, she eyed the entrance and spotted a familiar man standing by the doors. A young red-haired man with a hairy beard was standing next to him. Eboni trembled as she instantly felt perspiration form on her forehead. She fanned her face with her hand as she took a deep breath.

It was him! He's here!

When the martial artist spotted her, he displayed a warm smile. "Hello," his voice said to her across the main floor.

"Hi," Eboni said to him.

Clad in a black gi and a black belt, her hero looked every part of a martial artist. The man with him, an obvious student, was wearing the same traditional uniform used for martial arts practice and competitions except for the one he was wearing that was beige with a black belt.

Eboni walked up to them, eager to thank him yet again for his selfless protectiveness. "What's your name?" she asked curiously. "You ran off so fast that night I didn't get the chance to introduce myself."

The martial artist folded his arms and traced along his goatee with his left thumb. "I'm Lorenzo," he told her. "I never got your name either."

"Eboni," she said and took a sip of her vodka and cranberry.

"This is Kurt," Lorenzo said to her as he gestured towards the red-haired man on his left.

"Pleased to meet you, Kurt," Eboni said in a friendly tone and sipped a little of her drink.

"So, how are you doing, Eboni?"

"I'm doing fine. So, what will you gentlemen like?"

"Long Island Iced Tea," Kurt told Eboni.

"The same thing," Lorenzo said.

Eboni smiled gladly. "Coming right up for you both," she told them.

Lorenzo and Kurt walked to the middle of the bar as Eboni grabbed a hold of multiple bottles of liquor.

Eboni made Kurt's drink first. She placed it right in front of him on a black napkin. She made Lorenzo's beverage and placed it beside him as his eyes seemed to pierce through her.

"I was just thinking about you just before you came in here," Eboni said to Lorenzo.

Lorenzo smiled. "Thinking of me?" he asked her. "What are you doing thinking of me?"

Eboni shrugged her shoulders as her heart pounded against her chest. "Thank you for rescuing me from that hoodlum," she said and took another sip of her drink. "I could never thank you enough. I can't stop thinking about it."

"I'm happy I was there to prevent that man from robbing you," Lorenzo said, offering a friendly smile.

The way he had appeared from out of nowhere, annihilated the suspect and returned her belongings to her. And her planting his cheek with the sweetest of kisses. His cheek had been so soft to her lips. She had begged another before he had departed. A part of her still wanted to kiss him on the cheek now.

Eboni took a deep breath in order to slow her pulse. Their smiles met each other as he lifted his glass and sipped his drink through the thin straw.

Lorenzo's smile quickly faded, replaced by an impassive look. Eboni stared into his eyes and thought, *when he smiles, he's so gorgeous.*

The sound of the violin played. Eboni peered towards the center of the restaurant where Stuart stood playing classical violin music. She saw patrons as they got up from their seats, moved up to Stuart, and placed money on the floor beside and in front of him.

"You have excellent drinks," Kurt said to her.

"This is a beautiful restaurant," Lorenzo added.

"Why thank you," Eboni said delightfully.

****

"Why did you reconsider that day?" Buck quizzed Jocelyn.

Jocelyn watched him in his black vest he wore over top of a pink shirt, buttoned at the collar. His sporty sun shades made him look cool and somewhat cute. He appeared no different from he had all of those years ago in college when they were lovers. His angry eyes hid behind his dark glasses. But his clenched teeth revealed how angry he was with her.

"I couldn't do that to my husband," she retorted.

"But you sent me a text message the night before saying to meet you at the Times Square Hilton," Buck said. "You were pretty adamant about what you wanted us to do. I spent a lot of money on that hotel room."

"Listen, Buck! I thought it was what I truly wanted. When it was time to do it, I couldn't. My husband refuses me when I need him the most. But I couldn't bring myself to cheat on him. I love him to death. I couldn't do that to him. He's my husband and the father of my two children."

"Damn!" Buck exclaimed. "I wanted you, Jocelyn!"

Her usual day was to wake up in the morning at Six O'clock in order to be at work by Eight. Since her husband was off to the dojo by the time she got up, she hardly ever fixed him breakfast. She would cook Joy and Lori breakfast and iron their clothes for them to wear to school and take them to their school's daycare center two hours before kindergarten started. She would head to the Suites in the West Farms section of the Bronx and work there for six hours a day performing housekeeping duties. By the time her workday was over, Jocelyn would pick up her daughters from the same daycare center at their elementary school where she dropped them off. From there she would head home and start preparing dinner for her family. If Lorenzo wasn't home by Five O'clock in the evening, she would place his warm plate on the stove. And she would put his meal on a plate and stick it into the refrigerator if he wasn't home by Seven.

When her husband would finally come through the door, he would eat and meet her in the bedroom. Often Lorenzo didn't even look at her. He wanted to sleep, watch martial arts tournaments on DVD, or look at kung fu movies. And often it frustrated the hell out of her.

"Keep your damn voice down!" Jocelyn ordered Buck. "This is my job."

"Sorry."

He removed his shades. She saw his calm face and affable eyes looking at her. His abrupt smile showed her he was no longer pissed off at her.

"You can't ever come here while I'm working again," Jocelyn said to Buck.

"Okay," Buck said.

The door to the room opened from the other side, and Jocelyn clutched instantly at her heart as she spun to the entrance. Buck dove over the bed and landed on the other side of it, ducking down as a comely, well-aged woman who was old enough to be Jocelyn's mother walked into the suite.

"Pearl!" Jocelyn exclaimed, remembering their conversation recently.

"I was walking down the hall and thought I heard you talking to someone from inside the room," Pearl said, sliding her fingers playfully along Jocelyn's cheek as she examined the room.

"Oh, no!" Jocelyn said to her, thinking of a lie. "I was talking to myself about how badly a lot of our hotel guests leave the rooms so messy before they check out."

"That they do," Pearl said with a grin. "When you're finished here, I need your help in room 752. If I don't see you again today, have a nice evening."

Pearl showed Jocelyn a dazzling smile before she hurried out of the room. Jocelyn took a deep breath and closed the door. She shook her head and peered towards the bed.

"Okay, Buck, she's gone," Jocelyn whispered.

Buck popped up from behind the far side of the bed and smiled. "That was close," he said to her.

"Indeed, it was!" Jocelyn expressed. "Please leave and don't visit me here again."

Buck smiled crookedly and put his hands in the pockets of his trousers. He gave one last look at Jocelyn and opened the door. He turned around to look back at her. "When are we going to get to talk again?"

"Never," Jocelyn said, shaking her head as her eyes pierced through him. "I never want to see you again!"

Buck looked away from her. He showed her a disappointing smirk. He eyed her one last time and walked out of the room.

****

When Lorenzo came through the door, Jocelyn was sitting there in the living room on the sofa sipping red wine as she watched the nightly news. She was wearing a pink sheer see-through nightdress. When she glanced up and saw his smile, she greeted him with a smirk.

"I have good news," he said to her.

"What?" Jocelyn asked as he sat down next to her.

"The martial arts school is doing so well I've opened one in downtown Brooklyn," Lorenzo said to her. "I'm also going to start a bodyguard service."

"Well, I'm not too thrilled," Jocelyn voiced, frowning at him.

"How come?" he questioned.

She eyeballed him. Lorenzo had a strange, yet inquisitive look in his eyes. He focused away from her and took a deep breath.

Jocelyn peered at him and frowned. "You're expanding your business, huh?" she questioned. "You don't have time for me and the kids as it is, Lorenzo!"

"Jocelyn, you've never supported my being a martial arts teacher. You don't even like the idea of me teaching our daughters basic self-defense. My school in Chinatown has been open for years, and you've never seen how I teach my students or even ask me about how I work with people or anything. You haven't even been to my school to visit me."

Jocelyn sipped her wine. "Lorenzo, I appreciate all you do," she said. "I'm just not into this martial arts world. That's your thing. I've always thought it's good you are teaching people discipline and how to be mentally tough. I think it's good for you to teach people how to defend themselves. And no, I don't want our daughters to hurt someone. I'm against them learning that stuff. And I appreciate you protecting us."

"But?"

"If we made love more, I might show a little more support for what you do," said Jocelyn, brushing her hair from her eye. "Your lengthy day at the dojo is the reason we aren't having sex regularly. You come through the door tired as hell and dragging your feet. You open your school at Six O'clock in the morning every day and close your operation at Nine O'clock at night. That's fifteen hours away from home. Away from me and our children. Because you're so exhausted late at night, our sex life is being severely neglected. You never take a day off. You never fulfill my physical needs, Lorenzo. And it's all because of this damn martial art of yours!"

"Jocelyn, I'm trying to triumph at something important. I'm trying to reach a goal."

"Why?" she asked, seeing a calmness in his eyes as he remained still.

"For one, this is something I love," Lorenzo explained to her. "I'm always on my purpose. Martial arts are my purpose."

Jocelyn looked at the glass of wine in her hand, "And?" she quizzed.

"Because I not only want to be well off financially, but I also want to earn a generous income so I can put both of our daughters into Ivy League colleges after they graduate from high school. I'm thinking about their futures as well. I want the absolute best life offers Lori and Joy. They are the primary reasons I work so long and hard."

"Lorenzo, I understand all of that. I want Joy and Lori to attend Yale, Harvard, Brown, or Dartmouth too someday, but I feel you can scale back your workload. I feel you can soften your work schedule."

Lorenzo bit his bottom lip. "So, you want us to make love more frequently?" he asked.

"Hell yes!" Jocelyn exclaimed bitterly.

Lorenzo cracked his knuckles. He devoted himself to Jocelyn always. He had fully paid for their lovely house in the Kingsbridge section of the Bronx with the money he had earned from teaching martial arts. Lorenzo enjoyed what he did. A martial artist is what he was. It was who Jocelyn had married, and that he would not change.

Other than providing and doing the essential things a husband does, what else could he do?

Lorenzo shook his head. "Maybe I can cut my hours down," he said, looking at her. "What if I hire a night school instructor and come home a little earlier? I can't do that every day, but I can do it some days. I hope that's good enough for you."

"For me, it's not perfect, but it's something," Jocelyn said to him. "I can't continue to feel sexually frustrated and angry."

Lorenzo frowned. "Angry?" he asked.

"Yes, angry!" she yelled. "If you can't make love to me, it's a major problem. If this continues, I'm going to have to divorce you. I'm very serious."

Jocelyn made sure Lorenzo eyed into her tortured stare. Her eyes were intense. Her lips pressed together. Jocelyn had had enough. As Lorenzo nodded, she hoped he finally understood what he had been doing wrong. Jocelyn closed her eyes and sighed. She took a few more sips of her wine.

"I'm sorry I haven't been giving our love life its proper attention," he told her.

"Apology accepted," Jocelyn said, a bit satisfied he had confessed his shortcomings and admitted culpability.

"Okay," Lorenzo said to her with a smile.

"You find me attractive, don't you, Lorenzo?"

"Yes, of course, I do, Jocelyn," Lorenzo answered. "But your attractiveness is not why I married you. I married you because I simply love you."

Taking a deep breath, Lorenzo took her glass of wine and sat down next to her. He put the rim of the glass to his lips and took a sip. He laid back into the sofa cushions and closed his eyes as he handed her glass back to her. Jocelyn touched his arm and lay back with him. She put the rim of the glass to her lips, sipped the last bit of wine, and placed her feet into Lorenzo's lap. Before long, they both fell asleep.

Lorenzo felt his wife's chin on his shoulder as she rubbed his abdominals from behind him. As much as he enjoyed Jocelyn's soft touch, and going all the way with Jocelyn in the kitchen only moments ago, it didn't prevent Eboni from entering his thoughts. Where would she be if the jackass who attempted to rob her pulled the trigger that night? What would have happened had he not been there?

He ran into her again, not expecting to only hours ago. Lorenzo remembered her eyes, lips, and thankful smile. He recalled her awesome beauty the night he defended her, and tonight too.

Eboni, Lorenzo said to himself as he dreamed about her.

Five

Chapter 5

As she tossed and turned, Eboni screamed, "No!"

"I want your money or your life," a cold, callous male voice said to her.

"Please, no!" she screamed helplessly, seeing the silver revolver aimed right at her.

The robber aimed the gun skyward and fired two shots.

Eboni shook as she stared into his cold blue eyes. She saw threatening anger that paralyzed her. "No," she said, dropping her purse to the wet ground.

The thug stepped forward and reached for her purse. His blazing eyes focused ahead of him as he picked up her valuables.

"Now I will kill you," he said, aiming his weapon at her.

"Please, no!" she pleaded, but the horrific sounds of repeated gunfire drowned her out....

Eboni sat up; her eyes alert as she wheezed. She looked down at the brown sheets, seeing she was in bed. She realized it had all been a bad dream as she peered up at the ceiling fan blowing cool air on her sweaty body. Only this time, unlike in actual life, there was no one to prevent the robber from taking what he wanted from her.

****

Eboni walked into *The Camelot* as the hustle of the noisy streets echoed all throughout SoHo just after midday. When she got inside, she noticed one customer sitting at the bar having a drink as he gazed up at the giant plasma screen television displaying sports highlights. With her bartender at the other end of the bar chatting with a group of customers, Eboni eyed the patron as he sipped his drink.

His caramel complexion was magnificent. His braided hair was down past his hefty, strong shoulders, just like she remembered. The brown martial arts uniform he had on fit him evenly. The nobleman's pectorals appeared broad and muscular. The gentleman's eyes were a rich hazel color.

She recalled his name. Lorenzo.

A commotion broke out across the room, and Eboni hurried over to the customers before a scuffle started. A master at averting brawls, Eboni could diffuse any situation with a little sugar in her tone. Just as she stepped away from the table her eyes peered across the room towards Stuart switching on his way to a table with a tray of drinks. Taking her eyes off of him, she noticed her gallant champion had departed. Her head turned left and right. Where did he go?

When she went behind the bar, Eboni immediately turned around to scan herself in front of a mirror behind a shelf. It contained a stack of napkins. Her dark hair glistened in a curled bun. Her caked-on make-up was splendidly flawless. Eboni eyed the thin golden necklace she wore around her neck for a moment before viewing the tan hooded sleeveless dress which covered her from her shoulders to below her knees.

She took in the restaurant's sight. She fixated at the black and gold marble floor briefly before darting towards a bronze 6'9 statue of King Arthur smiting a bronze 6'7 statue of Lancelot with Excalibur by the left side of a black spiral staircase leading upstairs. Eboni eyed the walls on both sides where colossal fish tanks displayed manta rays, newborn whale sharks, and various kinds of beautiful aquarium fish swimming about.

She smiled at the sight of her friend Stuart, in tight pants and all, standing in the middle of the room in a black shirt and a white bowtie, picking up his violin.

Eboni nodded to herself as she placed her hands behind her back. She walked out from behind the bar and saw a sea of humanity fill up her restaurant. She placed her hands by her sides and trudged upstairs to her office as violin music began to play.

****

Three hours later, Eboni still hadn't come from out of her office. Eboni stood up from sitting at her long, antique walnut desk and stretched. She walked over to the mirror and gazed at herself. Her reflection revealed a woman who was '5'8 and weighed around 140 pounds. Eboni reached behind her head and undid her curled bun. As her hair fell down past her shoulders, she stifled a yawn, her mahogany complexion still shimmering, probably from the skin cream she had applied within the past few hours.

Eboni slowly unzipped her dress from the back near her neck. Stepping out of it and posing, holding her left breast in her hand, she took in the sight of her wonderful image in the mirror in nothing but Stilettos and black panties. She checked her smile and removed her earrings. Standing on one foot and lifting her other leg up, she pulled her head back, striking one of her favorite poses, resembling a young Dorothy Dandridge but with fuller lips.

Eboni walked over to her desk, sorted through a pile of mail, and located a syringe vial. She grabbed ahold of it, turned the needle towards the side of her stomach, and shot herself with the first dose of insulin today. She knew she didn't monitor her blood sugar levels as she should. But she lived a mostly healthy lifestyle and followed her doctor's directions. It had been most difficult to avoid the foods she liked most like white rice, potatoes, pastries, and soda. These things would only spike her glucose levels, and she didn't need that.

She took her dress to a closet in the back where a dozen of other dresses she wore every night of the workweek were hanging on hangers. No sooner than she hung up the dress she had been wearing, she picked out another one to garb for the rest of the evening. As she looked at it, she admired its bluish cloudy color. Eboni put the dress on. She walked back to the mirror and inspected herself. The dress fit her rather tightly, but it fit her.

The dress showed much of her magnificently sexy legs. She knew it wasn't entirely appropriate for business. She knew damned well whatever wives and girlfriends came in here tonight would have to hold their husbands and boyfriends tight if they accompanied them.

Eboni looked at the earrings in her hand. She had forgotten she'd been holding them. She walked over to her desk, opened the top drawer, and placed them inside it. Eboni saw about a dozen matching earrings she could choose from. Once she picked an elegant pair, she put them on.

She went back to the mirror and eyed herself. No, she didn't need to put on any make-up; she thought. And she really didn't need to slide on any perfume. Maybe she just needed to put on a little eyeliner and some blush. Eboni applied a small amount, turned around, and eyed over her shoulder at her reflection in the mirror. Her face fell at the unwanted sight of her narrow ass. If only her butt was plumper, she'd be perfect, Eboni thought.

Eboni high stepped over to her desk, sat in the chair, and reached for the yellow pages leaning slightly against the wall. She placed the large telephone book in her lap, flipped through its pages, and quickly found what she was looking for. She saw the image of the surgeon she wanted to perform her surgery. He appeared Bolivian or Ecuadorian. She saw a link to a website, read a few testimonials by women he had treated, and smiled. She reached for the cordless phone on her desk and dialed a number.

"Dr. Ruiz's office," a woman's voice answered pleasantly.

"I'm considering injections of the buttocks," Eboni said simply. "I'd like to set up an appointment."

"The doctor is out of the office, possibly for months," the receptionist said. "He has countless patients awaiting the procedure you inquired about."

"Out of the office for months?" Eboni questioned.

"He has surgeries scheduled all over the United States and several countries with an extremely long line of patients. I can still schedule you for an appointment, miss," the receptionist continued. "It's just going to take a very long time for him to speak with you."

"I see," Eboni breathed out.

Time was on her side, she knew. She could always book the appointment well in advance and change her mind about having the operation done as the date neared. Eboni knew it was unwise to rush into it. Eboni booked her appointment.

Leaving her office, she returned downstairs to where her servers worked frantically taking orders and delivering food to multiple tables. The bar was completely full. The sound of a million conversations filled the place; silverware hitting plates all throughout. Stuart, her longtime friend, and a loyal employee was still playing the violin to the delight of the patronage.

Business is good. She couldn't recall the last time *The Camelot* was so busy two business nights in a row.

Signaling the bartender, she hurried to the bar. "Julio, make me a shot of Hennessey and a Bloody Mary," she said to the bartender.

Smiling, Julio quickly filled the shot glass and made the drink, and placed them directly in front of her. She put the shot glass to her lips and downed it in one gulp before taking her drink with her to the front of the restaurant. As she sipped her alcoholic beverage through a thin straw, she saw a familiar-looking man entering the restaurant with the same brown martial arts outfit he had on earlier.

Eboni's heart pounded inside her chest as her breathing quickened. She placed a hand over her heart and took a deep breath. She closed her eyes for a moment. Opening her eyes, she noticed eleven similarly dressed individuals were with him. Smiling, Eboni walked up to him.

"Hello, Lorenzo," she greeted. "Back again?"

Lorenzo turned around and eyed her. "Hi!" he said happily. "Yes, I'm back. This time I'm going to eat something."

"Follow me," Eboni said.

She led him into the Tingagel Room, where the only remaining available table was. They were all seated. Her eyes found Lorenzo, noticing he was looking at her legs.

"These are my students," Lorenzo told Eboni, his eyes finding hers.

Eboni nodded and waved to all of them. "Are these all the students you teach?" she asked.

"No," he answered. "I have precisely five hundred and thirty-four students," said Lorenzo. "The ones with me now are the ones who attended the school late evening."

"I see."

"This is a pleasant atmosphere," a teenaged female pupil said to Eboni. "I love the music of the violin."

"I'm glad you do," Eboni told her. "Thank you."

Turning her attention back to Lorenzo, she motioned for the server. When the server arrived with a stack of menus, Eboni took them.

"Here is the menu," she uttered with a smile. "At the front, you will see tonight's recommendations. Take your time and let me know when you are ready. If there is anything else you need, Renee, one of our best servers, will come to find me. Enjoy your dinner."

"Alright," Lorenzo said as he saw her place each menu in front of every chair.

Eboni focused on him for two seconds more. She wiped the oncoming sweat from her brow. Leaving him in capable hands, she strutted slowly from the backroom to the main dining area. She glanced back at Lorenzo, seeing his seducing smile as he watched her.

****

The place had cleared out. Only a few customers remained, and it was almost closing time. Unable to help herself, Eboni glanced back, capturing Lorenzo's seductive smile, watching her walk away as he stood outside of the Tingagel Room, sipping red wine. His clan of martial arts trainees had left. He was now alone. Grinning, she walked over to his table and stood in front of him.

"Can I get you anything else?" Eboni asked Lorenzo. "We're about to close in less than a half-hour."

Lorenzo looked up at her and smiled. "No, thank you," he said, running his pinky finger on the rim of his wineglass. "Can I say something?"

"Sure," she said.

"You are an exquisite woman," he said to her in that deep honeyed voice of his.

Eboni smiled happily. "Thank you," she told him.

Lorenzo's eyes observed her. His eyes scanned her up, down, and across. She wondered for a moment why he was analyzing her.

"Eboni, there's something about you," he said to her. "When I see you, I see someone different. When I look at you, I see a fine lady. I also see something more."

"Something more?" she quizzed; her face perplexed by his words.

"Yes," Lorenzo answered. "I don't want to be wrong, but you strike me as a woman of a certain type. What I mean is you're special."

"Special?" she questioned. "Well, sir, I'm not sure I know what you mean."

Eboni swallowed hard and playfully batted her eyes. Lorenzo chuckled. He placed his left hand firmly on her right shoulder, and his right hand on her other one. She looked up at his dreamy gaze, eyeing his thick lips, and for a second, dreamt of his chocolate kisses. A smile touched her lips at the thought. As she returned his stare, the tip of his ring finger lightly touched the side of her arm. He smiled at her and brought his hands down by his sides.

"On quite the contrary, it's you who are special," Eboni told Lorenzo.

She eyed his smile and enjoyed the sight of his handsome face. It was his calm demeanor, his ability to fight, and the charm that made him special. But how did he see her as the same?

"You don't have a husband?" he asked.

"No," she said. "I haven't been fortunate enough to have one of those yet."

"Well, I'm sure you'll get married someday. How old are you?"

Eboni eyed away from him briefly. She didn't enjoy discussing her age. Plus, it was none of his business. But since she'd enjoyed his conversation and was grateful for his patronage, she answered.

"I'm in my fifties," Eboni told him, looking at him. "And you?"

"In my thirties," Lorenzo said, folding his arms. "Tell me something about yourself."

"I like to travel, see the world when I can, and laugh."

"I see. So, what kind of man do you like?"

"Nice and handsome ones," Eboni said.

"Those types of men are everywhere," he said.

The server came to Lorenzo's table with the check. When he viewed it, he saw it was for $375.00. He reached down into his sock for his debit card and handed it to the server along with the check. As Eboni came closer to him, the server walked away.

"You mentioned traveling. Where have you traveled to?" he asked her.

"Greece, Poland, New Zealand, Canada, Spain, Mexico, London, Paris, Dominica," Eboni said all in one breath.

"I haven't been to any of those places you mentioned," Lorenzo said.

"You haven't traveled at all?" Eboni asked him.

"Only to China and Japan," he said, smiling at her.

"For martial arts-related stuff?"

Lorenzo nodded. "Yes," he answered.

"What made you get into the martial arts?"

"My mother loved watching Kung fu movies when I was a small boy," said Lorenzo, his eyes looking away from her and scanning the room. "It intrigued her. She and my dad agreed to enroll me in a martial arts school during my last year of high school because I didn't want to play sports. I stuck with it."

"What do your students call you?"

"Sensei," Lorenzo said, looking at her.

"Sensei," Eboni repeated softly.

Eboni figured a Sensei had to be a master teacher of one of the many forms of martial arts. Certain fighting arts were deadly, she knew. She admired his dedication to stick with something like that for so long. He apparently loved what he was doing. She loved to see people follow their passions.

"Do you work out a lot?" Lorenzo asked, looking her up and down.

"I ride my mountain bike and jog long distances daily," Eboni answered him. "I'm a diabetic so I have to do my cardio every day."

"You appear so robust," Lorenzo complimented. "And you look to be in your twenties. I would never assume you were in your fifties."

"Thank you," she told him. "I've always been very serious about my health and fitness."

Lorenzo nodded gleefully. "It's time for me to go," he said, seeing the server coming back with his debit card along with a receipt.

"You seem to see right through me as if you know me," Eboni conveyed to him.

"I can see what many people don't see when they see you," Lorenzo said, his eyes beaming at her as he showed her a handsome grin. "One day I'll tell you what I see."

"That sort of makes me feel naked," she said to him.

Lorenzo chuckled. "Did you ever consider doing stand-up comedy?" he asked her.

"No, I haven't, Sensai," she said sarcastically with a grin. "But I'm glad I could make you laugh."

"Laughter is healthy," he told her, letting out one last giggle.

"If you don't mind me asking, what's your wife's name?" Eboni asked, looking at the band on his ring finger.

"Jocelyn," Lorenzo answered.

"I bet she's beautiful," Eboni said.

Lorenzo nodded. "Yes," he answered her as he gave a fifty-dollar tip to the server and signed the receipt.

Lorenzo had a faraway look in his eyes, probably thinking about the woman in his life. Eboni could never see herself being married to anyone. She couldn't stay in a relationship longer than a couple of months at the most. She'd been deeply in love once, many years ago. But that was another lifetime.

Lorenzo gazed at her. "I have to go now," he told her. "It was nice seeing you again."

"Likewise, Sensei," said Eboni.

Lorenzo gave her one last look. He turned away and Eboni's eyes never left him as he walked out of the restaurant.

Six

Chapter 6

Lorenzo's eyes opened at the sound of one of his daughters crying. As he sat up in bed, the first thing he knew was he had a throbbing headache. He soaked in his own sweat. Lorenzo placed his head in his hands and took a deep breath. As he held his head, he could hear his wife's voice speaking calmly to their daughters just down the hall.

Lorenzo swung his legs around and slowly placed his feet on the floor. Still holding his head in order to ease his painful migraine, he stood up. Just as he was walking towards the door, Jocelyn came inside the room with Joy crying. Losing concern for his own misery, he knelt down in front of Joy and pulled her to him.

"What's wrong, Joy?" Lorenzo asked his little girl with a simple smile. "Why are you crying?"

"I had a nightmare, daddy," the little girl said, her small face melancholy as she gazed up at him. "I woke up crying and Mommy was there."

"Well, your bad dream is over now," Lorenzo said, hugging her.

Jocelyn knelt down beside Lorenzo and reached out for Joy. Joy hugged her as Lorenzo stood up. Lorenzo closed his eyes as he grimaced.

"Are you alright?" Jocelyn asked him, scratching the top of her head as she watched him with a concerned look.

"I have the most terrible headache," he said, wiping sweat from his forehead.

"And you're perspiring a lot," Jocelyn said.

"Yes, I'm not feeling well. I think I'm going to take the day off."

"Really? You never take days off, Lorenzo."

"I know, but this feels like the worse headache I've ever had."

"You want me to stay with you today?" Jocelyn asked him. "I can always call in sick myself. That way I can stay here and look after you."

Lorenzo smiled at the gesture. "I appreciate it, Jocelyn," he replied softly, "I really do. Call the Suites and tell them you are going to be late. Stay in bed with me for a little while longer before you leave for work."

"I will." She grinned towards him and returned her attention to Joy.

Lorenzo placed his hand on the doorknob and regarded her. "There is something you can do," he said.

"What's that?"

"Call Kurt and tell him I need him to instruct the students today. Kurt's number is pinned to the refrigerator."

"Is that all?"

"That's it," he said, leaving out of the bedroom.

Lorenzo walked down the hall and stumbled into the bathroom and found Lori brushing her teeth.

"Good morning, Daddy," Lori greeted him cheerfully.

"Good morning, angel," Lorenzo said with a smile, kneeling down to give her a hug.

Lori quickly left out of the bathroom, leaving Lorenzo alone. Lorenzo walked to the mirror and saw he was sweating profusely. He ran the cold water in the sink and tossed some on his face. He took a deep breath and sat on the edge of the tub and placed his face in his hands again.

Jocelyn opened the door to the bathroom. "I'm about to take the kids to school and come back," she said to him.

"Okay," Lorenzo said without looking in her direction.

"I'm not going anywhere until I know you're alright, Lorenzo."

"I'm fine," Lorenzo said as he stared in her direction. "Go ahead."

Jocelyn nodded and closed the bathroom door. Lorenzo stood up and walked out into the upstairs hallway. He stared down from the banister towards Jocelyn, taking Joy and Lori by the hand as they headed down the stairs. As he watched them walk through the living room towards the front door, he smiled tightly and headed back to the bedroom. Once he got there, he changed the sheets on the bed and despite his aching head, performed yoga for nearly a half-hour.

Lorenzo took a cold shower, hoping he would feel better afterward. By the time he stepped out of the shower, it seemed like his headache had gotten worse. Lorenzo climbed back into bed and dialed a number.

"Doctor's office?" a feminine voice answered on the other end.

"I'd like to make an emergency appointment today," Lorenzo said.

"Name?"

"I'm the doctor's son," Lorenzo said.

"In that case, just come into the doctor's office and wait," the clerk said to him.

Lorenzo made his way from Kingsbridge to New York Presbyterian Hospital on Broadway and 168th Street. Like most people he knew, Lorenzo didn't like hospitals. But since he had a father who was a doctor and hadn't seen him in months, he'd figure to go see him.

Lorenzo passed through the hospital's main entrance and hurried through a set of double doors. The passage led him past the emergency room directly into a narrow bright hallway where an elevator was straight ahead. The smell of ammonia and a wonderful lemon disinfect along with a pleasant aloe scent filled the air. Once Lorenzo got to the fourth level of the building, he walked down a long corridor. It led to his father's office.

He saw his father's office door straight ahead. When he got to the door, he saw his father's name written in bronze letters. *Dr. Xavier Royal Jr. M.D.,* it read.

Lorenzo pushed the door open and saw three patients sitting on a long sofa in the area outside of the doctor's office. A secretary sat behind a desk with a computer monitor on it, far off to the right. When Lorenzo approached her, the woman greeted him with a smile. Her shoulder-length hair was appealing. Her mascara was a bit much, and Lorenzo thought she'd look prettier without it.

"Lorenzo," the secretary said in a sweet, mature feminine voice. "I told your father you called."

"Where is he now?" Lorenzo asked.

"He's in his office doing a routine checkup on a patient. Sit down."

"So, how are you, Lydia?" he asked her.

"I'm doing well," she said to him.

Whenever he came here, Lorenzo wondered if his sixty three year old father was having sex with Lydia. She was beautiful, single, and approaching her forties. He could not believe she had been unmarried and working for his father for almost ten years without at least one encounter ever occurring between them. With his mother in North Carolina taking care of the elder members of their family for the past several years, he knew good and well his father was sneaking behind her back with young New York City women, including the ones who worked in his office.

Lorenzo took a seat on the end of the sofa and closed his eyes. It didn't seem like his migraine headache couldn't get any worse, but it did. And sweat still poured down his face. Before he knew it, Lorenzo had drifted off to sleep. When he woke up almost two hours later, he slowly gazed up only to see Xavier shaking him.

"Lorenzo, wake up," his father's deep voice said.

Lorenzo gazed up into his father's friendly face and saw a man with forever graying hair with eyeglasses displayed crookedly on his face. Lorenzo immediately stood up and gave his father a hug. He stepped back and noticed all the patients in the office had left. He looked over to Lydia, who was talking on the office phone at her desk as she leaned back in her chair.

"What brings you here?" Xavier asked.

Behind the lopsided glasses, Lorenzo saw a calm face with black bushy eyebrows which often made Xavier appear as a mad scientist instead of a doctor. The forming wrinkles on his still youthful face hinted at age-old wisdom and maturity from life's experiences. He saw a studious, intelligent-looking man. The playfully charming grin and the twinkle in his eye hadn't gone away as he aged. "I have a headache and I'm sweating," Lorenzo said, walking in front of him.

"Let me take your temperature," Xavier said with a warm grin, clapping Lorenzo on the back. "Follow me to my office."

Xavier moved ahead of him and led Lorenzo down a narrow corridor. Lorenzo noticed several doors on both sides of the corridor as they passed by them. Xavier opened the last door on the left and went inside a room with a light on. When Lorenzo followed him there, his father gestured to a chair next to a tall plant. Xavier checked Lorenzo's pupils first and took a thermometer from out of a thin casing and inserted it underneath Lorenzo's tongue. A few minutes later Xavier pulled the thermometer out of Lorenzo's mouth and studied it.

"Your temperature is seriously high," Xavier revealed to him and left the room.

He came back less than a minute later with a cold bottle of water, an ice pack, and two ibuprofen tablets. Xavier placed the icepack on Lorenzo's forehead as Lorenzo took the two tablets with the cold bottle of water.

"You have a fever," Xavier said to Lorenzo, grabbing a rubber glove from out of a box that was on a shelf just above Lorenzo's head. "Your body temperature should go back to normal soon. Now open your mouth and stick your tongue out."

When Lorenzo opened his mouth and showed the length of his tongue, Xavier nodded as he tapped Lorenzo's tongue with a gloved finger.

"What?" Lorenzo asked him.

"Nothing," Xavier said. "Everything is fine."

Lorenzo frowned and eyed Xavier oddly. Xavier left out of the room again and came back with a needle and syringe. He stretched out Lorenzo's arm and stuck the needle into it. Moments later, when the syringe was full of Lorenzo's blood, Xavier applied a Band-Aid to the needle mark on his arm after wiping it thoroughly with an alcohol-filled cotton ball.

"What am I Being tested for, dad?" Lorenzo asked Xavier.

"I'm checking your blood for infections," Xavier answered.

As Lorenzo looked at his father, Xavier returned his gaze. Xavier's grin disappeared as he squatted down in front of Lorenzo and peered up at him.

"How are Jocelyn and the children?" Xavier asked.

"They're all doing well, father," Lorenzo answered.

Lorenzo bit his bottom lip and looked away. Xavier followed his gaze and eyed him.

"Lorenzo, what is it?" Xavier questioned.

"Jocelyn is demanding sex from me every day," Lorenzo said to him. "I work so hard. I try to maintain my household and my martial arts schools. She doesn't understand I can't give her the love life she wants until I establish my enterprise. With all the students I've gained, a love life with Jocelyn is impossible. She threatened to divorce me if we don't start making love more."

"How often do you two have intimacies?"

"Not nearly enough. I told her I would scale back on my work schedule for the sake of our love life."

"It sounds like she's extremely frustrated. What are you going to do?"

"I'm not sure, father. What do you think I should do?" Lorenzo asked as he cocked an eyebrow.

"Well, you're running a very lucrative business, my boy. I know you love your family. I also know you love your vocation too. Which is more important to you?"

"They both are."

"You also have aspirations for your martial arts franchise to grow. If you do indeed love your career more, let Jocelyn go. It's that simple."

"I don't want to divorce Jocelyn, father. I love her and the children so much."

"Son, I know you do. But your love for them isn't the issue. There are many couples who love each other who are in marriages that aren't working right. If Jocelyn is unhappy because you're not available to make love to her, and if you can't remedy that by providing her with the sex life she wants, perhaps maybe you two should get a divorce and go your separate ways. Once you part with her you can pursue the happiness of having a well-respected expanded martial arts corporation and she can have a husband who will satisfy her when she needs it once she remarries. But things can't continue as they are. It's a very unhealthy situation for her. Something has to give. You should let go if you can't give her all of yourself, Lorenzo."

 "I don't want to let Jocelyn go," Lorenzo said, his face long as he thought of Joy and Lori.

"I'm going to send your blood to our lab," Xavier said as if he didn't hear Lorenzo's last remark. "You should hear something in the next twenty-four to seventy-two hours. I'll call you when your results come back. In the meantime, I want you to rest here and go to sleep. Your fever will have broken by the time you wake up."

"Dad, I love Jocelyn very much," Lorenzo said, looking at the wall.

"I'll be back shortly. Try to get some rest."

Xavier stood up as his smile shined brightly on Lorenzo. Looking at his watch, he placed a hand inside his pocket and walked towards the door. Looking back at Lorenzo one final time, he turned the light off and left from out of the room.

Lorenzo's bottom lip twisted as he hung his head. He battled against an oncoming tear as he thought of Jocelyn.

Jocelyn, I don't want to divorce you. But I can't give you what you want. Not now. But I love you dearly.

Lorenzo contemplated within the darkness as he leaned back into the chair. He closed his eyes and thought of martial arts, seeing himself delivering roundhouse kicks, sidekicks, and devastating punches to an imagined enemy. He concentrated on the rhythm of his own breathing, feeling tranquility and calm engulf him as he thought fondly of The Shaolin Monastery. Before Lorenzo knew it, he had fallen asleep....

A hoary Asian man appeared before him walking with a cane and a sword in his left hand as he glided down a steep, wide staircase exiting a grey stoned building with many monks behind him practicing mixed martial arts at the entrance of the temple. His face was extraordinarily weary with endless wrinkles as if he was the age of three ninety-year-old men. The tan hooded robe he wore sparkled. His flowing white hair which dragged behind him seemed to rise at the whistling swirl of a strong wind amid a beautiful tulip garden, and a vast aqua sea just behind the shore. Was this a dream? It had to be. He was dreaming of the Temple of Shaolin. And he was dreaming about his mentor.

Don't concentrate on your troubles, young Lorenzo, the old man said. *Instead, focus on the important things. Be attentive to your heartbeat and your inner peace. The outward conflict has no place with you. Don't allow such sorrow to live rent-free inside your head.*

Yes, Sensai, Lorenzo responded.

Remember your lessons, the old man went on. *Remember what I taught you.*

Yes, Master Kimlau Li, Lorenzo said, addressing his teacher.

The visual in his dream disappeared, being swallowed up by a beam of white light. Lorenzo opened his eyes and took a deep breath.

****

Jocelyn looked at herself in the guestroom mirror. She resembled Lauren Velez with her dark brown hair gorgeously styled in a ponytail.

"Jocelyn!" a woman's voice called from down the hallway.

Jocelyn thought of her parents, and a second later she smiled as Lori and Joy crossed her mind.

"Jocelyn, there you are," the woman said.

Lorenzo crossed her mind. When she returned home earlier this morning, Jocelyn had found her husband wasn't there. She'd called

Lorenzo's martial arts school *The Warriors of Wushu*, but he hadn't reported there today like he said he wouldn't. She had waited for him for three hours before heading to work.

"Crystal," Jocelyn said. "You need something?"

"One housekeeper on the next shift called off duty," Crystal said to her plainly. "I need you to stay."

Crystal was the Director of Housekeeping at the Suites where she worked. The woman was short and petite with a pretty face. She was half Russian, half Sioux Native American. There had been rumors Crystal was a lesbian or used to be. But whatever she was, Jocelyn knew her as a fair, but tough boss.

Jocelyn wanted to be home with her husband and children after work. She didn't want to work a double shift. But since she hadn't made overtime in a long time, she nodded. She knew she would have to call Lorenzo and have him pick up the children from school. Knowing him, he would either bring them to the martial arts school or take them to Coney Island.

"Okay, I can do it," Jocelyn told Crystal.

Crystal smiled and combed her fingers through her flowing auburn hair and walked out of the room. Jocelyn walked back to the mirror and stared at her reflection again. Despite her and Lorenzo making love in the kitchen sixteen days ago, she found him making time for their love life was still a pressing and ongoing issue.

How much more of this can I take? Nothing has changed!

****

Jocelyn worked her exhausting double shifts and caught a cab to her home in Kingsbridge. When she arrived there, she found Lorenzo on the sofa reading a storybook to Lori and Joy as they sat on the floor in front of him. She walked over to her husband to kiss him on the cheek, but his lips found her cheek first. She watched as he closed the storybook and dropped it on the sofa. He picked up the girls in his arms and took them upstairs. Within a minute Lorenzo rushed back downstairs and stood in front of her.

Jocelyn just looked at him. He displayed a bright grin. The friendly way he stared at her perpetually was curious. Jocelyn raised her eyebrows at him and smiled.

"What?" she asked him.

"You're very unhappy with me, aren't you?" Lorenzo questioned her.

"Why do you say that?" Jocelyn asked him, folding her arms as she eyed him.

"Jocelyn, we both know you're frustrated. Because of the time I'm away from home teaching martial arts, you're unhappy. It has had a negative impact on our cohabitation life."

Jocelyn nodded. "Yes, it has," she said.

"Despite what I said about easing up on my workload, I truly can't do that."

Jocelyn frowned and stumped her left foot on the floor. "Lorenzo, what do you mean?" she asked, walking closer to him and looking him in his eyes.

She looked at the clownish happy stare on his face as he regarded her. His pleasing eyes seemed to look straight through her. What the hell was he smiling for? Was this amusing to him?

"I can't ease up when my schools are becoming more and more successful," he told her. "Student enrollment at each martial arts school is between 96-100%."

Lorenzo's smile vanished as he put an arm around her shoulder. His soothing hand caressed her arm up and down as he looked into her eyes. Before she could say anything, her husband continued.

"Everything I do is for our daughters. We've been through this. I'm also trying to finish paying off on this house. As much as I try, I can't give you the love life you want. I'm sorry."

"Of course not," she uttered, the words coming out with an odd reluctance. "So, what does this ultimately mean?"

"Jocelyn, I love you," Lorenzo said as he removed his arm from around her. As she looked at him, she saw his eyes water. Next came an uncharacteristic flow of tears she had never seen from him during all the time she had known him. "We have two options," he said to her as he choked up.

Jocelyn hugged him and gazed into his handsome face. "Which are?" she questioned.

Lorenzo took a deep breath and said, "You're going to have to keep putting up with this or you're going to have to divorce me. It all depends on how unhappy you are."

Jocelyn placed her hands to her face and took two steps back as he still looked at her. "I can't do this anymore," she declared to him. "I love you, Lorenzo. But I can't do this anymore."

"Understood," Lorenzo told her. "I'll call my sister Olivia and have her draw up the divorce papers."

She took her eyes off of him. She tiptoed upstairs and went inside the bedroom.

Jocelyn placed a hand to her mouth. She closed her eyes as disquietude grabbed a hold of her. She took a deep breath and blew it out loudly.

As the room spun around, she hurried into the bathroom. There she grabbed her stomach and sat on the toilet as she thought of her husband.

Jocelyn thought back to six years ago when Lorenzo walked up to her and gave her a red rose and a dozen lollipops after she had stepped on the D train on her way to the Bronx without knowing who he was. It was the first time they'd met. From there they developed a respectful friendship, and a beautiful relationship followed. Before she was to go to Puerto Rico with her family and stay there for good, Lorenzo had proposed to her. She'd accepted. They had Joy and Lori, and the rest was history.

As she thought of her husband, tears fell from Jocelyn's face. "Lorenzo, I love you," she whispered to herself. "I truly, deeply love you."

Seven

Chapter 7

From his position, Lorenzo roundhouse kicked, back kicked, side kicked, jabbed, and performed a high knee lift before returning to his basic stance. Following his instructional lead, his students displayed those moves in unison as they paid strict attention to him. This is where Lorenzo loved to be. Here he could be no other than himself. This was his life. To teach the ancient art of self-defense to those who wished to know it.

This was where he could focus on something which was so much a part of his being. Here, only discipline and total focus existed. Only the complete fitness of mind, body, and spirit was essential.

Lorenzo stood upright, his expression serious and dark. "What do we learn here?" he asked his students.

"To fight, to fight, to fight!" they all said in one thunderous voice.

Lorenzo eyed to his left and saw an older man wearing a red necktie over a white shirt standing by the wall with his head down. The man's hands were resting in the side pockets of a faded pair of Lee jeans. When the man lifted his head up, Lorenzo noticed it was Xavier. Lorenzo quickly motioned for Kurt to stand in his place and teach the class. When Kurt came, he walked over to Xavier.

"Dad," Lorenzo greeted Xavier.

"Hello, son," Xavier said to him.

"Dad, what are you doing here?"

"Your test results came back," Xavier told him with a smug smile.

Lorenzo looked his father in the eye. "Follow me to my office," he said and turned around.

Xavier followed Lorenzo from the main floor, down a short hallway full of martial arts trophies along each wall. Lorenzo's office was on the right, at the end of the hallway across from the men's restroom. Lorenzo entered his office and sat down on his desk, and watched as his father sat down in a chair near the wall.

"Give it to me," Lorenzo said to his father.

"Well, son, you're totally healthy," Xavier said to him, removing his glasses. "I don't know where the fever you had come from, but there's no sign it will ever come back. Perhaps it came from you working too much."

Lorenzo folded his arms and looked away from his father. "Thanks for bringing me this good news," he said, looking down at a medal lying on his desk he'd won in a tournament while he was still a young white belt.

Xavier peered at Lorenzo. "Have you and Jocelyn talked?" he asked.

Lorenzo smirked. "Our marriage is over, dad," he said sadly.

Xavier got up from out of the chair and placed a hand on Lorenzo's shoulder. "Son, I'm so sorry," he mumbled, wiping his glasses against his shirt.

"I have no choice. My marriage with Jocelyn has run its course. She's unhappy. Divorce is the only cure for her discontent."

"You and Jocelyn have two daughters. If you and she split, it's going to affect them greatly."

"Lori and Joy will be fine," Lorenzo said, looking at Xavier.

"I know. But once they're solely with her, they'll have to adjust to not having you around every day," said Xavier, putting his glasses back on.

"Divorce is the only solution," Lorenzo told his father, forcing a smile to his face. "I love her enough to set her free. So, after our divorce, Jocelyn can focus on finding someone who can give her everything she wants. I can't do that for her. You were right."

"What do you think will happen when you two divorce?" Xavier asked.

"I'll pay her alimony and child support. I'll probably have the children every weekend. Jocelyn will remain single or find someone else. I'll find someone else too."

"Do you remember the time when your mother left me for another man?" Xavier asked him.

"Dad, what does your bit of ancient history with my mother have to do with Jocelyn and me?" Lorenzo asked.

"Nothing," Xavier answered. "It's just when people divorce; it reminds me of that dark time."

"Yes, I remember," Lorenzo answered, as he nodded. "She left you, and you had to take care of my siblings and me for five years until she came back to you."

"That's right," Xavier said. "Simone left me for another man. We were married. I was so hurt and angry I wanted to do unspeakable things. Although she was with that man intimately and romantically, I forgave Simone."

"I miss Simone," Lorenzo said to him. "When we got older, my siblings and I were never really close to her. But I miss her."

"That's why you call her Simone instead of mom. Your mother and I talk on the phone at least twice a week," Xavier said to him. "Simone always asks me about you."

"When will she be leaving North Carolina?"

"Your mother says she wants to come back to New York. But she hasn't decided when she'll return."

"Have you been with any other women since Simone has been away?" Lorenzo asked Xavier.

"No," Xavier answered while shaking his head.

"So, you haven't dated Lydia?"

"My receptionist?"

"Yes," Lorenzo replied.

"No," Xavier answered.

"Dad, don't lie to me. I've heard rumors about you and her."

Lorenzo's lip twisted as he looked at his father. He didn't like the idea of his father messing around behind his mother's back. If those rumors were indeed true, Lorenzo hoped Xavier had the guts to tell him.

Xavier took a deep breath. "Okay, son," he said, straightening his glasses on his face as he eyed Lorenzo. "Lydia came over to my house one night wearing very provocative clothes. She had a tall bottle of *Brugal,* and she got drunk. We talked about her problems with her boyfriend. She actually told me that night she always wanted you or Silas to ask her out on a date. Of course, you and Jocelyn had married, and Silas was still with his second wife. Lydia always had a crush on you and your oldest brother. Anyway, I offered her sound advice, and she broke up with her boyfriend days later. Nothing happened between Lydia and me."

"How long ago was this?" Lorenzo asked, cracking a smile.

"Four years ago," his father answered.

"So that was rumors I heard?" Lorenzo asked Xavier. "Did you ever tell Silas about this?"

"Lorenzo, let's change the subject. How much are you going to give Jocelyn in the divorce settlement?"

"I'm not sure, father. But she'll have plenty of support. I love her too much for her not to."

****

Lorenzo was inside *The Camelot* having lunch. But he didn't have an appetite. The cheeseburger and fries fixed on a plate in front of him had been practically untouched. The gloom had remained with him since he and Jocelyn agreed to part ways. And not interacting with his daughters every single day would be something he'd have to adjust to. He'd seen them every day of their lives since the day they were born.

Lorenzo wanted to stay married to Jocelyn. It would seem like a credible thing to do since it would further the stability of Joy and Lori. But would divorcing Jocelyn truly have any effect on his daughters? To remain a happy family would be a good thing. But Jocelyn hadn't been happy, and he was mostly to blame. She certainly deserved better. He did the best he could, considering the circumstances.

"Hey there," a familiar voice said from over him. "You, okay?"

Lorenzo looked up and saw Eboni smiling down at him. He smiled back at her. Lorenzo hadn't seen Eboni for weeks. Her kinky hair was down around her shoulders. The red lipstick she was wearing shined on her lips. She wasn't wearing any other make-up on her face, but she still looked beautiful.

"Hi, Eboni," Lorenzo spoke.

"You, okay?" she repeated as her beautiful brown eyes gazed at him. "You look like you were somewhere else."

Lorenzo took a deep breath. "I'm going through some things," he said to her.

"Like what?"

Lorenzo didn't want to dump his problems on Eboni. "My wife and I are divorcing," he told her.

Eboni's face fell. Before he could elaborate, she took a seat at his table and placed her hand on top of his. "Are you okay?" she asked him.

"I'm dealing with it," he said. "She's also dealing with it. It was one of those situations where one priority reigned over another one. It's really no one's fault. But I accept full blame. She deserves someone who can make her happy."

"I'm very sorry to hear this," Eboni said, rubbing his hand. "I'm sorry you're going through that. What are you going to do?"

"I spend so much of my time away from home teaching martial arts. When I get home at night, I'm so exhausted. I have no energy to make love to my wife. All I want to do is sleep. She and I have talked about me reducing my workload in order to make room for our love life. But I can't. Student enrollments in all of my schools are very close to one hundred percent. All the schools will be at one hundred percent student enrollment soon. Now is not the time to get lax. I have to keep striving for success."

"Lorenzo, this is not your fault," Eboni said to him. "Marriages are challenging. Your wife shouldn't only view the sexual side of your marriage."

Eboni's words soothed him like some sort of therapy. He peered into her lovely face. His eyes moved down to her prodigious cleavage. He shamefully looked away.

"I don't want her to be miserable anymore," Lorenzo said, glancing at Eboni. "We just reached something in our marriage, and it was so monumental we couldn't overcome it."

"I'm sorry," Eboni said to him.

Lorenzo looked in all directions, focusing on the enormously exotic fish swimming about in the humongous tanks. His gaze shifted to Eboni, eyeing him with a hand on her hip. He glanced back at the entrance as a group of patrons came through the front door and took a seat at the bar.

Much to the delight of the customers and a few of the workers, the quiet speakers came to life with the calming sound of *Motown.*

Lorenzo bit into his cheeseburger and fries before they got cold. As Eboni sat there watching him, he looked at her. His eyes followed from her forehead, past her face, down to her bosom once more. His eyes met hers, and she rubbed his hand again before she stood to her feet.

"I have to get back to work," Eboni said. "I'm there for you. Let me give you my cell phone number so we can talk sometime."

"Can I ask you a question?" Lorenzo asked.

Eboni leaned forward as two of her fingernails scratched and tickled the back of his hand. Her eyebrows rose as a slow smile turned up the corners of her red embellished mouth.

"What is it?" she asked him.

Do you have a man? He wanted to ask her.

"Who does your hair?" he asked instead, smiling back at her.

"Why do you want to know?" she asked, looking at him with curiosity as the smile left her.

"Your hair is exquisite," he told her. *Beautiful, just like you,* he thought of telling her.

"Thank you!" she said, the smile returning. "A guy named Stevie who works out of a hair salon in Chelsea does my hair."

Eboni's grin reappeared as she stepped away from the table. Lorenzo watched as she headed in the bar's direction. From the back of her, he noticed her sexy legs and graceful strut. When Eboni got to the bar, Lorenzo saw her pick up an ink pen. She wrote something down on a receipt and headed back in his direction.

Why was she giving him her cell phone number? Maybe she was just friendly. More than likely, running this restaurant preoccupies her and she truly didn't have time to talk at length and wanted to continue their conversation outside of *The Camelot,* where she had more time to talk.

Eboni walked back to his table and stood over him. She grabbed his hand, opened it, and placed the piece of paper in it. She closed his hand up and stooped down. Lorenzo regarded her. He eyed her lips, her hair, and beautiful earrings. His eyes met hers, and Eboni smiled.

"Call me, okay?" she said to him. "I always work late, so I'm only available after midnight."

Lorenzo smiled back at her as he studied her eyes, thinking of the amicable kiss on the cheek she gave him the night he saved her from the armed thief. "I'll call you," he said to her.

Eboni gave him one last look before she stood up. When she did, she pulled her skirt down slightly. She turned around and walked to one server standing by the entrance of the restaurant. Lorenzo could not take his eyes off of her.

He opened his hand and saw the piece of paper Eboni had placed inside it. He eyed the number with a 347-area code written on it. Smiling, he folded it back and put it into his pants pocket.

****

"Jocelyn, someone is here to see you," the front desk manager said over Jocelyn's two-way radio.

Jocelyn dropped the pillowcase she was holding, wondering who it could be. Usually, people didn't come to where she worked to see her. The only exception had been Buck, but he arrived unannounced when he came. He had come on the elevator to the floor; she told him where she'd be, and he'd visited her.

But when Buck came, he didn't notify the front desk. So, it couldn't be him. But if it wasn't Buck, who was it? Could it be Lorenzo? Did he have a dozen roses for her? Did he come to tell her he wanted to stay married to her? She knew it wasn't likely. But what if it was? Maybe he had thought things over again and came to tell her he'd reduced his schedule after all so they wouldn't have to divorce.

Jocelyn left out of the guest room and headed down the hallway. She stopped in the middle of the hallway and quickly took the stairwell down to the lobby. When she got there, she walked towards the front desk. Two of the clerks behind the front desk pointed over to the left. Jocelyn turned around to look and saw a man standing in front of a chair in the middle of the lobby.

The man had on a red Reebok sweatshirt and denim jeans. He had a large envelope in his hand. His dark brown-skinned complexion seemed to shine. Although he was an older man, he was very handsome. As she gazed at him, Jocelyn grasped it was someone she knew but hadn't seen in a long time.

"Xavier?" Jocelyn said delightfully as she walked in his direction, placing her hands on the side of her face as she smiled. "Estoy tan feliz de verte. You are looking quite good."

Xavier took two steps towards her. "Jocelyn," he said with a smile of his own.

"What are you doing here?" Jocelyn asked curiously.

"I came here for one reason," Xavier said to her. "I want to see you and my son work things out."

Jocelyn looked around the hotel lobby and pointed towards a door straight ahead by the elevator. "Follow me," she said to Xavier.

Jocelyn led Xavier to the door, punched in a four-digit combination to unlock it, and led him inside a small room. She looked up at the countless suitcases on the shelves inside the room as the door closed behind Xavier.

"You brought me to the bellmen's closet?" he asked her.

"We needed to talk somewhere more private," Jocelyn said to him. "What's this all about, Xavier?"

"You haven't talked to Lorenzo, have you?" Xavier asked.

Jocelyn shook her head. "No, I haven't," she told him.

"So, divorce is what you both want?" he questioned

"Do we have to talk about this? I'm working."

Xavier frowned. "We do," he said. "I just wanted to know from you if there was any way you and Lorenzo could work this out?" he asked her.

Jocelyn shook her head. "We had an enormous problem with our love life," she said.

"Lorenzo told me. He says you're miserable."

Jocelyn shrugged her shoulders. "I am," she said. "We're leaning towards divorce."

"I know."

"I can't continue to suffer. Lord knows I've been patient, and I've been faithful. I just think we should get a divorce."

She saw his bushy eyebrows move upon his head. He shook his head as he looked away from her. When Jocelyn touched Xavier's arm, he forced his gaze upon her.

"But you still love my son, don't you?"

"Of course, I love him, Xavier," Jocelyn answered him, becoming straight-faced. "I've been strong. I've prayed and I've hoped Lorenzo and I could come up with some kind of compromise. We can't."

"I love you as if you were my daughter," Xavier said to her and walked away.

Jocelyn watched as Xavier stepped from out of the room back into the lobby. She followed him and stopped as he went through the entrance at the front of the hotel to outside in the street. She watched him throw the envelope he'd been holding into the trash can outside the hotel entrance before he waved a cab down. Xavier got inside the taxi, and the cab pulled off. As she wiped away an oncoming tear, she felt a gentle hand on her shoulder.

"Jocelyn, are you alright?" Crystal asked as she approached.

Jocelyn turned around and smiled at her boss. Crystal stood there, eyeing her as Jocelyn hung her head. Crystal put her arm around her and led Jocelyn out of the lobby to the stairwell Jocelyn had taken before she had met up unexpectedly with Xavier.

"What floor are you working on now?" Crystal asked her.

"Second," Jocelyn said, eyeing the woman's visage.

A sharply intriguing new rainbow-colored Emo hairstyle framed Crystal's large forehead and median looks. She wore two small looped rings on each side of her nose. Her tan checkered vest she wore overtop a black blouse fit her loosely. She wore a matching skirt with nylon stockings. Her beige high heel shoes made her seem taller than she was.

When they got to the second-floor level, Jocelyn walked to her assigned guestroom before receiving the front desk's notification over the radio. Crystal sat down on the bed and stared at Jocelyn. Jocelyn sighed and took a seat right next to her.

"What's wrong, Jocelyn?" Crystal asked, eyeing her intensely as she placed her hands behind her back.

Jocelyn put a hand over her mouth. "My husband and I are ending our six-year marriage," she said in a muffled voice.

"What do you mean?" Crystal asked with a bewildered look.

Jocelyn shook her head. She closed her eyes. She fought oncoming tears as her eyes opened. Wiping a single tear as it fell down the right side of her face, Jocelyn told Crystal everything.

Crystal put an arm around Jocelyn. "I'm sorry this happened," she said to Jocelyn. "Is there anything I can do to help?"

"Probably not," Jocelyn said to her.

"If you need to talk, I'm there for you," Crystal said as she showed Jocelyn a smile.

Jocelyn closed her eyes again as Crystal stood up. "I appreciate that," she said, her left eye slitting open as she walked over to the other bed in the room.

Jocelyn took a deep breath and looked away from Crystal. She looked straight at the window with her mind swirling.

"I'll be in my office," Crystal said and left the guest room.

Jocelyn sighed and thought of her husband. "I'll always love you, Lorenzo," she said as she headed towards the bathroom with washcloths and towels in hand.

****

Lorenzo dialed Eboni's number. As he lay on the floor looking up at the ceiling in his living room, he heard his daughters playing noisily upstairs. He could hear them running up and down the hall as Eboni's phone rang. Joy and Lori stampeded down the stairs and ran past Lorenzo on their way into the kitchen.

"Hello?" Eboni answered on the other end.

"Hi, Eboni," Lorenzo said with a smile. "How are you?"

"Excellent," said Eboni. "Who is this?"

"Lorenzo," he said to her.

There was a momentary pause on the other end. Lorenzo stifled a yawn and immediately got up when he heard something break in the kitchen. He quickly rushed into the kitchen, only to find his daughters standing over two broken plates. He snapped his fingers at them and motioned for them to go back upstairs. Joy and Lori quickly ran out of the kitchen and headed back upstairs to their room.

"It's about time you called," Eboni said. "What kept you?"

"Nothing," Lorenzo answered, knowing it was only yesterday Eboni gave him her phone number. "I take it you're home now."

"Yes, I got in about an hour ago. I'm lying here in my bed looking at the television. What are you doing up an hour after midnight?"

"Just waiting for my girls to go to sleep," Lorenzo said. "They aren't going to school tomorrow so I let them stay up."

"So, your kids aren't with your wife?" Eboni asked.

"No, they're not," Lorenzo told her. "I'll give the kids back to Jocelyn tomorrow. We've alternated with the children every day. We figured this is the best way to help them adjust to me not being around every day once she has sole custody."

"So, your children are keeping you up?"

"Yes."

"What are your daughters' names?"

"Lori and Joy."

"Those are beautiful names."

"They're twins. Joy is the oldest by four minutes."

"You've told me about your daughters before."

 "I have."

"So, what year were you born?" Eboni questioned.

"I'm thirty-four," Lorenzo answered her.

"Almost eighteen years younger than me," Eboni said. "I like your southern cadence."

"Thank you," he said to her. "Are you from New York?"

Eboni let out a light chuckle. "Detroit," she told him.

Lorenzo yawned. It had been a long day, as usual. He only taught for a half-day before taking Joy and Lori to the Bronx Zoo after school let out for them. He had brought them into Manhattan for Dominican food before heading back to the Bronx and taking them to the playground.

"Tired?" Eboni asked.

"A bit," he responded.

"Go on and get some sleep. We can talk later."

"I'm okay, really," Lorenzo said. "I'm tired but not sleepy."

"So, what were we talking about?"

"Us," Lorenzo reminded her.

"Where are you from?"

"Charlotte," said Lorenzo

"North Carolina," Eboni said. "When was the last time you were there?"

"Five years ago. I went there with my wife for a family reunion while she was pregnant with our daughters. "

"What about other places in North Carolina?" Eboni asked.

"What about other places in North Carolina?" Lorenzo asked.

"Have you been to anywhere other than Charlotte?"

"Mainly Raleigh, Winston-Salem, and Greensboro," Lorenzo answered. "My siblings and I lived in those places while my father studied to become a doctor. My dad attended several universities when I was a child. Our extended family lives in those three cities."

"How many siblings do you have, Lorenzo?"

"Ten," Lorenzo answered.

"That's an enormous family. Are you the oldest?"

"No," Lorenzo answered. "there are eleven of us. I have two older brothers and four older sisters. I also have one younger sister and three younger brothers."

"When did you come to New York?"

"We lived in San Francisco before going to New York," Lorenzo said.

"Why San Francisco?"

"It was where my father could get the highest paying job after leaving Charlotte."

"Does your family mostly comprise doctors?"

Lorenzo smiled. "No," he answered. "I have a family full of *lawyers*. Daddy Vincent practiced law all over the east coast as a young man. He was the nicest grandfather anyone could ever have. When he died, my brothers and sisters wanted to become attorneys to honor his memory."

"How beautiful," Eboni seemed to say more to herself than to Lorenzo. "This Daddy Vincent was your grandfather?"

"Not actually. He was actually my mother's grandfather. He was my *great* grandfather."

"Did you ever practice law?"

"I did for three years until I started teaching martial arts. I still take on a case sometimes. But since opening a martial arts school, I don't have time for law anymore."

"I see. Where did you go to college?"

"When we moved to New York in 2001 after leaving California, I went to Columbia University," Lorenzo said. "I graduated and went to law school at Fordham University."

"I see."

"Were you born in Detroit?" Lorenzo asked her.

"My parents were," Eboni said to him. "Thorne, my older brother, and I were born in Calgary, Alberta, Canada. My family went back to Detroit, and we lived there for seven years. Coco, my baby sister, was born there. Months later, we came here to New York City. Before I attended college, we left New York and came to Hartford, Connecticut, where my mother and father live now."

"What are you doing now?"

"Nothing," Eboni said. "I'm still in my bed."

"You want to meet me?"

"Meet you? Now? It's past One O'clock in the morning."

"If you don't want to, it's fine. I'll eventually see you another time."

"Okay. I can meet you. Are we meeting somewhere?"

"Come to my home. Normally I would come to you, but my daughters are toddlers and it's late. If it were daytime, I would come to where you are and I would bring them with me. But it's nighttime, and it's too late for my children to be out."

"I see. I can come to you. Where do you live?"

"The Bronx. Take the 4 train to Fordham Road. I'll meet you there. Where are you coming from?"

"The Upper West Side," Eboni said.

"You live on the Upper West Side?"

"Yes," Eboni answered. "But it would be easier to take a cab."

"In that case, tell the driver to take you to Bryan Park on Fordham Road. I'll be waiting."

****

Lorenzo waited patiently for Eboni's cab to arrive. After he tucked his girls into bed, he left the house to go meet up with Eboni. As a father, he knew he shouldn't be out of Joy's and Lori's vicinity for more than a second, but he knew they would be alright. He and Jocelyn would go for long walks around the neighborhood whenever the girls fell asleep. To Lorenzo, doing this was nothing new. It felt different slightly, only because Jocelyn had moved out and was no longer around.

He saw bright headlights just ahead. A New York City yellow taxi appeared, a back window rolled down, and Lorenzo watched as Eboni paid the fare. When she stepped out of the vehicle, he instantly noticed Eboni was wearing a tightly fitted green dress to go along with these knee-high black leather boots. Her hair was down past her shoulders and she wasn't wearing hardly any make-up, just like the last time he saw her.

"Hey there," Lorenzo spoke as Eboni walked towards him.

"Hey yourself," Eboni greeted him playfully.

Lorenzo smiled and placed a hand on Eboni's shoulder as they walked down Fordham Road. "When was the last time you came to the Bronx?" he asked her.

Eboni smiled. "It's been a long time," she said. "I never came to this part of the Bronx, though. I remember I used to go to Yankees games years ago."

"You're a Yankees fan?" Lorenzo asked her.

"I love the Yankees," Eboni said. "I've been a Yankees fan all my life. What's your team?"

"New York Mets," Lorenzo answered her.

Eboni laughed. "Really?" she asked.

"Yes," he answered. "My entire family are Mets fans."

"So, does your family all live here in New York?"

"Most of them live in New Jersey in North Bergen just across the Hudson River," said Lorenzo. "They can't handle the hustle and bustle of New York. So, they live in Jersey City. I have two brothers who live in Brooklyn and one of my sisters lives in Harlem."

"Where does your dad live?"

"My father lives in New Jersey in Newark."

"With your mother?"

"Normally, they would live together. But my mother stays in North Carolina. She's taking care of family members there."

"Oh. Are your parents still married?"

"Yes, for almost forty-three years."

"Wow!" Eboni exclaimed.

"Do you have any children?" Lorenzo quizzed softly.

"No," she breathed, almost sadly.

"Did I say something?"

Eboni eyed him. "Every time someone asks, I think of the babies I lost," she said to him. "I lost one child when I was eighteen and lost another six years later. Both experiences were harrowing. My mother convinced me that having children wasn't an option. So, I had a tubectomy. The first child that I was pregnant with would be your age right now."

Lorenzo's eyes met Eboni's as her hands touched her hips. Her eyes watered, but she wiped away a fallen tear as she shook her head. "So, your mother wanted you to have a tubectomy because she felt it was the right thing for you to do?" he asked.

"Not the right thing, but the best thing," Eboni said. "If I would have become gravid again and lost another child, I don't think I would have been able to cope with it. Getting my tubes tied was the best decision."

"How often do you think of children?" he asked her.

"Not as often as I used to," said Eboni, looking ahead. "But I think about kids. I would adopt a child, but I'm far too busy these days to be a parent."

Lorenzo regarded her as he folded his arms. There underneath the lamppost, he saw a few strands of grey hair he hadn't noticed before as she looked away from him. His eyes admired the charm on her face while she seemed to wince from a grievous pain from long ago. But Eboni offered him a dainty smile, and the pair continued their stroll.

They passed by a quiescent Jerome Avenue and walked toward Grand Concourse. Since it was nighttime, the traffic wasn't hectic. Lorenzo and Eboni walked to the other side of Grand Concourse and continued down Fordham Road. Smiling, Lorenzo sat down on the curb and gazed up at Eboni.

"I don't want to go too far from home," he said to her. "I have to be getting back soon, and I can't leave my girls unprotected for very long."

Eboni nodded and took a seat on the curb next to him. "I want a beer," she said, looking across the Grand Concourse as traffic sped in both directions.

"I have beer back at my house," Lorenzo said to her. "I can fix you dinner if you're hungry."

"You cook?"

"I do now," said Lorenzo. "I can fix you a big juicy steak with some beans, okra, and potatoes."

"That's awfully nice of you," Eboni said, standing up.

Lorenzo eyed her long leather boots from the ground to her knees. His eyes studied her perfect breasts and lovely face. She looked at him and smiled. Lorenzo stood up as his eyes stared into Eboni's. Eboni looked away. But her eyes found him again.

"Are you undressing me with your eyes, Lorenzo?" she asked him.

"I wouldn't call it that," Lorenzo said.

Lorenzo breathed deeply. He let it out and breathed deeply again. He let it out again. It felt like the air had more oxygen. He had abrupt butterflies in the pit of his stomach. They weren't there a second ago. These were feelings he hadn't experienced since... why was he feeling this way? It felt immediate. It felt strong.

Lorenzo looked at Eboni. Yes, Eboni. Beautiful Eboni. Gorgeous Eboni. Exceptional Eboni. Flawless Eboni. There lied the answer. He was feeling this way because of her.

"What would you call it?" Eboni asked, looking into his eyes.

"I'm looking at a lovely cutie pie," he complimented.

"Thank you," Eboni said to him.

"You're very sexy," Lorenzo said to her.

"Lorenzo!" she said, showing a helpless smile.

Lorenzo glanced at her as he retook her hand. He guided her safely across the street and headed back the way they'd come. They walked slowly until they found themselves back in Lorenzo's neighborhood. He guided Eboni to his house on Kingsbridge Road.

When they got inside, Lorenzo gestured towards the sofa. Lorenzo turned on the television in the living room and gave her the remote control before disappearing into the kitchen. He fried a huge T-Bone steak, boiled okra, microwaved kidney beans, and cooked mashed potatoes, as he promised her. Before long, Eboni's food awaited her. Lorenzo went from the kitchen to the living room to find Eboni watching a late episode of *The Family Feud.*

"Dinner is ready," he said to her. "Follow me."

Lorenzo led his guest to the living room just outside the kitchen. Eboni took a seat at the head of the table as Lorenzo pushed two Stella Artois beers in front of her plate.

"Thank you very much," Eboni said to him, smiling as her relaxed eyes looked at him. "This is extremely considerate of you. Would you join me?"

"Oh, I'm not hungry," Lorenzo said, feeling his heart soften just by looking at her. "I ate earlier before I called you."

"Well, I can't drink both beers," she said to him. "I can share one of these with you."

"Guzzle them down," Lorenzo encouraged her.

Lorenzo smiled and sat at the table diagonally across from her. Before long, she had eaten everything on her plate and finished both beers. Lorenzo stood up and offered Eboni his hand. Smiling, Eboni took it. He led her back to the living room. They sat on the sofa and looked at the television. Another episode of *The Family Feud* was on. Lorenzo peered into Eboni's eyes, knowing full well he was still holding her hand. He felt an extraordinary yet powerful pull towards her.

"I've noticed the way you look at me whenever you come to my restaurant," Eboni said softly, removing her hand from inside his. "I know you're attracted to me."

Lorenzo nodded and stood in a martial art fighting stance. He looked down at her. His facial expression is unique and a lot more serious. "You want me to teach you how to defend yourself?" he asked.

Eboni gazed up into his eyes, stood to her feet, and quickly emulated the fighting stance he was showing her. Lorenzo got behind her and swept at her feet with his own in order to widen her stance. He stood in front of her, facing the front door. He looked behind him, removed his shirt, and tossed it across the room.

"Just watch me," he told her.

"Okay," she said.

Lorenzo got back into his stance, bent his knees, and brought his fists towards his abdomen. He threw a series of right hooks before stepping forward and extending his left leg. He threw a front kick, moved his left arm upward as if he was blocking an attack, and followed by throwing a side right kick.

"Now, you try it," Lorenzo suggested to her. "These moves are not even the linguistics of Wushu or its conundrums. This is just using your limbs to strike."

Eboni bent her knees, brought her fists below her breasts, and attempted one right hook after another. She stepped forward, extended her left leg as high as she could, and kicked forward. She lifted her left arm upward. As she tried to kick to the side with her right leg, she lost her balance. Eboni stumbled sideways as Lorenzo grabbed both of her wrists. Her hand reached for Lorenzo's muscular forearm, and as she fell backward, she accidentally pulled him down with her. Before she knew it, Eboni was lying down with her back to the floor, and Lorenzo was sitting on her stomach as he looked down at her.

He loosened his grip on her wrists as she held onto his forearm. They gazed at one another for a moment as Lorenzo ran a finger down and up her arm. He stopped and brought his hand up to her shoulder. The back of his hand caressed her neck. Eboni closed her eyes in response. Before she could open her eyes, she felt the back of his hand caressing the side of her face.

As Lorenzo's head moved down towards her, Eboni's head moved up to meet him. Their lips kissed softly. Lorenzo placed a hand on the back of her head as Eboni begged another. Their lips greeted one another again. Lorenzo reached under her dress and instantly massaged the back of her leg. Their lips touched thrice in a whirlwind kiss, and Eboni lifted herself up and pushed Lorenzo off of her.

"What are we doing?" she quizzed him. "I should ask, *what am I doing?*"

"What?" Lorenzo asked.

"Lorenzo, you're married!" she said, seeing the hulk-sized muscles on his body.

"I know," came his respectful reply.

"I don't drink another woman's cup of tea!" Eboni vocalized with serious conviction. "Never!"

Lorenzo eyed her bewilderedly for an infinitesimal moment. A smile touched his lips as he looked at Eboni. "You're right," he said to her, nodding his head. "I'm supposed to be teaching you a few martial arts moves. I'm sorry."

"Don't be," Eboni said, eyeing his sexy six-pack.

Eboni placed a hand on her hip. She closed her eyes and smiled. She took a deep breath and walked over to the sofa. Eboni sat down, put a hand to her forehead, and crossed her legs. She looked towards Lorenzo as he put his shirt back on. Lorenzo disappeared upstairs and came back quickly with a small green box in his hand. He gave it to her.

Curious, Eboni tore open the small box and looked down at a beautiful gold necklace. It displayed an engraved yin and yang symbol.

"Thank you, Lorenzo," Eboni told him as he sat on the sofa next to her.

Lorenzo leaned back and closed his eyes. Eboni gazed into the television screen, took her boots off, and put her feet up on the sofa. She placed her head on the arm of the sofa as his eyes blinked. Before both of them knew it, they had drifted off to sleep.

Eight

Chapter 8

"I love Lorenzo more than life itself," Jocelyn said, turning in her husband's direction and seeing him looking at her with a slight frown on his face.

Their marriage counselor, a short petite Peruvian woman named Martina with blonde cornrows, sat calmly behind her desk asking Jocelyn and Lorenzo questions about their feelings about one another. Jocelyn knew by the look on Lorenzo's face the two of them belonged together. They were perfect for each other. She knew he had been a devoted husband in every sense of the word.

"How do you feel about Jocelyn, Lorenzo?" Martina asked him.

"I love Jocelyn," Lorenzo said, looking away from Jocelyn. "At first I thought she would understand I had to work and hustle in order to take care of her and our family. Our sex life has suffered. But I feel she should be able to hold out no matter what."

"Lorenzo, you know I've always been a passionate person. You should have known it would cause a problem once your workload increased."

"Jocelyn, you're my wife. You know I'm trying to build a noble enterprise. You refuse to see the greater good."

Jocelyn frowned. She took a deep breath and eyed Lorenzo. "So, what am I supposed to do? Wait twenty or thirty years from now when you retire to rekindle a normal sex life with you?"

"Didn't we agree to divorce because of this?" Lorenzo asked. "Why are we even arguing? Why are we even here?"

"We're here to find out if we can truly solve this problem, so divorce doesn't become an option," Jocelyn said, sticking her neck out towards him as she stomped her foot on the floor. "I've always felt a deep, binding emotional connection with you, Lorenzo. I love you so extremely much and that alone prevented me from committing adultery. I've come very close a few times but because of the profound feelings I have for you and my deep respect, I didn't do it. My emotional connection to you means more. But I can no longer tolerate this physical neglect from you."

"My grandfather Xavier Royal Sr. was a goat herder, a fisher, and a hunter. He stayed away from my grandmother for days at a time. This was never an issue with them."

"Lorenzo, just stop it!" Jocelyn exclaimed, raising her voice.

Lorenzo stood up from out of the chair he was sitting in and walked around the office, looking at several beautifully artistic paintings on the wall. Jocelyn studied him. He seemed irritable to her as if he truly wanted to be somewhere else. Or maybe he tires of sitting next to her.

"I work hard to pay the bills, pay for the food, and keep a roof over her head because this is what a husband should do," Lorenzo said, a smile appearing on his face. "I learned this from my father. He raised eleven children."

"Okay," Martina said.

"How many women have a husband to protect and provide for them that would actually complain?" Lorenzo asked Martina, pointing towards Jocelyn as his eyes found her. "A lot of married people don't even have sex. I take responsibility for working all the time, and I'm also sorry for *not* fulfilling your needs. As I've told you before, I work long and hard in order to secure Joy's and Lori's future. The money I fight and claw for puts them in Ivy League colleges after they finish high school and to make us financially comfortable."

"I'm sorry for not being as understanding as you would like for me to be," Jocelyn said to him.

Jocelyn told Lorenzo a week ago she wanted to work things out, but both of them knew it was of little use. She had persuaded him to come to a marriage counselor's office in Corona, Queens, not too far from where she had been staying.

"You should be able to understand why I work so hard and so long, Jocelyn," Lorenzo said to her. "Sex isn't everything."

"It is to me! Do you realize how much closer to you I've always felt after we've made love?" Jocelyn yelled, shaking as her eyes damn near popped out of her head. "You literally cut off our love supply on purpose!"

"You don't understand, I'm just trying to be an upstanding father and husband," Lorenzo said to Jocelyn.

Jocelyn shook her head. "Upstanding husbands and fathers don't look at dirty magazines."

Lorenzo's eyes beamed at his wife. "So, what if I do?" he asked her.

"You gave those models more attention than you gave me," Jocelyn said to him.

"I didn't," Lorenzo said back to her. "You're lying now."

"So, you're not denying it."

"Yes, I had nude magazines because I didn't feel like having sex all the time."

"So, were you messing with anyone behind my back?"

"No, I wasn't," Lorenzo told her, shaking his head.

Martina looked at both of them as Jocelyn placed her head in her hands and shook her head.

"Lorenzo, are you attracted to someone other than Jocelyn now?" she asked in a relaxed tone of voice. "The question deserves to be asked here."

Lorenzo smiled at Martina and eyed Jocelyn. "I am," he admitted.

"Has your attraction to this other woman affected your love life with Jocelyn?" Martina asked him.

"No, it hasn't. My workload alone has affected my love life with Jocelyn."

"When was the last time you guys had sex?" Martina asked them, standing up.

"Just over a month ago," Jocelyn said. "We made love in the kitchen."

"I truly wanted to have sex with her more, but----."

Jocelyn stood up and cut Lorenzo off. "Are you kidding me?" she asked. "You were emotionally and sexually unavailable for months! Stop your lying!"

"Jocelyn, we've been through this!" Lorenzo exclaimed, closing his eyes. "I have to work long and hard in order to provide for my family!"

"A weak excuse!" Jocelyn retorted angrily, sitting back down.

"How could I be at fault for trying to provide for my family?" he asked, opening his eyes and looking at Jocelyn.

Jocelyn folded her arms as she rolled her eyes at him. "You just don't get it," she said to him.

"You actually want me to be sorry for that?" he asked her.

"Not exactly, Lorenzo. What I want from you is to admit to me and to yourself you don't care about sex life with me."

Lorenzo shook his head. "You know that's not true!" he yelled.

"Yes, it is true!"

Lorenzo looked at Martina and Jocelyn. Jocelyn could see the obvious frustration and the strain on his face of him continually defending himself to her. "I can't do this anymore," he said to her.

"Lorenzo, I'm sorry!" Jocelyn shouted.

The room filled with silence. Martina and Jocelyn were both looking at Lorenzo. But Lorenzo appeared to stare into the wall by the door as they awaited a retort from him. His tortured gaze disappeared.

"Lorenzo, Jocelyn apologized to you," Martina said, walking around her desk.

Lorenzo bit his bottom lip and shook his head. He pounded both of his fists on Martina's desk as his eyes found Jocelyn. "I love you, Joce-lyn," he said, stepping quietly towards the door. "I can't be with you. It's better if we both go our separate ways and start over with a clean slate. What did we think we would accomplish by coming here? We had already agreed to end our marriage."

"I know," Jocelyn told him. "I was desperately hoping we could save our marriage. Now I see it's not possible."

Jocelyn's heart skipped a beat as she peered directly behind Martina's desk at a large framed aerial view of Skellig Michael on the wall.

"This has been really stressful," Lorenzo said. He looked at his wife. "Jocelyn, I'm tired of going through the discussion of me being sexually unavailable. This isn't getting us anywhere."

Jocelyn quickly stood to her feet as she wiped her tears. "You're right," she said to him. "We should end this."

"You can have custody of Lori and Joy. I'll pay you alimony and child support. But the house remains with me. You'll be hearing from my sister Olivia in a matter of days."

Lorenzo opened the office door and walked out. Jocelyn's bottom lip quivered when she closed her eyes, fell to her knees, and shrieked as she buried her face in the blue carpet on the floor.

Her life with him was nothing more than a memory now. Despite being married to him for six years, did she ever really know him?

It took Jocelyn an hour before she could get up.

****

*

The wind blew, lifting the crumpled leaves and sending them into the direction of Church Street. The bumper-to-bumper traffic in both direc-tions had been mainly because of a head-on collision between two auto-mobiles in the center of the nearest intersection. A whistle blew from the female traffic guard as she motioned for pedestrians to cross. The irritat-ing sounds of different horns blasted and roared amid the frantic scene of impatient drivers cursing and swearing as they sat frustrated in unmoving traffic.

As Lorenzo watched the unfortunate event, he saw Olivia walking with a group of pedestrians as they made it safely across the street. He waved his hand in the air, and when she spotted him, she rushed over.

"You sure picked a noisy spot," she irritably said to him.

His older sister appeared casually. She wore a simple white blouse and a long black skirt with white pinstripes. She wore simple black slippers. A brown briefcase was in her right hand. Her lengthy silky dreadlocks, as she always had on display, hid beneath a sizable black bucket hat as he took in the sight of her winsome face.

"Tribeca Park is usually quiet during this time of day," Lorenzo said, walking toward a bench.

Lorenzo sat down. Olivia sat next to him and looked at him with a blank stare. A smile touched her lips.

"So, what happened in the marriage counselor's office?" Olivia asked.

"Jocelyn and I couldn't come to a resolution," Lorenzo told her, smirking as he shook his head. "I think the right thing to do is to grant her a divorce. She and I have talked about it before, anyway."

"What was the problem, Lorenzo?"

"A lack of a sex life," he told her, still smirking as he watched two squirrels run up a nearby tree. "With trying to expand my business, and my schools growing greater and greater in clientele, I just didn't have time for Jocelyn. I wanted to gross a couple of million dollars before I hired more instructors and stepped away from teaching for a while. But Jocelyn wouldn't have it."

"I'm sorry, Lorenzo," Olivia said, eyeing him sadly. "I remember the day you and Jocelyn got married. You looked so happy. It pains me deeply that you and she are parting ways."

Lorenzo looked up into the grey, cloudy sky. There was a ray of sunlight trying to peep through. Abruptly, he felt a raindrop hit his nose as he thought about Jocelyn. Lorenzo hung his head, sniffed the air. Despondently, he rested his head on his forearm. Soon Olivia was leaning over him, holding Lorenzo with her chin on his shoulder as she rubbed his back.

"You love her, don't you?" Olivia asked him.

Lorenzo wept a moment longer, wiped his tears, and held his head high. "Yes," he answered her.

"Are you sure you want to get a divorce?"

Olivia looked right at him- sort of right through him. Lorenzo shook his head repeatedly and peeked away as they heard a clap of thunder.

"It's the right thing to do," he told Olivia, forcing a smile to his face. "Jocelyn's unhappy. If she's frustrated and displeased, it would be unfair of me to request her to wait until I'm finished building my martial arts franchise. Jocelyn is a wonderful woman who deserves to have someone who can accommodate her. I can't right now."

Olivia nodded as she dried Lorenzo's tears with her hand. "What are the stipulations for a divorce between you and her?" she asked, crossing her legs as she forced a smile to her own face.

"Jocelyn gets the children, I get the house, I pay child support until the kids are eighteen, and I'll give Jocelyn alimony."

"I see." Olivia's face became expressionless. "I'll file a petition with the Bronx County court. The petition will state the grounds for divorce. It could take up to three to five months until you get a court date."

Lorenzo nodded as his melancholy ethos returned. "Okay, Olivia," he said as he stood up.

Olivia got to her feet. "Will you be, okay?" she asked him.

"Olivia, I'm a big boy," Lorenzo assured her. "I'll be fine."

Olivia put her briefcase on the bench. She wrapped her arms around him in a warm clinging. She picked up her briefcase and stepped away from him.

As she walked away, Lorenzo watched her go. He felt two drops of rain hit his face again. As he watched Olivia get into the back seat of a taxicab on Church Street, a clap of thunder sounded. He took his eyes from off of the cab, becoming drenched in the unforeseen heavy showers, the rain hitting the ground, appearing as innumerable dimes in the street.

Nine

Chapter 9

Eboni reached for the bottom lock. As she secured the heavy door, she smiled. As soon as she turned around, she saw a masked bandit with a nickel-plated firearm. Shivering fear crippled her. As she looked in both directions of Mott Street, she threw a punch to the side of the thug's head. The man stumbled backward. When Eboni implemented the right-sidekick that Lorenzo had shown her, she followed up with a front kick to his chin, and the bandit fell to the ground.

The gunman quickly scrambled to his feet. Just as he aimed his revolver at Eboni, she side kicked him again on the side of his neck. Her right elbow smashed down on his wrists and the gun fumbled from the criminal's grasp, and as he threw a straight punch at her, she intercepted it in the palm of her right hand. Eboni lifted her foot and delivered another front kick to the side of his ribs. As she watched him wince in pain, Eboni circled around him. The robber disappeared and a split second later his gun vanished....

Eboni fell out of the bed and bumped her head on the floor. Her right hand touched the side of her head. The volume of her hard breathing echoed just barely over the sound of her heart pounding inside her chest. She stood up and sat on the edge of the bed. As her breathing slowed, she discerned the dream she was having of being robbed at gunpoint was reoccurring.

But in this last one, she had fought her mugger back. But why was she having different variations of the same dream stemming from an actual occurrence?

"I won't be seeing him again," Eboni whispered silently to herself.

****

An ocean of pedestrians flooded Mercer Street. Just up the street, there was a festival of some sort taking place. South of Houston was always busy. Today Mercer and the surrounding streets throughout the neighborhood were unusually active and loud. Nearby, about a block away on Prince Street, a fair was taking place.

As Eboni walked inside *The Jaguar Lounge,* the latest song quickly swallowed the *sounds of the noisy streets up* by The Fray. As she stood at the entrance, she saw the bar wasn't busy. Only three people sat at the bar with a drink of some sort in front of them. Eboni would always come here to have a drink every Wednesday before she opened up her restaurant.

Farther back to the side, a restroom door opened and Eboni saw a familiar man walking out onto the main floor. He walked in her direction seemingly and took a seat at the end of the bar. Smiling, she recalled falling asleep on his sofa just weeks ago in a beautiful house in a Bronx neighborhood she had never been to before.

Eboni walked up to Lorenzo and placed her hand warmly on his shoulder. He gazed up at her and smiled. Pulling up a barstool next to him, she caught sight of anguish and melancholy on his face. It appeared Lorenzo was uptight or immensely distressed about something.

"Eboni," he said.

"Lorenzo, are you alright?" she asked curiously, placing her hand on top of his and rubbing it as she sometimes did.

"Why do people end up with the wrong people?" he asked her, as his speech slurred. "Why is it people have to get divorced so much these days? Why can't they have a marriage of longevity like their parents and grandparents?"

Eboni looked at him. Lorenzo appeared sullen and lost. She didn't have the answers to the complicated questions he asked her, but Eboni knew something was wrong and it must have had a lot to do with this woman Lorenzo was married to.

"Bartender, another shot of whiskey, please!" Lorenzo said aloud.

"Lorenzo, what's troubling you?" Eboni asked him gently.

"Jocelyn and I are divorcing," he said, the words spilling out. "She calls me and wants me to come to some marriage counselor's office in Queens. I agree to discuss our marriage. She needs someone to be more sexual. I need her to understand how much my personal goals mean to me. We had agreed to end the marriage. We struggled to find some common ground just to see if there was any way of us staying together. There wasn't."

Eboni took a deep breath. "Divorce?" she asked him.

"Yes," said Lorenzo.

The bartender placed a shot glass of Maker's Mark in front of Lorenzo. Smiling, Lorenzo took the glass and threw it back like it was nothing. He slammed the shot glass on the bar and looked at her. For a moment Eboni wondered how many shots he had. Whenever he came to her restaurant, Lorenzo never ordered shots. Maybe this was his way of trying to forget his marital misfortunes.

As she watched Lorenzo, she wondered if he would cry. He looked so sad and full of emotional turmoil. She couldn't even know what he was going through.

"I poured my heart and soul into that marriage!" he told her aloud, slapping his hand on top of the bar. "To work as hard as I did and to come up so short. It seems like the last six years of my life were for nothing."

"It's not the end of the world," Eboni said, smiling at him when he peered at her.

"What are you doing here?" he asked, looking her in the eye.

Eboni watched as Lorenzo seemed to undress her with his eyes like he sometimes did. He regarded her cleavage for a few seconds and eyed her glistening legs. She knew she must've looked good today because she received a few compliments on her way over here.

"I stop by here from time to time to get a drink before I open up shop," said Eboni, seeing Lorenzo's eyes had met hers again. "Why are you here?"

"I was putting up some martial arts school fliers around the neighborhood before heading to Chinatown and felt I needed a few drinks and shots," Lorenzo said to her.

"What will it be, Miss?" the bartender asked her.

"I'll have a Bloody Mary," Eboni said to the bartender.

The bartender quickly fixed her drink and placed it on a napkin in front of her. She paid for the beverage, eyed Lorenzo, lifted her drink, and sipped it. Sliding her arm around him, she scooted her stool closer to him. He looked at her and took a few deep breaths.

"Are you really okay, Lorenzo?" she asked him.

"I'm fine," he told her, a smile appearing on his face.

As she gazed ahead, she felt something moist on the side of her face. Her head turned in Lorenzo's direction. Her eyes looked at him as a smile touched her lips. The gentle kiss on her cheek he'd just given her made the room spin rapidly as if she were a little girl on a speedy merry-go-round.

"What was that for?" she asked him.

"You gave me a kiss on the cheek before, so I wanted to do the same," Lorenzo said.

"But why?" she asked with a grin as the spinning room seemed to slow down.

Lorenzo stumbled as he got up, took hold of Eboni's hand, and lifted her up from off of the stool. He stepped closer to her until her breasts touched his chest. He gently placed her face in his hands and kissed her lips. Eboni studied him, smelling the fresh stench of alcohol on his breath as he smiled at her.

"Because your beauty is intimidating, and because I like you a lot," Lorenzo confessed to her, feeling what she perceived as his nervous heartbeat pulsating against her breasts.

Lorenzo smooched her bottom lip, forced his tongue into her

mouth, and kissed her passionately. Eboni trembled as her mind went blank. She took part in the kiss and slithered her own tongue around in his mouth. The breaking of a glass snapped them both from their tender moment.

Lorenzo looked to the floor and pointed. "You dropped your glass and broke it," he said to her.

Lorenzo's devastating kiss had knocked Eboni out. She gazed up at him and reached inside her purse for three five-dollar bills. She threw the cash on the bar, grabbed Lorenzo by the hand, and walked outside.

The noisy streets filled Eboni's ears again. People were screaming. Music was playing. Sirens sounded. The noise was deafening. Eboni walked Lorenzo down three blocks until the noise seemed to quiet down. When she turned to face him, she looked up at him.

"Do you know what you're saying?" she asked him.

Lorenzo smiled. "I want you," he said as his speech slurred.

"Lorenzo, I like you a lot," Eboni said as people walked hurriedly past them. "Let's not rush into anything."

Eboni felt an uncontrollable warmth in the pit of her stomach. She eyed him, seeing his eyes looking from her and down the street.

"What do you mean?" Lorenzo asked her breasts.

"I---," she began, but she saw he was too drunk to understand anything she said, and tomorrow or the day afterward Lorenzo probably wouldn't remember bumping into her today.

Eboni felt his lips on her cheek again. The sound of his smooch was eccentrically stentorian. She could hear her heart blasting inside her chest as her breathing quickened. In an instant she looked down at both of her hands, watching them as they quacked.

Please do it again! Eboni thought. *Maybe I should kiss his cheek too!*

She quickly peered down at her watch. It was a little past noon and Eboni looked at him. She had to get to her restaurant to open it up.

"We'll have to continue this later, Lorenzo," she said and hurried toward Mott Street.

****

Stuart was playing the violin as patrons left from out of the front door. Staff members were standing around talking. The bartenders were counting money, and several chefs were all sitting around the bar having a drink or two. Eboni walked towards the entrance of *The Camelot* and placed her hand on the lock. Just as she was going to bolt the door, she saw Lorenzo approaching the door with a box of Godiva chocolates in one hand and a beautiful white rose in the other. Smiling, she opened the door for him and let him inside.

"You just made it," Eboni said.

He was wearing a beige three-piece suit with a black dress shirt opened at the collar. He had on dark shades but it was nighttime now and unless he wore them to look cool; she didn't see the logic in him having them over his eyes. Lorenzo also displayed a smile, appearing far happier than he was earlier in the day when she last saw him. From the looks of it, Lorenzo was sober, like she was used to seeing.

He removed the shades from his face as he stood in front of her. "You look beautiful tonight, cutie pie," he told her.

Eboni smiled. "Thank you," she said. "Do you remember bumping into me at the *Jaguar Lounge* earlier today?"

"No," he told her. "We saw each other today?"

"You were very drunk," said Eboni.

If he didn't remember seeing her less than twelve hours ago, he certainly remembered nothing they said to each other. It was too bad Lorenzo didn't remember telling her he wanted her. Eboni knew Lorenzo liked her. The way he looked at her body sometimes, she could tell.

"I was?" he asked her.

"You kissed me and told me you wanted me," Eboni said. "You were going through something because of the situation with your wife."

"Soon to be ex-wife," Lorenzo put in. "The fact of the matter is I like you, Eboni. I wish you were my sweetheart."

Eboni smiled. But her smile soon disappeared as Lorenzo quickly stepped into her personal space. He kissed her lips gently. Her entire body shook as perspiration flooded her face. Her heart skipped a beat as she closed her eyes. Eboni turned around to see if any of her workers were looking at her. They were all talking amongst themselves and hadn't noticed.

"This is for you," Lorenzo pronounced, handing her the box of chocolates along with the exquisite white rose.

"Thank you very much," Eboni said to him as she received his gifts.

A chef came to Eboni with a burger and French fries on a large plate. She took it and eyed Lorenzo as the chef walked off.

"Lorenzo, I have something very important I want to tell you," she said, looking up at him.

His cell phone started ringing. Lorenzo pulled his cellular phone from his pants pocket and answered it.

"Yes, angel," he was saying to whoever it was he was talking to. "Daddy will be home in a little while. Just fix some cereal and watch cartoons. Daddy will be home soon. Okay. Bye-bye."

"Your kids?" Eboni asked.

"My daughter, Joy," he said, placing his phone back in his pocket. "She and her sister are waiting for me to come home. I hired a baby sister to watch over them. They both miss their daddy."

"Lorenzo, we need to talk," Eboni said to him. "Follow me to my office."

She smiled while securing the door to the restaurant. Eboni turned around and headed towards the stairs. As they both climbed the stairs, Eboni could feel Lorenzo's hand land on her shoulder. When they got upstairs, they walked down a short, narrow passageway until Eboni came to a stop at a door in the middle of the hallway. She opened it, held the door for Lorenzo, and turned the light on when they both walked inside a bright office.

"Have a seat," Eboni said to him as she sat at her desk.

Lorenzo flopped down into a comfy leather chair in front of her desk. "What do we need to talk about, Eboni?" he asked her.

"It's about me," she said as she saw Lorenzo get up.

He seemed to look around her office as he walked over to a window with a plant on the window seal. He picked up a tall bottle of brandy that was next to the plant and looked at it.

Eboni walked to the closet and grabbed a royal purple blanket from the top shelf and spread it out in the middle of the room. She went behind her desk, grabbed ahold of five candles inside a glass casing, along with a lighter, and placed the candles farther apart on top of the sheet. She lit each candle as she smiled.

"Come join me," she offered.

"What about you?" he asked her as he opened the bottle.

Lorenzo sat in the lotus position in front of her and studied the beautiful office. He looked down at the candlelight as Eboni watched him.

Eboni placed the box of chocolate candy, the rose, and plate of food on the sheet covering the floor and sat down.

"Hit the lights," Eboni told Lorenzo.

He immediately unscrewed the top and put the bottle of brandy to his lips. He closed his eyes at the strength of the liquor. Lorenzo got up and walked over to the entrance. He turned the overhead lighting down low. The candlelight lit the room halfway. Eboni gazed at their shadows on the wall behind her desk.

"We should have a drink while we talk and eat," Lorenzo suggested.

Eboni got up and walked over to the closet. She reached for two glasses from off of the top shelf and took them over to a little brown freezer on the other side of the room by the window and opened it. She retrieved an ice tray, cracked the ice, and placed several ice cubes into both glasses. Eboni slowly walked over to Lorenzo. Lorenzo poured her a full glass of brandy and poured himself an equivalent amount.

"What's on your mind?" Lorenzo asked her as they both sat down on the sheet close to one another.

"I'm interested in martial arts," Eboni said as she removed her open-toe high heels she was wearing.

Lorenzo took two bubbles of his drink, finishing it quickly. He poured himself another glass and began sipping on it. "Is that what you wanted to tell me?" he asked Eboni.

"Yes," she said to him.

She watched as he gulped down his second full glass, while she hadn't even taken one sip of hers yet. Lorenzo poured himself a third glass. Eboni tore the cheeseburger and gave half of it to Lorenzo.

"Why are you interested in martial arts?" he asked, taking a bite.

Eboni's eyes blinked. "The way you came to my defense that night," she said, remembering the incident and the related dreams which followed. "After you taught me just a minute's worth of kung fu inside your living room, it boosted my confidence. It felt like I took a step into a bigger world."

Lorenzo smiled fondly at her. To Eboni, he seemed so relaxed and comfortable. She took her eyes off of him as she grabbed the other half of her cheeseburger.

"With time and intense training, you'll have your black belt," he said as he scooted closer to her.

"Really?" Eboni questioned in a disbelieving tone as she gaped at him.

Lorenzo smiled as he eyed her. He placed his chin on her shoulder. Eboni rested her head on his. Lorenzo put his arm around her as Eboni took a few sips of the alcoholic beverage. Her glass slipped from her grasp as she stood up on her knees and faced him. She gazed down into his calm stare. Her eyes focused on his ebony lips. Those lips found hers in a warm, passionate kiss that seemed to last forever.

"So, despite being married to this lady, Jocelyn, you have no trouble admiring other women?"

Lorenzo nodded. "Yes," he answered. "I mean no."

Lorenzo took her by the hand and gently rubbed her knuckles. Her heart throbbed as she bit her bottom lip.

"How do you feel about those that will condemn you for loving me?" Eboni asked, seeing his finger traced along the back of her hand. "They will criticize us for our age gap relationship."

"The only person who would condemn us is my father," Lorenzo said to her, his hazel eyes sparkling in the dimmed office. "Maybe my mother as well. But my father, for sure."

Eboni stared at him. The way he looked at her seemed so over-friendly. His eyes remained glued to her. His smile appeared so pleasing to her. She didn't know what he was thinking or what he was feeling, but he had set aflame her heart today. The small flame had spread into a raging inferno all throughout her being.

"Eboni, you're a Queen to me," Lorenzo confessed to her. "You're a goddess. And a Queen and a goddess are more than worthy of my adoration and protection. Only two women rule my world- my mother Simone and now you."

The beam of candlelight flashed before her as Lorenzo embraced her and kissed her again. Eboni's heart raced as she lay on top of him. They devoured each other with blissful, yet hungry kisses. She wrapped her arms around him as he looked up at her. Her lips and tongue journeyed down his neck. Lorenzo moaned in pleasure as he caressed the small of Eboni's back.

They lifted themselves up and sat. As she stared into his eyes, she felt the wildfire raging within her again. But it disappeared. She saw a playful calm in his eyes as he looked back at her.

Lorenzo took off his beige blazer and unbuttoned his shirt. Eboni licked the insides of her mouth as she combed his chiseled chest with her eyes. Butterflies swirled in her tummy, and her eyes closed at the abrupt, fierce excitement she sometimes felt whenever Lorenzo was near her. She kept her eyes shut until she regained total control of her emotions.

Eboni peered down and spotted the white rose and *Godiva* chocolates he had given her. She tore the plastic from around the box. Lorenzo took the lid off of the box of chocolates, reached into the box, and grabbed three chocolates. He gently stuffed them into her mouth as she held the white rose.

****

"Bedroom life," Xavier said as he looked around the South Street Seaport with a straight face, his hands behind his back as the wind blew Jocelyn's long hair into his face. "I know to some people sex is a big deal. Some couples don't engage in it."

"But most do," Jocelyn said to him. "I need someone who will take care of my needs, and Lorenzo needs someone who can look past his workaholic ways."

"Two of my other children have divorced - my daughter Dana and my son Silas. Out of my eleven children, only my youngest son Vernon has never married."

"People can stay married for years before they find out they aren't right for each other," Jocelyn said, shaking her head as she thought of Lorenzo.

"Jocelyn, you and Lorenzo *were* right for each other. You two just ran into a situation you both couldn't overcome."

"I suppose."

Xavier could see the bitter disappointment on Jocelyn's face. It was the anguish blended in with a rigorous letdown of a failed marriage, and it was nobody's fault. It was the strained result of two people who loved each other, but the steps they took to make their marriage ultimately succeed were different. Jocelyn saw only the short term. Lorenzo saw nothing but the long term. Jocelyn wanted Lorenzo to be everything to her in the present. Lorenzo wanted Jocelyn to wait until the future when everything would be grand and full of total comfort. They saw different things and wanted different things.

Xavier and Jocelyn caught sight of a dozen crows soaring through the air. They blended in with the six large seagulls flying in the opposite direction. Xavier walked to the edge of the seaport and gazed out into the East River. Jocelyn walked up beside him and saw a few bobwhites walking around in the dirt as they chirped. She wished she had breadcrumbs or a few worms to feed them, but she didn't.

"Will you be heading back to Puerto Rico to rejoin your family after the divorce proceedings, Jocelyn?" Xavier asked her.

Xavier looked at Jocelyn. Her appearance struggled to maintain joy, and he could see clearly her countenance was lamenting.

"No," she answered. "I want to stay right here. I love New York. Life is grand where I am."

Ten

Chapter 10

"I'm thinking of having a silicone injection operation," Eboni said as she looked Lorenzo in the eye.

He peered at her for a moment before returning his gaze to his plate of chicken, rice, and asparagus. Regarding her, he grabbed his chalice filled with white wine and placed it to his lips. He took several sips and focused into his plate again. This was the first time she had mentioned to him her intentions to have a bigger butt.

"Did you hear what I just said?" Eboni asked him.

"I heard you," he said to her as he placed his chalice on a napkin in front of him. "I was just thinking of something to say."

They were out on a date at *Al Di La Trattoria*, a beautifully exquisite restaurant in the upscale neighborhood of Park Slope. Living way up in the Bronx, Lorenzo told her he didn't have time to come to Brooklyn as much as he wanted, although he had a martial arts school in Bedstuy. Eboni didn't get to Brooklyn much either. She always worked every day and never took a day off except for her birthday and perhaps a day or two during the year in between.

"Well?" she asked.

"Does it really make much difference?" Lorenzo asked her, cocking an eyebrow. "Your perfect breasts, sexy legs, and pretty face overshadow your horizontal ass."

A smile touched Eboni's lips, and she chucked. "Is that supposed to be funny? Describing my ass as horizontal? I just want to have this operation," she said. "It means so much to me."

"Yeah, but why?" he asked her. "Truthfully, I don't think you need it. I like you the way you are. Besides, silicone is poisonous. Sometimes these types of surgeries can backfire. I wouldn't want something to go wrong and you end up mutilated."

"I've thought about that too," Eboni answered back.

"Why don't you like your ass?"

Eboni nodded. "Obviously it's too narrow," she said.

"No, it isn't," said Lorenzo. "It's fine just the way it is."

"You really think so?" she asked him.

"It's your body," he said, poking at a slice of chicken with his fork. "I have no say-so in the matter."

For as long as she had been an adult, Eboni loved the way she looked. She enjoyed the compliments from many men over the years. But she just never liked her butt. Her natural breasts caught stares whenever she walked down any New York City street. But she felt she was lacking something else.

"Can I ask you a question?" Eboni asked him.

"You can ask me anything," Lorenzo said to her.

"If you could choose whether I got silicone injections, which would you choose?" Eboni questioned.

"It's your body," he repeated, his cheerful grin now appearing.

"That's not what I asked you, Lorenzo," she said irritably.

"I would prefer you not do it," he said to her.

"Why?"

"Eboni, if you eat plenty of meat and potatoes and work on your glutes at the gym, you would have an amazing gluteus maximus."

Eboni stared at him. He hadn't looked at her since she brought up her pending operation. Judging by the slightly sullen look on his face, he didn't want to discuss this at dinner. Her gaze narrowed to the grey shirt and matching bowtie he was wearing.

"Lorenzo, how did you become so tough and so brave?" Eboni asked him, changing the subject.

His eyes gazed at her. A smile appeared on his face. She heard a chuckle from him as he looked away from her. His eyes gazed at her cleavage just for a moment to where her beige vest fit her loosely. She wore compatible slacks along with casual black flats. Her made-up face made her appear amazingly glamorous. Eboni styled her hair in a rare fashion, an upswept ponytail, instead of her usual kinky strands.

"I'm not really tough," he told her, looking down into his plate once again. "I have a lot of fortitude. You can mistake that with being tough."

"It just seems like you have no fear," Eboni said, smiling at him.

"They taught me fear is your opponent. Fear is an avowed enemy to us. Long before I entered a dojo, my great grandfather Daddy Vincent taught me not to have fear."

"How did he teach you to be fearless?" Eboni asked.

Lorenzo's eyes connected with her again. "When I was four years old, Daddy Vincent would take my siblings and me hunting with him. We would leave Charlotte and head to West Virginia. We would climb Spruce Mountain during the day and go camping afterward. At night while my sisters stayed with a female guide and listened to stories around the campfire, a male guide, and Daddy Vincent would take me and my five brothers on a trip far up into the sky."

Eboni smiled and looked at him. Lorenzo smiled as he told her this story from his childhood. Whoever this Daddy Vincent was, Lorenzo obviously loved him.

"How did you and your brothers get far up into the sky?" Eboni asked Lorenzo, seeing his smile grow larger when he eyed her.

Lorenzo continued. "Daddy Vincent would pilot a helicopter that lifted us to about 35,000 feet in the sky," he said, his eyes looking up to the ceiling as if remembering. "Whenever a full moon appeared, it looked so scary because we were so close to it. Anyway, we would skydive from out of the helicopter and descend to earth in a free fall. At about three hundred feet before impact with the ground, we would activate our parachutes and land safely on our feet."

Eboni frowned. "That sounds really crazy!" she exclaimed with a chuckle. "And you did this at four years old?"

"Yes," Lorenzo answered her.

"How many times did you skydive from a helicopter?"

"About twenty times," he said to her.

"No wonder you fear nothing," she said to him, shaking her head. "When was the last time you did it?"

"About a year after I attempted it the first time," Lorenzo answered. "It was the same year my family left North Carolina and came to San Francisco. I never went skydiving again."

Eboni looked away from Lorenzo, her eyes scanning the front of the restaurant as she imagined herself skydiving from the top of a skyscraper. She focused on Lorenzo again, and his returning smile caused her to titter once more.

"You thought about it, didn't you?" he questioned her, leaning across the table.

She peered into his now emotionless, handsome face. "Yes, I did," she admitted to him plainly.

"We can do it together," he suggested to her. "My student Kurt Peters, who you've met, goes to a skydiving center in Orange, New Jersey, ten times a year. We can go there too."

Falling to the earth at the speed of free fall sounded so insane. But perhaps it wouldn't be that drastic a dive like it was when Lorenzo was a child. Maybe they could activate their parachutes long before they were three hundred feet from colliding to the ground. It would be wonderful if they could slowly float in the sky from way above and drift benignly to the turf.

"Okay, Lorenzo. I'll do it. Let's go skydiving together."

Lorenzo, elated, reached his hand across the dinner table. Eboni stretched her own hand as she intercepted him. As she held his hand inside hers, he looked at her seriously.

"I know you have your concerns and your fears about this," Lorenzo said to her. "You would be foolish not to. Just know I'll be up there in the heavens with you."

Eboni nodded as she removed the act of skydiving from her thoughts. Her thoughts drifted to the here and now, and what possibilities there were for the two of them before this beautiful night was over.

A young Filipino man wearing a maroon vest and matching bowtie came up to the table holding a large basket of red roses. Lorenzo reached for one and gave it to Eboni. Lorenzo gave the young man a ten-dollar bill before he stepped into the direction of the table beside them. Eboni put the rosebud up to her nose as she smiled and hit Lorenzo with a sideways glance.

"The rose is beautiful," Lorenzo said to her. "Just like you."

"Thank you, sweetie," Eboni retorted.

"What about your relationships with men?"

"A fleeting hope," Eboni said to him. "Just because I have good looks doesn't mean I get treated with respect. I've been the side piece, the other woman, but hardly ever his number one. I had one man in my life. He fully committed to me."

"How long ago?"

"About thirteen years ago. He didn't stay with me because I couldn't give him children."

"Thirteen years ago, was when your last relationship was?"

"Yes," Eboni answered.

"What about your parents?"

Eboni sat up straight. "I try not to think about them," she said to him.

"Why?"

Eboni shook her head. "I haven't always gotten along with my father," she said, looking away towards nothing in particular. "My mother and I are on again, off again."

Eboni placed the rose on the table. As Lorenzo stared at her, he could see pain. How much it hurt; he couldn't tell. Her bottom lip trembled as she frowned.

"When was the last time you reached out to them?" Lorenzo asked.

Eboni's eyes darted towards Lorenzo. Her torturous frown hit him. A single tear slid down the right side of her face.

"My father is such a bastard!" Eboni told Lorenzo. "How dare he treat me like that? I didn't deserve it!"

Treat her like what? What was she talking about? What wasn't she telling him? She seemed upset. He felt he would not push her parents. It was something he didn't need to know.

It was apparent to Lorenzo a long-ago scar that Eboni's father had produced hadn't healed. Or was it something else?

"I haven't seen my parents in twelve years and I try not to think about them," Eboni said as she wiped away her tears.

"I think you've mentioned your siblings before," Lorenzo said.

"My older brother Thorne lives upstate in Syracuse," Eboni said, a delightful smile appearing on her face. "He comes down here to New York City mainly for Gay Pride every year and stays with me for a few days. Our younger sister Coco lives in Toronto. She calls me at least twice a week."

"I would love to meet them one day," Lorenzo said.

Eboni shook her head. "That would be nice," she said as she scraped whatever bit of food that remained on her plate.

Lorenzo smiled at her and reached across the table. Eboni looked at his hand for a moment and took a hold of it. As he eyed her, Lorenzo brought her hand up to his lips and kissed it. He kissed it a second time before letting go of it. As her heartbeat raced faster than normal, Eboni thought about standing up from the table and walking around to where Lorenzo sat just to kiss him.

Lorenzo finished eating and placed his plate to the side. Before long, Eboni ate the last bit of food. When the server brought the bill to their table, Lorenzo paid for it while Eboni left a generous tip. When they walked out of *Al Di La Trattoria,* they both saw the dark sky and the moonlight.

"Where to now?" Eboni asked him.

Lorenzo shrugged his shoulders. "I don't know," he said to her.

Eboni looked at her watch. It was just past 9:30. They had been inside the restaurant for over an hour. Eboni waved a cab down and she and Lorenzo got into the back seat.

"Where to?" the cab driver asked them.

"Manhattan, midtown," Lorenzo said. He looked at Eboni as he put his arm around her. "You want to catch a movie?"

Not looking at him, Eboni shook her head. "No," she answered. "Let's go to *Platgina*."

"What's *Platgina*?" he asked.

"It's a hookah lounge not too far from Times Square," she said to him. "I have a few friends who are belly dancing tonight."

"Belly dancing?" Lorenzo asked her with a plain face, his voice gentle and yet curious.

"Many people will be there," Eboni said to him with a wink of her eye. "Male and female belly dancers will perform there tonight."

"Let's go there," said Lorenzo, winking back at her as he smiled.

"It's really entertaining, Lorenzo. You'll enjoy it."

The cab driver took the Manhattan Bridge from Brooklyn. As they sat quietly in the backseat, Eboni glanced over at Lorenzo. He had a bewildered look on his face. For ten minutes he hadn't said a word. Eboni placed her hand in his lap and massaged his thigh.

"9th Avenue and 40th Street!" Eboni shouted to the cab driver.

They remained quiet for the rest of the ride. Soon enough their cab came upon 9th Avenue heading south. Eboni reached inside her purse as the taxi pulled along the side of the street at the corner of 40th Street. She gave the cab driver money for the fare and tipped him as Lorenzo stepped out of the backseat. She stepped out of the cab and took Lorenzo by the hand. They reached the front of *Platgina* where a short line of people stood. Eboni focused up into the night sky as she felt Lorenzo's hand on the small of her back. The bouncer checked their IDs at the door and they walked into a noisy, filled club with luminous people standing around laughing and talking. As she walked ahead, she eyed behind her at Lorenzo trailing.

He caught up with her as she took an available seat at the bar.

Eboni ordered herself a cranberry and rum. She stood and motioned for Lorenzo to sit down on the barstool. When he did, she sat down on his lap as the sublime bartender behind the bar dressed simply in a brown dress and beige hijab with a matching veil pushed the drink over to her.

"When does the show start?" Eboni asked the bartender.

"Less than twenty minutes," came the bartender's reply.

As she looked in the direction of the dressing room, Eboni caught sight at one of the sleek female dancers walking towards the stage in front of the audience. It was a lady Eboni had never seen before. As the thin woman stooped over to pick up a black microphone from off the floor, she felt someone tap her shoulder. When Eboni gazed up, she saw a dancer wearing a euphoric grin. Her olive complexion gleamed. The lady's eyes were big and brown accompanied by glitter that sprinkled onto her face which could have been easily mistaken for sweat. Many believed that oily hair was an adversary to a woman's appearance. But the length of her dark hair, and the neat way it draped over her left shoulder, made her hair appear ravishing.

"Rahima Zubair," Eboni said with a smile.

"Eboni Law," Rahima Zubair said cheerfully. "How are you? I haven't seen you in so long. Where have you been?"

"Ladies and gentlemen, the show will begin in fifteen minutes," the beautiful performer who picked up the microphone said to the audience.

"I've been doing well," Eboni said to her, embracing the lady warmly.

"You look damn beautiful, girl!" Rahima said to her. "How is your restaurant doing?"

"We're busy every day," Eboni said. "I'm pleased with how things are going."

Rahima turned her attention towards Lorenzo. "And who is this fine black man here?" Rahima asked Eboni.

"This is Lorenzo," Eboni said.

"Pleased to meet you, Lorenzo," Rahima said. "Eboni and I go way back to college."

"It's nice to meet you," Lorenzo told Rahima. "You're awfully pretty."

"Why, thank you, sir!" Rahima said. "I'll see you guys after the show."

Rahima stepped away and disappeared behind the curtain leading to the dressing room. Eboni took a sip of her drink and offered some of it to Lorenzo. Lorenzo sipped her drink as his powerful arm fastened around her waist. She looked behind her and puckered her lips. Lorenzo kissed her. Eboni turned around and leaned back comfortably against his body and felt Lorenzo wrap both of his muscular arms securely around her in a loose embrace.

About fifteen minutes later, the show started. Darbuka drum music touched the ears of the audience and Eboni watched as her friend Rahima Zubair came from behind the curtains wearing a headdress and a veil doing her dance. She wore a black dress and a pair of white pumps. She placed what appeared to be a silver dollar on her stomach and stood sideways as she flipped the coin up and down her stomach until it flipped into her bra. The sound of noisy cheers came from the crowd as Rahima left the stage. She walked around the room with two-stage lights illuminated on her.

When Rahima's performance was over she took a bow to the delight of a cheering crowd and headed back behind the curtains where she'd come from. Within the next forty-five minutes, more talented female and male belly dancers delighted the audience.

Lorenzo finished the rest of Eboni's drink for her. When she saw he had drunk it all, she ordered another one. She and Lorenzo shared that one as well. Soon the crowd dispersed and Rahima came back over to them with her headdress and veil in her hand.

"Did you guys enjoy the show?" Rahima asked them.

"It was fantastic!" Eboni said.

"Well, I'm off work now, Eboni. Do you guys have any plans for tonight?"

"No," said Eboni. "Why?"

"Maybe we all can hang out and have some drinks," Rahima said, sneaking a quick look at Lorenzo. "I was hoping we could go somewhere like old times."

"Of course," said Eboni, a beautiful smile forming on her face. "I'd love to catch up with you."

"We can go to the Lower East Side," Rahima said. "Remember how much we used to go there when we were in college?"

Eboni smiled as she nodded. "L.E.S.," she remembered fondly. "I haven't been there in so long. I've been away from there for too long."

"When was the last time you were there?" Rahima asked her.

"It's been many years," Eboni told her.

"It was years before I married Ahmed and had two children," Rahima said. "What the hell do you do with your time?"

"I've just been living life, Rahima," Eboni said. "I was never really into the New York City nightlife much. Before I started my restaurant, I was a server and a bartender at a bar in Queens. I just haven't had the chance to go hang out in the Lower East Side hardly in the past decade."

"You know what's going on in the world, don't you?"

"Of course, I know what's going on, Rahima."

"I've never been to the L.E.S., although it's very close to my school," Lorenzo told them as he broke his silence.

Eboni stared at Lorenzo carefully, looking for any signs of objection from him. But Lorenzo didn't show any. Surely, if he objected to going with them, he surely would have said so. But he didn't.

The three of them left *Platgina* and hiked several blocks to the F train at Bryant Park. The subway cruised to Broadway and Lafayette. As soon as they emerged from the subway station on East Houston, Eboni saw the crowded streets with countless people. Rahima led them through a street full of people all the way to Ludlow. The three of them entered *The Wild Kangaroo* delightfully. Lorenzo paid their cover charge, went through the entrance of the Aussie bar, and they all walked right into a loud party.

Eboni saw Rahima approach a table by the window as a beautiful piano melody played through the loud hand-clapping of the patronage. She took a seat. Lorenzo and Eboni each took a seat across from her.

"So, how did you guys meet?" Rahima asked, her eyes looking from Eboni to Lorenzo.

"At Eboni's restaurant," Lorenzo answered, looking up to the left as if remembering. "So, how long have you guys known each other?"

"I met her in 1985 during our freshman year of college," Rahima retorted happily.

Lorenzo regarded Eboni. "You guys have known each other for a really long time," he said to her.

"Yes," Eboni told him. "Rahima used to be in a relationship with my brother Thorne before he introduced me to her."

"Long before Thorne dumped me for a guy," Rahima added.

A slender server came over to their table" Can I get you guys a drink?" he asked them.

"Bourbon and ginger ale," Lorenzo told him.

"I'll have an Apple Martini," Eboni said to the server.

"Zombie please," Rahima said.

The server smiled tightly at them and walked away. As Eboni's eyes followed the server to the bar, she felt Lorenzo place his arm around her.

"When was the last time we saw each other before tonight?" Rahima asked Eboni.

"About four years ago," Eboni answered. "We went to Coney Island for a Brooklyn Cyclones game. We also went to a birthday party in the East Village and got completely wasted."

Rahima chuckled. "I remember," she said. "We both were so drunk we passed out on the A train and woke up the next morning at 207."

"Damn," Lorenzo said to them. "You guys must have partied extra hard."

"We did," Rahima said.

"I'd never been so inebriated in my life," Eboni said." Seeing you again sure brings back memories."

The server came back and placed their drinks in front of them. As the piano melody ended, a rhythmic drumbeat sounded. Rahima looked at them before looking out of the window towards Ludlow. Eboni placed her own arm around Lorenzo and rubbed his shoulder as she lifted her glass.

"To old times," she said and touched glasses with Rahima and Lorenzo.

"Cheers," Rahima said.

"They set my divorce date," Lorenzo told them.

"You're married?" Rahima asked Lorenzo.

"For a while longer, yes," Lorenzo told her. "It's unfortunate. But it's something that has to happen."

"What happened?" Rahima asked him.

"Nothing too major," Lorenzo said to Rahima. "Jocelyn and I ended the marriage peacefully. It's nobody's fault. Jocelyn and I just strongly disagreed on something. It's better for her and me to move on and go our separate ways."

Rahima nodded and looked behind them by the window. Eboni followed her friend's gaze towards a group of men and women singing merrily on the far side of the bar.

They sat quietly for the next few minutes enjoying their liquor. The rhythmic drumbeat ceased, and the DJ played a popular song by Gym Class. The pub was three times more crowded than it was before they came. Eboni finished her drink and got up from the table.

"Where are you going, love?" Lorenzo asked.

"To the ladies' room," Eboni said.

As she walked in the direction of the women's restroom, Eboni saw men of all ethnicities inside the club breaking their necks to look at her. Even a few women had turned their heads looking at her.

When she entered the women's restroom, she saw two women kissing against the wall. Eboni quickly took her eyes from off of the lesbian couple and entered the farthest bathroom stall. As she unzipped her pants, she peeped down into the toilet and thought of Lorenzo. When she finished using the restroom, Eboni hurried to the sink and washed her hands, noticing the lesbian couple who were kissing when she arrived had gone. Eboni let her hair loose as she headed back to her table where Lorenzo and Rahima were sipping their drinks.

Eboni retook her seat and looked across the table at Rahima. She had walked in on the continuing conversation going on since before she had got up from the table.

"Yes, I've never seen belly dancers before," Lorenzo was saying. "I really enjoyed your show."

"Well, come back to *Platgina*," Eboni heard Rahima say.

"Maybe I will," Lorenzo said, half smiling as he tapped the table with his finger.

"You want another one?" the server asked Eboni when he walked up to their table.

"Yes, I'll have another," she told him.

"Me too," Lorenzo responded.

"I'll just have a Guinness," Rahima said to the server.

As the server stepped away, Eboni felt Lorenzo place his hand in her lap. He caressed her thigh wonderfully as she put her arm around him. As Lorenzo finished up his first drink, she could feel his hand rubbing her arm up and down.

"Lorenzo, you talk with a southern tongue," Rahima said. "Where are you from?"

"Charlotte, North Carolina," Lorenzo said to him. "And you?"

"Strictly the United States although my great-grandparents came here from Tripoli," Rahima said to him.

"So, what do you do?"

"Martial Arts expert and teacher," Lorenzo said, reaching into his pocket for his wallet. He pulled out several of his business cards and gave Rahima one. "I have a martial arts school opened in each borough. You should come and bring your friends. You can never go wrong with knowing self-defense. I can teach you how to kick someone's ass if they give you problems. I teach a blend of martial arts. Taekwondo, jujitsu, Judo, aikido, and others. I have seven black belts in seven different disciplines. I give special lessons in Krav Maga and Wing Chun every Thursday night."

Eboni smiled. "I've thought about visiting your school in Chinatown for a while," she said to Lorenzo, trembling in a bit of ecstasy as Lorenzo continued to caress her. "I just haven't done it yet."

"Sounds fascinating," Rahima said to Lorenzo as she read the business card. "I'll definitely mention your school to several of my friends. And I'll come by one day."

When the server came back with their second helping of drinks, Eboni thirsted for her Apple Martini. She quickly took the glass from the server before he could settle it down in front of her. Lorenzo quickly sipped his second ginger ale with bourbon, and Rahima just eyed the cold bottle of Guinness placed in front of her.

"So, where do you live now, Eboni?" Rahima asked her.

"West End Avenue and 88th," Eboni said.

"I live in New Jersey now in Hoboken," Rahima said.

As time wore on, the night got old. They stayed inside *The Wild Kangaroo* for another two hours near closing time. The three of them socialized and enjoyed continuous drinks courtesy of the bartenders working the bar.

"I'm going to head home," Rahima Zubair said with a radiant smile. "Eboni, it was wonderful seeing you again. Lorenzo, it was nice meeting you."

Both Eboni and Lorenzo waved to Rahima as she got up from the table. She blew them kisses and stumbled towards the front entrance. Eboni watched her friend rush from out of the saloon, and eyed Rahima through a side window, never taking her eyes off of her until she disappeared down Ludlow Street.

"You ready to leave?" Eboni asked.

"Yeah," Lorenzo said, drinking the rest of his bourbon and ginger ale.

To Eboni, Lorenzo appeared very sober. They both got up from the table and held hands as they left out of the bar. As they walked down the street towards East Houston, Eboni placed her head on Lorenzo's shoulder. She placed her arm around him. They walked slowly and caught a yellow New York City taxi a half block from the Bowery. In the backseat, they sat cuddled up.

"Where to?" the taxi driver said.

"Upper West Side," Eboni said to him. "88th and West End Avenue."

"Make that Riverside Park," Lorenzo said to the taxi driver.

In about fifteen minutes, the cab got on 11th Avenue where it turned into West End Avenue. Before they knew it, they were on Riverside Drive and 87th Street. The cab driver had stopped the cab and Lorenzo reached into his wallet and paid the fare.

When they got out of the taxi, Eboni and Lorenzo held hands as they walked across the street to Riverside Park. The park was dark, empty, and quiet. Lorenzo walked Eboni over to a park bench and sat down. She sat next to him and crossed her legs. She handed the red rose to him and leaned over. Her face rested on his chest for a moment before she looked up at him.

His mouth dove for hers as he placed his arm around her. Eboni's lips confronted Lorenzo's in a passionate kiss. To him, her tender kiss tasted like strawberries- and tasted like something sweeter.

Eboni broke from the kiss, and she placed a hand over his chest. "Your heart is beating quite fast," she said to him.

Lorenzo was about to say something but didn't. He goggled down at Eboni as she eyed joyously up at him.

"I love you!" they both proclaimed to each other simultaneously.

As Lorenzo affectionately kissed her bottom lip, Eboni quickly got up. She took three or four steps back, turned sideways, and stood firmly in some sort of defensive stance that was unknown to Lorenzo.

"Finish what we started in your house," Eboni said, her eyes watching him.

Lorenzo got to his feet, lifted his hand up near his chest, and said, "Forward kick my hand using both feet. Now kick with mean intentions!"

Eboni's face darkened as she did as Lorenzo instructed. She focused on the hand before her, making repeated contact with it using both feet as she kicked. As he moved his hand from high to low, and from side to side to give her angles, she became more determined to strike her moving target forcibly with her foot. The astonished look on Lorenzo's face revealed how shocking and surprised he was at how accurate she was with her blows.

"Stop!" he said, bringing his hand down to his side. "Now, work on your sidekick using both feet."

Eboni delivered sidekick after sidekick, using her left leg and foot. As she continued to do it, she felt an uneasy burn to her muscle in her left quadriceps.

"Opposite leg and foot," Lorenzo said, feeling showers falling from the night sky.

Eboni lifted her right leg and kicked sideways at the air continuously. Within three minutes of landing on an imagined opponent, she fatigued, the both of them becoming soaked by the heavy rainfall.

"All you need is practice," he encouraged her. "But with Wushu, there's so much more to learn."

"I can imagine," Eboni said, hunching over with her hands on her knees as she panted.

"Straighten up," he instructed her.

Taking a last breath, Eboni stood erect. She focused on Lorenzo. As she eyed him, she became oblivious to the downpour. What had started out as a simple date on this night had ended in martial arts lessons.

"Think of somebody you despise attacking you," Lorenzo said to her. "In displaying Wushu, display how you would counter-attack them.

Eboni closed her eyes, feeling the raindrops splatter onto the top of her head. She remembered the icy blue eyes of the robber piercing through her. She remembered trembling with fear, with dread as he pointed his gun at her. Eboni recalled his threats to do physical harm to her unless he gave her what he wanted. She remembered the not-so-distant memory of feeling vulnerable and helpless- and thankful. Thankful a flying kick from out of nowhere had thwarted the robbery attempt.

"I vow to never be that powerless to protect myself ever again," Eboni whispered faithfully to herself.

She opened her eyes and lifted her wrists in order to block his oncoming blows. She jumped vertically, throwing a front kick that landed on the gunman's jaw. After delivering two sidekicks to the gut and chest, the assailant went tumbling backward. She repeated the exercise eight more times and stood over the perpetrator as he struggled to get up. Rain soaked his ski mask as he held his ribs. As soon as Lorenzo touched Eboni's shoulder, the image of the outlaw disappeared.

"Did you see him?" she asked, looking at Lorenzo, his face soaked with rain.

"See who?"

"The man who I just took on," Eboni told him.

"The person who you despise attacking you?" he asked her.

"Yes."

"No, I didn't," he said, looking at her oddly. "But your form needs a lot of work. You also have to learn more control. But you did well for someone doing this for the first time."

"Thank you, Sensei."

Lorenzo looked at her for a second longer and turned his back to her. He made a fist and lifted it above his head. Standing on his right leg, he lifted his left leg and stretched it outward. He turned on his leg, faced her, and put his left leg on the ground.

"Everything I do, you do also," he said to her with a friendly smile.

Eboni nodded, seeing Lorenzo stand firmly in a basic stance. He performed seven straight punches and followed those up with wide kicks. As she kept up with his even pace, it rained even harder. But she kept her focus on him, imitating every move he did. Every punch, kick, and blockage for defense, she emulated him precisely.

"I could see emotional pain when you were engaging your imagery opponent," Lorenzo said, his smile widening. "Use the pain as a source of strength. Use it as a motivational tool. Don't identify the pain with the person who caused it. Rather make it work for you by using your pain as an asset to fight well. By doing that you will accomplish two things; you'll rid yourself of the emotional pain and you'll become ten times the fighting warrior before you began learning."

Eboni regarded him, pressing her lips together as she folded her arms. "Yes, Sensai," she said to Lorenzo as lightning shot through the sky above.

He got back into his stance and performed basic offensive moves. Eboni imitated him and observed him as meticulously as she could. When he restarted, she knew his offensive strikes well enough. She could perform each kick, punch, and knee lift, and backward elbow strike at the same moment he did them as if she were reflecting him in a mirror.

"You saw the robber, didn't you?" Lorenzo asked as he turned to face her. "You've dreamt about him."

How could he possibly know that? She looked at him wide-eyed. She wanted to question him, but she paid him her strict attention.

"When you saw his gun and his mask, you acted with hesitation, didn't you?" he questioned her.

Eboni nodded as drops of rain splattered onto her head. "Yes," she honestly answered.

"When the moment comes, a martial artist acts," Lorenzo said. "Whenever you pause in a situation like you were in, you are feeding into the robber's idea of fear. The last thing he wants is for you to engage him in combat. The gun he holds is his threat against you, and he thinks you are defenseless. Your skill and defiance will surprise him. Your mission is to make him regret pulling that gun out on you. Your duty is to use martial arts as an extension of your will to alter his mindset from one of disrespect to respect. Leave him with the thought of his own folly after you've engaged him. The robber should fear you, not the other way around. Instead of being paralyzed by fear and succumbing to his imposition, your duty as a martial artist is to not only thwart his attempt, but you must also leave him to wallow in his pain."

Eboni thought back to the robbery attempt again. She remembered seeing the hand holding the gun. Without thinking about it, she thought about delivering a quick elbow to his throat, face, or even a front kick to the armed hand. Something she knew the robber wouldn't have expected.

"The robber is just scum," the master said directly to her. "You are a true martial artist. There is a vast difference between you and the robber. When he confronts you with his firearm to intimidate you, you remain calm. While he imposes on you, you remain calm. A true martial artist doesn't have to show her dignity as the robber does. You just respond with the kick, or chop, or punch, or high knee, or elbow at the moment you need to do it. You do what is needed and no more."

"Yes, sensei," said Eboni.

Lorenzo went on. "Martial arts are not about fighting," he said with a smile. "It is a fine art and a way for you to construct your confidence through compassion, patience, respect, and humility."

Eboni nodded. "Yes, sensei," she said. "Is that how you could defend me against the bandit?"

"Yes," he answered her, as rainwater dripped from his forehead into his eyes.

Now she understood him. Eboni thought she knew Lorenzo. But she didn't really know him until now. She had known him as her friend and companion. But this part of him was new to her. She thought back to the night in the Bronx when he started showing her how to strike. But now his wisdom and keenness were new to her. She had just become his student.

"Now, I want you to wait for me to come to you. I'm going to reach in your pocket like I'm taking what belongs to you using my right hand. I want you to grab hold of my wrist using your left hand. Lift it above my head, place your right heel behind my left heel, and force me to the ground by reaching for my throat with your left hand."

Eboni placed her hands on her hips and nodded. As she watched Lorenzo approach, she closed her eyes. His footsteps splashed against the wet ground as he came closer. She bit her bottom lip, hearing sirens from nearby. She felt Lorenzo's hand reach into her left pants pocket. Eboni instinctively grabbed his wrist, lifted it above his head as her right heel pinned his left heel. Her left hand quickly clutched Lorenzo's throat as she shoved him backward. Lorenzo tripped and fell.

"And in a real-life situation, you want to deliver a punch to the face," Lorenzo said, smiling at her, seeing her matted wet hairs sticking to her forehead.

"Of course," Eboni said, returning the smile, feeling her confidence grow as she opened her eyes. "I mean yes, Sensei."

"We'll go over what you did here tonight before we go to bed," he told her.

She saw him eyeing her strangely as she collapsed on top of him. Her breasts rested on his chest as she felt his arms embrace her.

"What is it?" she asked, sneaking a peak to the darkness in the rainy sky.

"Eboni, you're so captivating," Lorenzo mentioned to her in a whisper.

Before she could bring her eyes from the dark sky to ogle down at him, she felt his lips on hers. Here in the rainstorm, his kiss was the sweetest her lips had ever tasted.

Eleven

Chapter 11

"Tomorrow's the big day," Eboni said as she soaked in her warm bubble bath.

She gazed up at Lorenzo, seeing his sparkling silver yin and yang necklace similar to the one he'd given her around his thick, muscular neck, her nostrils breathing in the pleasant cherry scented candle and jasmine incense that filled the bathroom.

Lorenzo sat at the edge of the tub and watched her. She eyed the blissful sight of his big biceps, beautiful deltoids, and pleasing broad, chiseled chest. Lorenzo handed her the glass of red wine he'd been holding as she bathed. She reached for the glass, put it to her lips, and took a few sips.

"Yes," Lorenzo answered. "My divorce date has arrived."

"Do you still love her?" Eboni asked, taking another sip of wine.

"Of course," Lorenzo answered plainly, as he looked at her. "I had two children with her. She was a wonderful spouse. I care about her a great deal."

"But do you still *love* her?"

Eboni's voice sounded eager, and her tone hinted insecurity.

Though she had asked him with a straight face, he could see straight through her concerns. She wanted to be the only woman in his life without question. From the time they had known each other; their friendship had blossomed into a feverish relationship. Still, Eboni wonders if she was his queen, and he was her king.

"Romantically?" Lorenzo asked, now looking at her with one eye closed. "No, I will always care about her, as she's the mother of my children. Jocelyn's not a part of me anymore. Eboni, you rule my world now like God rules the solar stars."

A smile touched Eboni's lips. Lorenzo reached across the tub for a tall jar of shampoo. He poured a portion of it into his hand and placed his palm on Eboni's scalp. She chewed inside her cheek as Lorenzo began washing her hair. Eboni closed her eyes and took a deep breath as he thoroughly massaged her scalp.

"This is extremely sweet," Eboni told him. "I didn't know men did things like this."

"I do it," Lorenzo said. "I go that extra mile like a real man to show you how much I care."

Eboni giggled. "I see," she said, and finished her wine.

Lorenzo stood up and grabbed a hold of the showerhead. He rinsed her hair completely and turned the water off. He reached for her New York Yankees towel on the back of the bathroom door as she stepped from out of the tub. Lorenzo wrapped the towel around Eboni and grabbed her hand as they left the bathroom.

A short time later, after she had dried off, Eboni lay back on the sofa with her elbows propped. Lorenzo sat at the other end of the sofa with Eboni's feet in his lap as he polished her toenails a crimson red.

Lorenzo took in the elegance of her apartment. In the living room Calloway, Ellington, and Kitt graced the walls with a dozen waxed Motown records. A small flat turntable sat on the cocktail table in front of the sofa. The waxed records of Duke Ellington, Count Basie, Buddy Bolden, Louis Armstrong, and Earl Hines leaned up against it.

The spread-out thick rug was a light blue, with dark blue spaces in it from footprints. Unlike the bathroom, the air smelled of a sort of pleasant, lime-scented fragrance. The fancy curtains near the windows were white and azure.

"Thanks for letting me spend the night," Lorenzo said to her.

"I'm glad you're here," Eboni responded with a smile.

"I should get to bed," he said to her after he finished making her feet look pretty.

"You want to sleep in my bed and I sleep out here?" Eboni asked him.

"Sure," Lorenzo said to her as he got up.

Lorenzo walked towards her bedroom. Eboni quickly got up and followed him. She moved in front of him, peered up, and kissed his lips.

"Good night, Lorenzo," Eboni told him.

"I'll see you in the morning," Lorenzo said and walked inside her bedroom.

The bedroom door closed, and Eboni slowly walked back into the living room. She walked into the small dining room and sat at the table. She eyed Lorenzo's suit, shirt, and necktie he'd be wearing into the courtroom tomorrow draped over a chair across the table. Taking a deep breath, Eboni closed her eyes. She put her head down on the table. Before she knew it, she had fallen asleep.

****

The teenage girl ran behind Eboni. She saw three shadowy figures standing still, looking in their direction. Eboni didn't know why the girl was using her to shield her away from three bodily shapes she couldn't quite make out, but she knew the adolescent female was in trouble. Eboni turned to look at the girl, seeing she was shivering with fear.

The girl looked up at her, and Eboni could read her emotional appeal for protection as tears streamed down her innocent face. Eboni waited for the child to speak, but she remained quiet.

Eboni turned towards the tenebrous silhouettes as they approached her simultaneously. As her gaze narrowed, she bent her knees and assumed a martial arts stance....

Eboni woke up, looking in all directions. She saw framed pictures of Babe Ruth and Dave Winfield on the wall by the door. There were various New York Yankees banners on the wall, on the opposite side of the room. On top of the dresser, where a glass jewelry box was, stood a blue bottle of New York Yankees perfume.

She saw she was in her bedroom. Her thoughts shifted back to the recent dream. It had linked her previous dreams to a past event. But this new one had no foundation. Could it have been a precognitive dream? Was it a prophetic dream of a future happening?

Eboni quickly got out of bed and hurried to the living room. She spotted Lorenzo in front of the kitchen entryway, sitting in the lotus position with his hands on his knees. Lorenzo's eyes were closed. He opened them and stared in her direction.

"Did we sleep in the bed together?" she asked him with a lovely smile. "Did I hop in the bed with you last night?"

Lorenzo smiled and shook his head. "I found you on the floor by the table at Four O'clock this morning when I came out of the bedroom to get a glass of water," he said debonairly. "I carried you to your bed, and I slept out here."

"I was exhausted," Eboni said, placing her hands on her hips.

"You must've been," Lorenzo said to her.

"What time is it?" she asked him.

"Just after nine in the morning," he told her, scratching the right side of his face. "I have to be at the courthouse in the Bronx in two hours."

"You better get ready," Eboni suggested.

"You should go out there with me, Eboni."

"I guess I could open the restaurant an hour later," she said. "I can't stay for the entire proceeding. But I can certainly go out there with you."

****

Jocelyn walked up the enormous staircase, which led to the entrance of the Bronx County Courthouse. As she walked through the doors, a few men's eyes dropped on her. She smiled to herself, wondering if their watchful compliments were because of the classic black sheath dress she wore or were these men admiring her big calves as she took a step after step in her matching high heels. As she moved through a crowd of people on her way to the courtroom, she spotted Lorenzo with three women by the middle elevator in the lobby. One woman was his sister Olivia, and the other was her own lawyer, Cressida. But who was the other woman with her soon-to-be ex-husband?

Jocelyn looked at the woman from head to toe when she approached them. She was sporting a pink off-the-shoulder top. Tight navy-blue pants brought out the provocative shape of her legs. The woman also wore a pair of sandals. Jocelyn also saw the dame had a ladylike white bonnet on her head. Jocelyn watched as Lorenzo kissed the woman on her cheek as she approached them.

"Good morning," Jocelyn said to them all. "Hi, Lorenzo. Is everyone ready?"

"Hola, Jocelyn," Lorenzo said.

"Lorenzo, who is she?" Jocelyn asked him.

"Let's head to the courtroom," Olivia said, pulling Lorenzo by the arm.

"I'm Eboni," the unknown woman answered Jocelyn.

Jocelyn eyed her as Eboni extended her hand. In an instant, she saw the woman's beauty. In a flash, Jocelyn took in the woman's friendly smile, eyes, nose, cheekbones, and the noticeable flat mole on the right side of her face.

Jocelyn eyed the woman skeptically, knowing in her heart that this was the woman who had replaced her in Lorenzo's life.

"Eboni is my friend," Lorenzo said.

Jocelyn looked at Eboni's hand. Her eyes moved back up to meet the woman's gaze. Making a tight fist as she pressed her lips together, Jocelyn frowned and turned her back. Gritting her teeth, she stepped away and followed both counselors to the courtroom. She turned back and saw Lorenzo kissing Eboni.

****

Lorenzo looked from Jocelyn and her attorney to the judge. Looking back on his marriage to Jocelyn, Lorenzo felt he was a spectacular husband. He did his absolute best to create happiness in her. He created the conditions in his house to bring out of her what he thought God had put in her for him. He maintained her so well. He maintained her spiritually. He maintained her intellectually. He covered her morally. He protected her from physical harm. He took good care of her and their daughters. He did all the things a husband should do regarding his wife. He tried to maintain her well. He tried to find ways and means to become the man in his own house. And it still wasn't enough.

A tear escaped from his left eye, and he turned toward his sister. Olivia looked in his direction. She frowned slightly and placed her hand on his back.

"You okay, Lorenzo?" Olivia asked him. "What is it?"

He regarded her with long black dreadlocks flowing all the way to her lower back. She wore a long black and red dress.

Olivia and Jocelyn were the only two people he ever cried in front of. It always came back to the conclusion of his marriage to Jocelyn.

"I'm sad because of the finality that I'm parting ways with Jocelyn after today," Lorenzo said to her. "Thinking back on the life I had with Jocelyn makes me want to cry."

Lorenzo wiped a few of the tears from his face. He looked in Jocelyn's direction and frowned. An intense regret replaced his sadness. Was it something that just didn't work out in the long run? Or did Jocelyn and Lorenzo just grow into two separate directions?

"Dry your eyes, Lorenzo," Olivia said calmly. "You'll find a woman far better than she ever was to you."

But he already had found a better woman. He had told no one in his family about Eboni yet. They would learn of her soon enough.

"Mr. Royal, I see in the language where it says there's something about child support," the judge said sharply.

The judge, a lovely Cuban woman with blonde hair with dark brown streaks, and a serious facial expression looked towards Olivia and Lorenzo.

Lorenzo looked towards the judge. "Yes," he said, forcing a jovial expression onto his face.

"I have expressed it. Jocelyn will keep custody of the two children and she will receive child support from Mr. Royal," Cressida told the court.

"Can you provide a record for the court in writing, counselor?" the judge questioned Cressida.

Cressida opened a small briefcase and retrieved a tiny document. She approached the bench and presented it to the judge.

Lorenzo's gaze found Cressida, seeing her bald head, wide hips, and white stockings covering her lower legs and weighty thighs. She wore a classy brown denim skirt. It came about six inches short above her knees. She also sported a white shirt buttoned to the collar and a black necktie. And she had these safari boots on.

The female judge looked at Jocelyn. "The house in the Bronx is also in question," she said, taking the information. "Mrs. Cortez-Royal, how long did you live with your husband and children in that home?"

"For five years," Jocelyn answered.

"Where did you live before that?"

"We lived with our kids in an apartment in University Heights in the South Bronx."

"And there are two little girls involved," said the judge.

"Joy and Lori, my daughters," Lorenzo said.

"Is the house paid for, Mr. Royal?"

"Yes, Your Honor," Lorenzo said as he turned around, only to see Xavier entering the courtroom. He turned back around to focus on the judge. "I paid off on the house just recently."

"Mrs. Cortez-Royal, why do you want to live in the home once you're divorced from your husband?"

"Lorenzo and I agreed he will keep the house," Jocelyn told the judge, appearing mirthful.

"And in a divorce settlement, you're seeking the custody of your children?"

"Yes".

"In the language, it says here both you and your husband are seeking a divorce for irreconcilable differences," said the judge. "You want to explain, Mr. Royal?"

"It's no one's fault they are divorcing," Olivia said to the judge, her face homespun. "They had some issues and those issues in their marriage were far too great for them both to want to continue the marriage."

"Despite the grounds on which you are seeking a divorce, Mr. Royal, would you be willing to grant the house and the children to Mrs. Cortez-Royal?"

Lorenzo straightened his necktie, scratching the bridge of his nose as he smiled. "Certainly, although it's not what we agreed upon," he said. "I want to say for the record I take responsibility for neglecting Jocelyn and working long hours, which led to her frustration with our love life. I want to give Jocelyn alimony to keep her secure after our divorce."

The judge nodded towards Lorenzo. "I'll take it into strong consideration, Mr. Royal." She turned towards Jocelyn. "Mrs. Cortez-Royal, would you say Mr. Royal is an exemplary father to your children?"

"Lorenzo is an excellent father," Jocelyn admitted.

"Mr. Royal, would you say Mrs. Cortez-Royal is an excellent mother to your children?" the judge asked.

"I'd say so," Lorenzo responded.

"What kind of work do you both do?" the judge asked.

"I'm a housekeeper at a hotel in West Farms in the Bronx," Jocelyn said.

"I'm a martial arts instructor," Lorenzo said.

"I've seen statements from your check stubs, Mrs. Cortez-Royal. You are earning close to $23.00 an hour where you work. Do you feel it's enough to live on and support two young children?"

"Yes, Your Honor."

"Mr. Royal, I've seen the bank statements over the past three years pertaining to your martial arts schools and a bodyguard service. You earn over $100,000 annually. There's no doubt here you can support your children if you're granted full custody of them. Do either of you have a problem with paying child support if I granted the other custody?"

"No," Lorenzo and Jocelyn said simultaneously.

The judge stood up to her full height as she looked over the bench at Jocelyn and Lorenzo.

Jocelyn and Lorenzo eyed one another. Lorenzo quickly took his eyes off of her and looked at Olivia.

"I'm going to my chambers to make my decision there," the judge announced professionally. "There will be a fifteen-minute recess."

****

When the judge came back from her chambers fifteen minutes later, Lorenzo was staring off into space as thoughts of Eboni came to his mind. Olivia sat quietly beside him. His thoughts of Eboni vanished as the judge retook her seat behind the bench.

"My ruling is simple," the judge said to them all. "Because of Mr. Royal's and Mrs. Cortez-Royal's grounds for divorce, the possession of the house will stay with him. Custody of the children will remain with Mrs. Cortez-Royal because I think while children need both a mother and a father, I feel mothering a child is a few steps more vital than fathering a child."

Lorenzo nodded and peered in Jocelyn's direction. Jocelyn waved to him.

The judge went on. "Mr. Royal, you may claim your children every weekend. But primary custody will be with the children's mother. Mr. Royal, the court will regulate you to pay child support for your two children until they are eighteen years of age. You will also be totally responsible for everything they need when they are in your custody. In addition, Mr. Royal, you will pay Mrs. Cortez-Royal $1,000.00 a month in alimony for three years."

The judge hit the bench with the gavel.

"Congratulations, Jocelyn!" Cressida exclaimed as she stood up.

As soon as Lorenzo stood up, Olivia embraced him. Lorenzo felt a firm hand on his shoulder. He turned around and saw Xavier smiling at him.

"Hello, dad!" Lorenzo said.

"Hi, father!" Olivia said to Xavier.

Xavier put his arms around Lorenzo and Olivia. "We should celebrate," he said, looking at them. "I don't have any appointments scheduled for another few hours. "

"Where should we go?" Olivia asked.

Lorenzo walked over to Jocelyn as she stood next to her lawyer. She was smiling brightly. He waved his hand. Jocelyn gazed up at Lorenzo.

"I want the very best for you, Jocelyn," Lorenzo said to her with a straight face. "Despite everything that happened, I still care about what happens to you."

Jocelyn found her voice, taking a deep breath as she watched him sadly. "I want the same for you too, Lorenzo," she said to him. "There's no reason we still can't be friends."

"I agree," he said, extending his hand to her.

Jocelyn's melancholy face turned gleeful as she peered up at him. She extended her hand, and Lorenzo gave her a loose but enthusiastic handshake.

As they looked at one another, Lorenzo peered into her gaze, seeing the same remorse he'd been feeling since the day he had left the marriage counselor's office. They both knew the only thing for them to do was to look ahead.

"Felicitaciones!" Lorenzo told her wholeheartedly, as they gave one another a hug. "Take good care of my girls."

"You know I will," Jocelyn assured him.

****

Lorenzo looked out at Rivera Avenue, seeing light traffic travel in both directions as he, his sister, and his father walked inside *Inez's Sports Bar*. When they went inside, they walked right up to the bar. One plasma screen television was on televising a New York Yankees road game against the Texas Rangers.

When they walked up to the bar, a woman with dark skin, high cheekbones, and dimples working the bar greeted them with a beauteous smile.

"Good evening," she said. "May I help you, please?"

"Whatever you want is on me," Xavier told Olivia and Lorenzo.

"Six shots of your best whiskey and a Brooklyn Lager," Lorenzo said to the bartender.

"Screaming Orgasm," said Olivia.

"I'll have two Coors Light," Xavier said.

As the three of them found stools, the bartender reached for the Jameson bottle on the shelf behind her. They scooted their stools close to each other. The bartender served Lorenzo his six shots and beer and fixed Olivia's drink.

"You said earlier I would find someone better than Jocelyn," Lorenzo said to Olivia. "I have already."

"Who?" Xavier asked, eyeing Lorenzo.

"What's her name?" Olivia said, her eyes big and beautiful, and her smile jocund.

"Her name is Eboni Law," Lorenzo told them, reaching inside his pocket for his wallet. He pulled a picture out and gave it to his sister.

Olivia took the photo and held it close to her eyes. "She's striking," she said, handing the picture to Xavier. "She was at the courthouse with you today. I met her."

Xavier too looked at the picture. "She's ravishing," he said, as his bushy eyebrows arose. "This woman is extremely beautiful. She has a nice pair of jugs too."

"Dad!" Lorenzo said, snatching the picture away from Xavier.

"I'm sorry, son," Xavier said. "It's just the image of being so gorgeous. Now you can certainly forget about Jocelyn."

"I'm moving on. I'm going skydiving with Eboni soon."

"How long have you known this woman?" Olivia asked.

"For ten months," Lorenzo answered. "We've dated. We've gone out. She's also spent a little time with Joy and Lori."

"What kind of work does she do, Lorenzo?" Xavier asked.

"Eboni is a restaurant owner in Soho," Lorenzo told him.

"Where does she live?" Olivia asked him.

"On the Upper West Side along West End Avenue," Lorenzo said. "Dad, you and I should go to her restaurant one day so you can meet her."

"I'd like that," Xavier said, as he reached behind him for one of his bottles of beer, which sat to the side of him.

"This Eboni is very kind," Olivia said to Xavier. "I can tell she has a lot of class."

"I spoke to your mother," Xavier said to both Olivia and Lorenzo. "She'll be returning to New York next week."

"Really?" Olivia asked. "We haven't seen her in a long time."

Lorenzo's thoughts drifted back to Eboni. As he thought of her, he reached for the one-shot glass on the bar in front of him. He took the shot and threw back two more before he reached for his beer.

"Lorenzo, did you hear me?" Xavier asked him.

Lorenzo's gaze found Xavier. "Huh?" he asked.

"Did you hear me?"

"No, I didn't."

"I said your mother is returning to New York next week," Xavier repeated.

"I feel strongly about her," Lorenzo said as if he didn't hear his father.

"What?" Xavier asked, hitting Lorenzo with a bewildered stare.

"I like Eboni a lot," Lorenzo told them with a straight face.

Olivia frowned as she looked at him. "I'm so glad for you, Lorenzo," she expressed. "How can you move on so fast? I'm sure Jocelyn would object."

Lorenzo eyed his sister. "Olivia, my marriage was quite sluggish," he said to her with a straight face. "You get married, have children, relate to one another for a few years, and find out at a later time just how incomplete you are as a married couple. Jocelyn and I were not in sync."

"I liked Jocelyn so much," Olivia said, her eyes piercing through him.

"Jocelyn is a daughter to me," Xavier said, his eyes looking at Lorenzo, a confused grin on his face.

Lorenzo peered at Olivia. "What it comes down to is I'm trying to extend my business," he said to Olivia. "It's difficult to make the money, put food on the table, be a father, a fully devoted husband, and give her the attention she deserves. It's like trying to have the strength of a thousand men."

"I understand, little brother," Olivia said, putting her hands behind her back as she stared at Lorenzo in disbelief. "But I still think you could've made it all work if you tried."

"I tried," Lorenzo told her.

"This really saddens me," Xavier said, shaking his head.

Lorenzo took a deep breath and said, "My plate is totally full. I teach so many people daily. Mixed martial artists have even approached me to train them for their fights inside the octagon. Things are going excellent. I'm living my dream."

Lorenzo looked at them. He closed his eyes as he reached for another of the shot glasses full of whiskey. He threw it back and eyed towards the entrance out at Rivera Avenue.

"I'm thrilled for you, Lorenzo," Olivia said, her shoulders slumping as a half radiant smile emerged on her face. "I'm sorry for the tribulations you and Jocelyn went through. But I am happy you are achieving your goals and accomplishing things beyond your wildest dreams."

"Thank you, Olivia," he said to her.

"I don't like it because you moved on so fast," Xavier told Lorenzo. "I have a feeling this Eboni woman is not right for you."

"Stay out of it, dad," Lorenzo said and sipped his beer. "Just stay out of it."

"I'm just a concerned father," Xavier said with a smile.

"Please, father," Olivia said to Xavier. "Don't interfere in your son's life. Lorenzo is right."

"You were already bonding with this woman while still married," said Xavier, shaking his head as he looked up at the baseball game on the plasma television.

"Jocelyn and I have come to an understanding," Lorenzo said to his father. "I love Eboni. I'm going to be with her whether you like it."

"Very well," said Xavier.

"Dad, you of all people should know how challenging marriage is," Lorenzo said, shaking his head.

"Carson and I have an open marriage," Olivia told them, turning her head and focusing thoughtfully up at nothing in particular. "Both of us have cheated. I've said nothing, but our marriage has been on life support for a while now. We're both seeing other people."

"I did not know," Lorenzo said with concern. "You've kept this all to yourself?"

"I have until now because it's difficult to talk about it," Olivia told Lorenzo. "It's hard for me to discuss it even with family. It's easier that way for me and Carson."

Xavier folded his arms and looked at her. "An open marriage?" he questioned.

"I have serious offers from a few respectable ladies in the Manhattan prosecutor's office."

"What?" Xavier asked, an irritable disturbance on his mug. "Ladies?"

Lorenzo's eyes located Xavier. "Dad, leave Olivia alone," he said to him. "It's her life. She just told us something she really didn't want us to know."

Olivia smiled. "That's all I'm going to say about it," she said.

"Live free, Olivia," Lorenzo said to her.

Xavier stood up. "I can't believe I'm hearing all of this," he said, throwing his hands in the air. "I have to head back to the office. Congratulations on your divorce, Lorenzo."

Xavier placed a five-dollar tip on the bar and left it out. Lorenzo saw the two beers his father had ordered, barely touched.

"They're really female lawyers in the Manhattan prosecuting office that like you?" Lorenzo asked Olivia.

Olivia nodded. "Yes," she said. "Several."

"Are you seriously considering them?"

Olivia looked at her wedding ring on her ring finger as the smile left her visage. "Lorenzo, I'd rather not discuss it with you," she told him

Lorenzo downed the final three of his shots before grabbing his beer. Right now, he felt a small buzz as he gazed up into the plasma television and saw the Yankees and Rangers tied in the middle of the fourth inning.

"Do you think father will give you and Eboni space?" she asked him. "Or will he try to fix your life for you?"

Lorenzo struck her with an uncharacteristically stony stare. "Dad better be careful," he said, folding his arms. "I will not tolerate him disrespecting me or Eboni. I've already made my choices. Dad better watch his step. He better leave Eboni and me the hell alone."

****

Lorenzo took the N train to Prince Street. As he walked to *The Camelot*, Lorenzo whistled joyously. He placed both hands in his pockets as he walked down the sidewalk, passing countless people on the way to his destination. Once he got to Eboni's jam-packed restaurant, he quickly took a seat at the bar.

"Bruce Lee, how's it going?" Stuart asked him, a goofy smile on his face.

Lorenzo smiled. "Hello, Stuart," he said. "Where's my lady?"

"Eboni is on the other side of the restaurant taking orders," Stuart said. "I'll tell her you're here."

Lorenzo waved a hand. "No," he told Stuart. "Don't alert her to my presence. She'll see me, eventually."

When Eboni arrived at the bar, Lorenzo eyed her. Eboni noticed him and smiled. Eboni sashayed across the room in a short, dark denim skirt. Her black pumps and matching tights made her legs appear impossibly long. Her breasts and nipples pierced through the lightly faded New

York Yankees tee shirt she had on. She didn't look fifty-one. She looked twenty-nine.

"How did it go?" she asked him as she set a tray of empty glasses on the bar.

"I kept my house," Lorenzo said, eyeing her. "Jocelyn got the kids. I'm now officially divorced."

"Lorenzo, I'm happy for you," Eboni said and kissed his cheek.

A short time later, once all the customers and employees had left, Lorenzo and Eboni were alone, sitting at the bar, sharing a tall glass of gin and grape juice. As Lorenzo looked at Eboni from the hair on her head to the sexy high heel shoes on her feet, he licked his lips. Smiling, he pulled her to him and kissed her lips.

Eboni looked at him. "What was that for?" she asked him plainly.

"Eboni, my feelings for you are very strong," Lorenzo divulged to her. "I enjoy our time together. If I could, I'd give you my last breath. Whenever I'm away from you, I constantly think about you." He peered down to the floor and over to the statues of King Arthur and Lancelot by the twisting staircase. His eyes focused on her as he smiled. "As I told you before, you rule my world. I want you to rule my world always. Words can't describe how much I love you."

Lorenzo saw her eyes looking at him as she got up off of her stool and stood in front of him. Her eyes blinked repeatedly. Her eyes dampened, appearing as a pond full of water before a flow of tears ran down her face.

For a moment, Eboni peered at him curiously. But once Lorenzo touched her inner thigh and kissed her forehead tenderly, she smiled brightly as he wiped away her tears. As he watched Eboni pull her shirt over her head, Lorenzo's desire grew as he looked at her two firm, round breasts.

"I want you," Eboni said to him, throwing her shirt across the bar.

Lorenzo bent down to one knee. He kissed her stomach and licked her navel in circles. Eboni delightfully squealed. His tongue traveled up towards her abdomen and came back down to her belly button.

Lorenzo's tongue glided counterclockwise inside Eboni's navel as her eyes closed.

Eboni stooped down and lifted Lorenzo up. As they stared into each other's eyes, Eboni unfastened his belt and opened his pants. As she pulled his pants down, she trembled.

She pulled him by his arm as she walked him towards the back of the restaurant. She turned and playfully eyed him, wanted to fill him throughout her as thoughts of carnality and love mixed.

As she sat on the edge of a table in the back, she pulled Lorenzo down on top of her, hugging his body with her legs.

Twelve

Chapter 12

Eboni's eyes opened at the sounds of dishes breaking. Her head was resting against Lorenzo's chest. The next thing she was cognizant of was she was in the protective custody of his warm embrace. His fingers were through her hair only because he was very fond of stroking the hairs of her head gently every night before they fell asleep.

Eboni lifted herself up and got out of bed. Putting her red silk nightgown on, she hurried to the kitchen only to find Lori sweeping up the pieces of a bowl she'd broken. Eboni stooped down to kiss the little girl on the nose. She took the broom and dustpan from her and finished cleaning up the tiny mess Lori had created.

"What are you doing?" Eboni asked, showing the child a toothy smile.

"I wanted to make some cereal," said Lori, looking away from Eboni.

"Just take a seat at the table and I'll make some for you."

For the past few months, Lorenzo had been living with Eboni in her Upper West Side apartment. Lorenzo had put his house in the Bronx up for sale. Since Eboni had three more years remaining on her lease, she'd decided she didn't want to live alone anymore. Getting to know Lori and

Joy wasn't as hard as Eboni thought it would be. She had found both girls to be the same yet different. Lori was always so nice and playful but it was taking Joy a little more time to warm up to her. It was too bad she only saw them Friday through Sunday.

Eboni shook the remaining contents of cornflakes into another bowl and poured milk in it. She took it to the dining room where Lori was sitting patiently at the table. Smiling, Eboni placed the bowl in front of the little girl.

"Thank you," Lori said joyously, gazing up at Eboni as she smiled.

"You're welcome, sweetie," Eboni responded, handing her a spoon. "What are you doing up so early?"

"I went to sleep, and I woke up," Lori said to Eboni. "I just couldn't go back to sleep."

"I see."

Lori took the spoon and began eating her cereal. As Eboni smiled at Lori, she wondered about Joy. Was the other twin still sleeping? Or was she up far before sunrise like her sister? Eboni had never known either of them to be up so early when they were under her roof.

"Where is Joy?" Eboni asked.

Lori looked at her. "She's still sleeping," she responded.

"Lori, does Joy like me?"

"She likes you," the little girl said. "She hasn't said a lot to you because she sees you with daddy and daddy and mommy aren't living together anymore."

Eboni nodded. She watched as the little girl stretched and yawned. "Is that the only reason?" she inquired, rubbing her hands together.

"Joy feels you are trying to take our mommy's place. I told her it wasn't true. She's confused why mommy and daddy aren't together anymore. I'm confused too. I had a friend at school whose parents went through the same thing. So, it doesn't bother me as much as it bothers Joy. But Joy likes you very much. She told me herself."

Lorenzo's ex-wife would always be their mother. The only thing Eboni could do was accept the role of being an extra parent since Lorenzo was their father and she was now with him.

"Do you like me, Lori?" Eboni asked.

Lori's smile expanded when she dropped her spoon into the bowl of cereal. "I like you a lot," she said to Eboni.

Eboni showed a bright smile.

****

Eboni sat behind the desk in her office. As she eyed meticulously all the bottles of liquor printed on the inventory sheet for the past month, she thought of Lorenzo. Trying to concentrate, Eboni placed a beautifully polished fingernail on the sheet as she continued to run down the list of alcohol.

Eboni gently placed the sheet down on her desk and frowned at the assortment of mail she hadn't looked at since it arrived two days ago. She saw a manila envelope addressed to her from STZ, a foreign subsidiary of the New York City Bank. She tore open the envelope and immediately unfolded a piece of paper inside and read a letter. Her eyes concentrated and her face frowned. A drop of sweat poured down from the middle of her forehead.

> *Dear Ms. Law,*
>
> *I am sorry to inform you we can no longer afford you an excess loan of $800 a month. The realtor who owns the property of your place of business has informed us the monthly rent is increasing by $600. I met with my associates about lending you another $250 a month because of the confidence you've provided us by always paying back our loans to us in a timely manner. I humbly regret to tell you we can no longer issue loans anymore. We thank you for your business for the past year and wish you all the best.*
>
> *Sincerely,*
>
> *Wyatt G.S. Schottenheimer, National Bank of Belgium*

Eboni closed her eyes and took four deep breaths. She trembled as beads of sweat formed on her forehead. Her bottom lip twisted as she balled up the letter in her hand and tossed it across the room.

She walked to the window and looked down at people walking in both directions down Mott Street.

Knock-knock.

Damn. Someone was at her office door.

"Who is it?" Eboni asked, a slight frown on her face as she looked irritably at the door.

"It's Stuart," a voice somewhere between masculine and feminine said.

What does he want?

Eboni rushed to the door. Taking a deep breath, she opened it. She pulled Stuart inside her office and closed the door back.

"What is it?" she demanded, seeing a dozen of roses in his hand attached to some kind of long black casing.

"Eboni, were you busy?" Stuart asked her.

Eboni smirked and shook her head.

"What is it?" Eboni asked him a second time.

"We're reaching full capacity," Stuart told her, his eyes fixed on hers. "And it appears Bruce Lee had these flowers sent to you along with this."

Eboni focused on him and took a deep breath. Stuart frowned as he approached her. Eboni shook her head as he gazed at her. She nodded and took the flowers and a thin curved black casing from him. She smelled the roses, smiled, and pulled what appeared to be a glistening chrome sword out of the long case.

Eboni looked at Stuart for a moment as she brought the blade up to her eyes. There was some kind of a Japanese inscription on the left side of the sword's handle. She reached for the inventory sheet she had been holding only moments ago, tossed it into the air, and swung the silver blade down and across. The sheet of paper became four pieces before they floated in the air and landed on the floor.

Eboni's smile grew larger as her heart melted inside her chest. Her eyes sparkled as her cheeks burned. She felt her skin tingle throughout her body. While her eyebrows lifted, she flashed her teeth at Stuart. She thought fondly of Lorenzo kissing her, holding her, and caressing her.

"Eboni," Stuart said softly as he touched her shoulder. "Eboni, what were you doing when I came in?" he asked her.

Eboni dropped to one knee and gazed up at him. "I have to be honest with myself," she said to him, placing the Katana sword on her desk next to the roses.

"What are you talking about, Eboni?"

"Stuart, I'm not going through with my butt injection operation," she told him as tears flowed down her face. "I thought it was something I really wanted. I guess I don't."

"Eboni, did something happen?" Stuart asked her.

"No," she answered. "I have to learn to embrace my narrow ass the way it is."

Stuart looked away from her. "Eboni, what is it?" he asked her.

Eboni stood up. "I see I'm sexy just the way I am," she said to him, shaking her head.

"Of course, you are," he said, his eyes meeting hers.

Eboni forced herself to smile as Stuart approached her. As they locked gazes, he smiled back at her. "I never really thought I needed butt injections anyway," she said. "Lorenzo told me I'm fine without it. I don't need a big butt."

"You really love Bruce Lee, don't you?" Stuart asked her.

"Yes," Eboni said as she placed a hand over her heart. "I love him. I love Lorenzo unconditionally."

"So, you have more appreciation for your body?"

Eboni nodded. "Yes," she said. "Having an ironing board backside is not the end of the world."

Stuart laughed and placed a hand on Eboni's shoulder as he stood in front of her. "Yes, Eboni. I'm not saying who, but a few of the servers and at least two bartenders think you're one of the most beautiful women they've ever seen."

Eboni took another deep breath. "I don't want to know who," she answered. "All I care about is how Lorenzo feels about me."

She focused away and closed her eyes again. This time she took two deep breaths as she shook her head. Stuart's gaze quickly found her.

"Eboni, is there anything else?" her friend asked. "You look down-trodden somewhat."

Eboni took a deep breath. She peered down towards the sword on the desk and picked it up. Many emotions flooded her heart abruptly. She looked at her reflection on the chrome sword and turned her mouth up into a smile.

"We might go out of business, Stuart," she said, forcing herself to eye him.

Stuart sat on the dispersed envelopes on her desk. "Going out of business?" he questioned with a bewildered look on his face.

"I just opened a letter from the bank in Belgium saying the property owner is raising the rent and they no longer can give me loans even if I have a good track record of paying the bank back. I don't know what I'm going to do."

"Ask another bank!" Stuart suggested.

"I don't have a solid relationship with any other bank," Eboni said, wiping sweat from her brow as she tried to force herself to smile. "Besides, I tried to get a loan from three of them before we opened fifteen months ago. They said no. I deal with banks in foreign lands only to assist in any business venture."

"Which country was the bank located in?"

"Belgium."

"Where's the letter?" Stuart asked, his expression intense.

Eboni pointed to a wrinkled piece of paper on the floor by the closet door. Stuart went over to it and picked it up. He immediately regarded the letter and nodded as he placed it on her desk by her Louis Vuitton purse.

Eboni peeped up into the ceiling and closed her eyes. She knew it would take a miracle for her to stay in business. She knew she would need help and fast. There was only one person she knew who could aid her. She only hoped he could prevent this disaster.

"Eboni, what are you going to do?" Stuart asked her as she placed the sword back on her desk.

Eboni shook her head. "I don't know," came the helpless reply.

****

Eboni entered the dojo. It was the first time she had been to any of Lorenzo's martial arts schools. She met with security and signed in at the front desk. When she proceeded on down a short corridor, she heard nothing but quietness. As she made her way onto the main floor, Eboni noticed there were no students there. There was just Lorenzo.

She watched him for several minutes performing Chi. The way he did it was so effortless and beautiful. Watching him doing Chi was like seeing poetry in motion, full of artistry and grace. Eboni put her hands together and clapped.

"Hey," he spoke when he noticed her.

"Hey," Eboni spoke back. "Thank you for the roses and the sword."

"You're welcome, my love," Lorenzo said to her. "I want to teach you how to wield your sword when you're ready to learn."

Eboni smiled and put her hands on her hips. She walked out into the main floor and viewed ahead of her. She turned and looked at Lorenzo.

"It's funny to see you here," Lorenzo said to her with a cheerful smile.

"Do you remember when we went to Brooklyn for dinner and I mentioned my butt operation?" she reminded him.

"I remember," he said to her.

"Do you remember what you said to me?"

"I recall saying you don't need this operation," he answered her.

"You said that."

Lorenzo gazed at Eboni. "Are you having second thoughts about this surgery?" he asked her.

Eboni nodded and put her hands on her hips. "Yes," she retorted. "Sometimes I look at my ass in the mirror with and without panties on and I feel it's not big enough. I guess I've been struggling with the thought of my ass being flat."

Lorenzo smiled. "Think of the things that can go wrong," he advised her. "As my father would tell you, a lot of these silicone injection surgeries have disastrous consequences, and women have regretted getting it done. Even implants are unnatural."

"You also told me to eat a lot and work my glutes for satisfying results," Eboni said.

"Either do that or just leave it alone. But having silicone injected inside your butt shouldn't be an option. You don't want a synthetic ass."

Eboni snickered. "I know," she said.

When Lorenzo finished doing his Chi exercises, he walked up to her. He kissed Eboni's lips and guided her through his school. Her eyes looked up towards the walls, seeing dozens of pictures of students performing martial arts. When he led her through a corridor on the opposite side of the main floor, Eboni saw more pictures of older students hanging on the walls.

Lorenzo walked slightly ahead of her. He opened a door on the right and went inside what Eboni had thought to be a room. When Eboni followed him, she saw a desk, furniture, and countless framed pictures of a much younger Lorenzo with an old man all over the walls.

"Welcome to my office," he said to her. "It's not as exquisite as your office."

"Lorenzo, this is really nice," Eboni said in awe as she smiled. "Who is the old man in all the pictures with you?"

"Master Kimlau Li," Lorenzo answered. "He was my teacher."

"Is he still living?" she asked.

"Yes. He's ancient. I haven't seen Master Kimlaui Li in ten years. But a few people who work here in Chinatown who knows him have mentioned he lives in a senior's home on Staten Island."

Eboni took a seat on a small sofa and crossed her legs. Smiling, Lorenzo sat right beside her. As they regarded each other, Eboni's heart raced a little. Lorenzo placed a hand on her inner thigh and kissed her lips fervidly. Lorenzo buried Eboni under an avalanche of kisses.

"I told my father about you recently," Lorenzo said. "You've already met my sister Olivia. I think she likes you a lot."

"But your father has a problem with me, doesn't he?" Eboni instinctively asked.

"Yes, he does," Lorenzo told her. "But it's his problem."

"Lorenzo, I don't want to come between you and your father."

"I'm the type of man who draws simple lines in life. If my father has a problem with my life, and the choices I make in my life, no matter what those choices are and who they involve, he's not my father," Lorenzo said as his eyes watched her.

"What did he say?"

"My father can control as my younger brother Thaddeus will tell you," Lorenzo said wearing a slight frown. "He doesn't know how to respect the boundaries of his children. He tries to interfere not just in my life, but all of my brothers' and sisters' lives too. And he's so unapologetic about it. If you meet him, he's going to give you a hard time."

"I'm so sorry," Eboni said.

"Don't be," Lorenzo said, cheerfully grinning at her.

Eboni shook her head, displaying an uncharacteristic frown as she pressed her lips together

"No class today?" Eboni asked. "There's no one here except us and the security guard at the front door."

"I taught a couple of classes earlier this morning," Lorenzo said. "For whatever reason not too, many students showed up today."

"Oh."

For a moment, Lorenzo's office was silent. As they both looked at one another, Eboni wondered what was on Lorenzo's mind. This would be the perfect time to do something spontaneous, she thought. But she knew Lorenzo well enough to know when he was thinking about sex and when he wasn't.

"Lorenzo, there's a good chance *The Camelot* could close," Eboni told him.

Lorenzo's eyebrows arose. "Why?" he asked her, placing a hand firmly on his chest.

Eboni told Lorenzo about the letter from the bank. When she finished telling him how hard it would be to get another loan from a different bank, he reached out for her and held her in his arms. Tears that slipped from out of her eyes were dry cleaned by his bright smile.

"Eboni, how much is the rent there?" Lorenzo asked.

"It was $1200 a month," she told him. "They are increasing it to $1800 a month. My apartment is close to $2,200 a month. I---"

Lorenzo cut her off. "I'll pay $900 of the rent for your business every month," he offered. "If you can also pay $900, you'll have the monthly rent covered for *The Camelot*. With my help, you would keep an extra $300 a month. You can use it to start an account at a different bank. At this different bank, if you add $300 a month, you'll be eligible for a loan in less than six months, probably."

Eboni peeked into Lorenzo's angelic stare. He looked so innocent. He looked so friendly.

"Why would you do something so gracious like that for me?" she asked him.

"You really have to ask me?" Lorenzo asked, eyeing her lips.

"But why?" she asked him again.

Lorenzo swallowed. "Because I love you more than you know," he told her. "And you wanted me to help you. That's why you brought this to my attention."

"You're so sweet," Eboni said, both of her hands touching his arm.

"Are you ready to meet my father?" Lorenzo asked her.

Eboni smiled. "Yes," she answered. "I'm up to it. I would love to meet your father."

"I'm not sure what to expect."

"What do you mean?"

Lorenzo scratched his mustache and placed his hand on Eboni's knee. "I'm not sure how he is going to treat you or me," he said, shaking his head. "But if my father gets out of hand, I'll deal with it. I won't allow him to disrespect you."

Eboni smiled. "Do you think he will?" she asked.

"I know my father."

Eboni eyed away thoughtfully. She turned back towards Lorenzo as his smile blazed like rays of sunshine onto her. She returned his smile, wondering how their meeting with Dr. Royal would go.

"But," he said, taking her hand.

"But what?" she asked, glancing at him as they walked side by side down the hall until they reached the main floor.

Lorenzo stooped down and removed her feet from her shoes. She followed him onto the main floor where the lessons in martial arts took place. The floor felt soft beneath her feet.

"But allow me to give you a crash course in Taekwondo and Jiu-jitsu," he said to her.

Eboni bowed to acknowledge the sensei. "Teach me everything," she said to him.

Lorenzo walked up to her. He waved for her to approach him. As soon as she got close enough to Lorenzo, he reached down and grabbed her left leg, pinned it between his ribs and forearm, and placed his left hand on her shoulder as he blocked her lower right leg with his lower left leg. Eboni fell backward with a slight push and before she knew it, she was lying on the floor looking up at him.

"It's a simple takedown," he said to her.

"Similar to what you taught me the night when it was pouring rain," she said.

"Similar, but not the same," Lorenzo said, smiling as she got up. "Now I want you to take me down."

Lorenzo went over it with her slowly. Eboni did exactly as he told her and took him down as he did her.

"And then punch you in the face," Eboni remembered him telling her.

"Correct," he said to her. "Now I'll teach you to set up the armbar submission hold. I'll also go over with you how to trap the forearm and lock the elbow when someone comes at you with a gun or a knife. But first, let's revisit those side and front kicks."

"Yes, sensei," Eboni said humbly.

Two hours later, Eboni peeped to her clothing she had tossed aside as she sat up. She looked down to the loose triangle chokehold she had Lorenzo in like the back of his neck rested comfortably on her inner thigh. All she had to do was compress the back of her lower leg against his throat, and she could choke him unconscious.

Perspiration dripped from her forehead down her face. From out of the corner of her eye, she saw her breasts fall and rise with every breath she took. Eboni eyed down to Lorenzo, and she saw he hadn't broken a sweat. Of course, he hadn't. His style of teaching required no energy. But learning and doing everything right did.

"You're fun to teach," Lorenzo's voice echoed, his hand rubbing Eboni's left hip.

"I enjoy it more each time you teach me," Eboni said, looking down towards him,

Eboni reached behind her for her purse, opened it, and retrieved a long thin syringe. She removed its top and stuck the needle full of insulin in her arm.

"Okay, my love," Eboni said softly. "I want to meet Dr. Royal."

"Let's shower first," Lorenzo said.

"You lead the way."

****

Jack Johnson's restaurant in midtown Manhattan on 30th Street was at full capacity. Lorenzo entered, dressed in a grey suit and black necktie. Eboni walked behind him, dressed modestly with loose-fitting blue jeans, a sky-blue blouse, and a pair of black textiles bow accented loafers on her feet. An aqua headscarf adorned her head, hiding most of her hair.

"Do you see him?" Eboni asked Lorenzo.

She watched as Lorenzo looked in all directions. He nodded in response to her and pointed into the back of the room. A party of two sat near the wall. Lorenzo took Eboni by the hand and slowly walked in their direction.

"Father," Lorenzo said when he and Eboni approached them. "Hello, Olivia."

"Have a seat, Lorenzo," Xavier said nonchalantly as he watched Eboni.

"It's so good to see you and Eboni again," Olivia said to him.

"It's good to see you too, Olivia," Lorenzo addressed his sister as he and Eboni sat across from her and their father.

"So, this is the person you're with now?" Xavier asked Lorenzo as he looked at Eboni.

"Yes, father," Lorenzo answered.

"Just explain something to me. Why do you have flings with married men?"

Eboni frowned at Xavier. "I don't," she said, keeping her tone even as she replied calmly.

"But you know Lorenzo had a struggling marriage, and you took full advantage," Xavier said to Eboni, a simple grin on his face.

Eboni shook her head. "I didn't take advantage," she said.

"Tread lightly, father," Lorenzo warned.

"Lorenzo and I have been friends for a while now," Eboni went on. "The night I met Lorenzo; Someone almost robbed me at gunpoint when I was closing my restaurant. He was there and botched the robbery attempt. He started coming to my restaurant. We became friends. As for him belonging to some else..."

Lorenzo had cut Eboni off. "She doesn't have to explain herself to you!" Lorenzo exclaimed as his fist punched the table.

"Lorenzo, it's okay," Eboni said to him, placing her hand on his forearm and stroking it.

Lorenzo looked sternly at Xavier. His facial expression seemed to soften when he turned to Eboni. Lorenzo took her hand and held it and placed their held hands on the table. He wanted to make sure they noticed it. Xavier kept his eyes on Eboni.

Eboni went on. "I mean no disrespect, but this is really none of your damn business," she said to Xavier, feeling her patient and kind disposition changing. "It's truly none of your concern. I have done nothing wrong. Your son made the choice to be my companion and champion.

Why are you trying to cause a problem? You risk alienating Lorenzo if you keep this up."

Xavier looked back at Eboni. His eyes glazed towards Lorenzo. He saw Lorenzo looking at Xavier angrily.

"I envy Eboni," said Olivia, pulling at two of her silky dreadlocks. "She's one of the most beautiful women I've ever seen in my life. I feel like a little sister to her already."

"I like her spirit," Lorenzo told Xavier.

"Lorenzo, you could have made things work with Jocelyn," Xavier argued as his eyes peered at Eboni. "I doubt seriously if you and she tried hard enough. This new woman is far too old for you. She's older than all of my children."

Lorenzo frowned as he stood up. "I've heard enough from you, dad!" he told Xavier in a hostile tone of voice. "At least I never committed adultery. You should be ashamed of the many times you've cheated on my mother."

"Both of you stop now!" Olivia exclaimed; her face serious.

"I LOVE THIS WOMAN!!!!" Lorenzo exploded.

"Lorenzo, I'm disappointed," Xavier said to him.

"Father, why are you fighting against me?" Lorenzo asked Xavier.

"Son, I want you to be happy."

"Act like it, father!" Olivia said to Xavier.

Lorenzo frowned. "Just stop it," he told Xavier. "Eboni has a great heart, father. Her heart is full of love and her spirit is full of life. I am committed to her, and she to me."

"Lorenzo, Lorenzo, Lorenzo," Xavier said more to himself than to Lorenzo.

"Dad, stay out of my love life!" Lorenzo said with conviction. "I don't care for your approval or your blessing. You can keep up this nonsense and risk losing a son. Or you can come to grips with it. It's your choice."

"I brought you into this world, Lorenzo. I can take you out."

Lorenzo's frown got darker. "Are you threatening me?" he asked Xavier.

"Both of you please shut the fuck up!" Olivia hollered as she scowled.

In response, Lorenzo stood up and said, "Hiyahhh!" as his hand came crashing down on the table. The table broke and leaned sideways as two plates fell onto Xavier's lap while other plates, silverware, and glasses all came colliding to the floor.

Eboni turned around, seeing all eyes inside the restaurant were focusing in their direction. Servers and diners had to stop what they were doing just to watch the spectacle Lorenzo and Xavier were putting on.

A smile danced around Eboni's lips. Her eyes widened as her heart fiercely pounded inside her chest. Eboni had felt Lorenzo's love. Here, with this display of his honor and strength defending her and their union.

"You have to be insane!" Xavier shouted as he looked up at Lorenzo.

Eboni gazed at Olivia. Eboni peeked towards Lorenzo's father. Xavier's bottom lip trembled as his breathing seemed to quicken. His eyes looked away from Lorenzo for a moment as he remained silent. When he eyed Lorenzo again, Xavier stood up.

"I'm sorry, son," Xavier said softly as a man wearing a suit and necktie approached their table. "I'm so sorry. I didn't mean to upset you to this degree. If this woman is who you truly love you will have my blessing."

"Hello," the man in the suit and necktie spoke. "I'm the manager. Is everything okay here?"

"We're fine," Eboni said as she stood up. "Just a minor family quarrel but everything is under control now."

"The table and several dishes are broke," the manager said to Eboni. "I'm afraid I'm going to have to ask you all to leave."

"It doesn't have to come to that," Eboni put in. "We'll pay for the table and the damaged dishes." She quickly reached inside her purse for a checkbook and an ink pen. She wrote a check for $500.00 and handed it to the manager. "We would like to be seated at another table."

The manager examined the check and nodded. "Fair enough," he said. "We will reseat your party at another table shortly. But no more fighting!"

But Lorenzo's eyes blazed at Xavier still. Lorenzo let out a deep breath and eyed away from his father. He sat down in the chair he had vacated and placed his face in his hands as he took a series of deep breaths. The manager watched them until he disappeared into the kitchen.

Eboni exhaled, thankful this bickering between them had ended.

"Lorenzo, look at what you did to the table," Olivia said, covering her mouth with a hand. "Stop acting crazy."

Eboni watched as Lorenzo sat back down and grabbed her hand. He lifted their held hands in the air for all to see. Xavier nodded to them.

"Very well," Xavier said to the couple.

"Both of you look great together," Olivia said to Eboni and Lorenzo.

Lorenzo and Eboni smiled at each other.

Thirteen

Chapter 13

Chapter **13**

Jocelyn sat on the edge of the bed. She blinked her eyes repeatedly as she stared down at the clean folded towels and washcloths inside a small plastic basket. But as she tried to focus on work, her ex-husband took over her thoughts.

How do I pick up the pieces? How do I go on? Oh, Lorenzo, I miss you!

She sighed as she thought about her daughters. It gratified her to have custody of Joy and Lori. They were never far from her thoughts whenever they were away from her on the weekends. She thought about them every second of every hour of every day during the three-day period when they were with their father. But she couldn't help but bathe in the sorrow of not seeing them every single day like she once had. Just having them five days a week wasn't enough. Jocelyn wished they could be with her all the time. She felt a tremendous void every time she met with Lorenzo at Queensboro Plaza every Friday to give him the children.

Jocelyn shook her head and closed her eyes. She continued to recall her marriage to Lorenzo. She remembered the good times of having him come home to her Latin dishes and salads after he spent an entire day working very hard. She was reminiscent of the joy, the laughter, and the genuine love they had for each other. But wasn't she trying to move on? Why couldn't she?

Damn! I need to say goodbye to the past! She thought.

A tear slid down her face. Before she knew it, she was lying face down on the bed with her head buried in the pillows as tears overflowed. She embraced the pillow and cried harder. As she wiped away her tears, more tears flowed

"Jocelyn?"

The voice was immediate and unexpected. The voice startled her. But she buried her face deeper into the pillow and ignore it as her crying became louder. Jocelyn heard the door to the room close, and the sounds of footsteps on the shallow carpet seemed to get louder as they came in her direction.

"Jocelyn?"

The voice called to her once again. She knew the voice. She knew it well. She knew full well it was Crystal's voice. Jocelyn felt a gentle hand on her shoulder. When she turned around and gazed up, she saw Crystal looking down on her with a concerned gaze.

"Jocelyn, what's the matter?" Crystal asked, sitting on the edge of the bed.

Jocelyn turned around and sat up next to her. She placed her face in her hands for several minutes before she could regain her composure. Crystal's hand wiped Jocelyn's face as she sought where to begin. It was something she truly didn't want to discuss with her boss. But Jocelyn felt if she just talked about it to whoever, it could prove emotionally beneficial. Talking about her pain, her impatience with a distant husband, her personal drama, and whatever regret she still felt could prove therapeutically helpful.

Crystal placed her arm around Jocelyn's shoulder and pulled her close to her. To Jocelyn, it gave her a sense of comfort. It made her know whatever was on her mind she could share. She knew she had to let go of it here and now or else it would continue to haunt her. To say goodbye to six long years wasn't possible.

"What's wrong, Jocelyn?" Crystal asked her.

"I----," Jocelyn began. "I miss my husband."

"What do you mean?"

Jocelyn told Crystal everything.

"Are you sure he's in a relationship with the woman you saw him kiss in the courtroom?" Crystal asked her.

"Yes," Jocelyn told her.

"Well, Jocelyn, you can't look back now," Crystal advised. "What's happened has happened and no matter what the impact of what's already happened, give a nonchalant attitude towards it. If you don't, it will continue to eat you up inside. You and your husband divorced for a good reason. You both agreed to conclude the marriage because *you* were the unhappy one."

"You're right," Jocelyn said as she sobbed. "I can't continue to put out all of this negative energy. I'm just trying to cope with not having my husband with me, and the fact he's quickly moved on."

"It takes time," Crystal said to her. "It's going to take a while to get used to life without him. As for your husband moving on as rapidly as he did, you needn't concern yourself with that. He did what was best for him. He lost you too."

Jocelyn gripped the other woman as Crystal rubbed her back. Crystal too held onto Jocelyn. They unfastened themselves from each other and Jocelyn eyed away.

"After your divorce was final, did the two of you speak?"

"Yes," Jocelyn said as she wiped her watery eyes. "We wished each other well, and he told me he and I would always remain friends. We shook hands that day before we parted ways."

"I think that's positive."

"Have you ever been married?" Jocelyn asked Crystal.

"Yes," Crystal answered as she nodded.

"What happened?"

"I wrecked a ten-year marriage. It's the one thing in my life I wished I could take back. My husband loved me. I loved him too. My situation was identical to yours somewhat."

"You had needs he wasn't fulfilling?"

Crystal smiled. "Yes, like in your case," she admitted plainly. "My husband used to travel to Denver for business on the weekends. One Saturday, he canceled his flight and returned home. He caught me in bed with my lover. My husband filed for divorce soon after."

Jocelyn's eyebrows arose as her chin dropped. She peeped at Crystal's face, seeing lasting shame. Why did Crystal go into such graphic detail?

"I wallowed in self-pity for a long time before I could forgive myself," Crystal said, slumping her shoulders as she looked away.

"How did you feel afterward?" Jocelyn asked.

Crystal shrugged her shoulders. "I wish it never happened," she said, bringing her focus back on Jocelyn. "Before I got caught, it was all about the moment with my other lover. But after my husband found out, my marriage was over. When my husband caught me, he called me every degrading name."

"How did it make you feel?" Jocelyn asked her boss, eyeing her from her extravagant Emo hairstyle to her face.

Crystal smiled and shook her head. "Like I did something wrong," she answered.

"Did you continue to see him?"

"You mean the other gentleman? I saw him for the next year," Crystal said, a tiny smile on her face as she remembered. "Eventually he found a woman and settled down."

Crystal's narrative about her unfaithfulness was so similar to Jocelyn's story except for Jocelyn never crossed that line. "I had an older friend who was a lesbian," Crystal went on. "She was the next chapter in my life."

As Jocelyn wiped away her drying tears, she looked in Crystal's direction. Crystal was staring at the wall across the room for several moments before she returned Jocelyn's gaze. As she did so, a mind-bending thought took a hold of her.

Maybe I should try the same sex. Maybe I need to find a woman with who I can connect on a deeper level.

"So, you were a lesbian?" Jocelyn asked for her own confirmation.

"I still am."

Jocelyn put her hands together. "Believe it or not, I had heard you were a lesbian when I first started working here," she told Crystal.

Crystal nodded. "It's no secret I like women," she said with a smile.

"How long has it been since you've been with a man?" Jocelyn asked.

"Years and years," Crystal said, smiling as she regarded Jocelyn again.

"You don't like men anymore? Not even a little?"

"I love men," Crystal said. "I even fantasize about one or two. I'm more intrigued by those who are the same sex as me though. I'm extremely attracted to femininity."

"I see."

"Have you ever been with another woman?" Crystal asked curiously.

"One time during my junior year in college," Jocelyn answered. "It happened many years ago."

"She made you feel wonderful, didn't she?"

"She did."

"Another woman whether she's bisexual, or a femme knows how to please," Crystal said, looking away towards the window. "She knows your body because hers and yours are virtually the same. She knows what buttons to push. She knows how to send you into total bliss. She knows how to push you past the heights of ecstasy until you reach the point where you don't even want a man."

Crystal placed a gentle hand on Jocelyn's arm and smiled at her. Jocelyn returned the smile and looked across the room. She took several deep breaths and eyed the engraved line on her ring finger. It had served as a depressing reminder of what once was. But it also served as the perfect emphasis to what could await her in the future.

"I have to return to work," Crystal said. "Focus on what lies ahead in your life. But take it one day at a time and you'll be fine, Jocelyn. It was nice talking to you."

Jocelyn smiled. "Thanks for being there," she whispered.

"You're welcome," Crystal said, touching Jocelyn's shoulder.

Crystal gave her a smile and got up. She waved as she walked to the door. Giving Jocelyn one last look, she walked out of the guest room and headed down the hallway. Jocelyn stood up and walked towards the door. She came outside of the room and stared down the hall just in time to see Crystal entering through a side door leading to a staircase.

Jocelyn smiled as she nodded to herself. The smile turned brighter, the gloom of melancholy disappearing. The longing for Lorenzo was still there, but she knew Crystal was right about several things. She had to get out more. She had to meet new people. She had to forget about the past. And last, she not only had to deal with the outcome of her marriage, but she also had to move on. Yes. She had to move on.

****

Jocelyn hurried to the West Farms subway station when her workday was over. As she walked across the street, she heard a horn blowing loudly.

"Jocelyn!" a familiar feminine voice called.

Jocelyn turned around and immediately saw Crystal behind the wheel of a blue Ford Explorer. The vehicle stopped at a red light on the other side of the intersection. Jocelyn adjusted the strap on her purse over her shoulder and walked across the street in Crystal's direction.

"How far do you live from here?" Crystal asked when Jocelyn came to her vehicle. "I'll take you home."

Jocelyn wanted to say no. But heading to Queens from the Bronx on the subway was an awfully long commute. It would take her almost two full hours to get home. In an automobile, the time to get from West Farms in the Bronx to her neighborhood in Queens took less than a half-hour.

"I live just off of Queens Boulevard in Forest Hills," Jocelyn answered.

"Get in," Crystal said in a friendly tone. "I'll take you home."

Jocelyn got into the passenger side of the truck and placed her purse down by her feet. Crystal turned to look at her and drove on when the light had changed. She soon merged onto the highway, and drove over the White Stone Bridge into Queens, taking Northern Boulevard down further than she should have. When Jocelyn noticed it, she turned to Crystal as the woman continued to drive.

"Do you live in this borough?" Jocelyn asked Crystal.

"I don't," Crystal said.

"You've driven down further than you should have," Jocelyn said.

"You wanted to go straight home? There's a club in Astoria I wanted to go to."

Jocelyn thought about the twins. She just wanted to get home and kick her feet up and spend time with them. Hanging out at a club with her boss was going way outside the boundaries of professionalism. But Jocelyn knew she needed to do what Crystal suggested earlier. She needed to get out more. She needed to learn to get her mind off of the things she couldn't control. Home could wait. For now, Jocelyn was curious about this place where Crystal was taking them.

"No," Jocelyn answered calmly. "We can go wherever you want."

Crystal turned off of Northern Boulevard and smiled. Soon enough Crystal made it to 31st Street and parked her truck right across the street from a go-go bar called *Lounge Electra*. When they stepped out of the truck, Jocelyn took a deep breath and slung her purse over her shoulder while Crystal put a pocket mirror up to her face and did her make-up. They walked through the front door of the club to the sounds of Katy Perry.

Jocelyn recalled a distant memory of her and Lorenzo riding a beautiful brown horse at the Bronx Equestrian Center years ago when she was six months pregnant with Joy and Lori. She fought an oncoming tear and smiled at the song. Why did the song remind her of this memory? Perhaps it was the fondest of memories of her and Lorenzo when they were together.

But a haunting image came back to her. Lorenzo and Eboni were standing by the elevator kissing. He seemed to be so into it. Before turning around and walking behind Cressida and Olivia, Jocelyn saw Lorenzo holding Eboni's face in his hands as he kissed her passionately. Before a tear could slide down her face, Jocelyn shut her eyes tight and bit her bottom lip as she tried to block the troubling depiction from her thoughts.

One girl was dancing on stage. The bar was empty except for a few men sitting at a table far in the back drinking beers and talking.

"Usually during happy hour there are more people here," Crystal said.

"Maybe more people will arrive after happy hour," Jocelyn said.

"Crystal!" a female's voice screamed over the music.

Crystal and Jocelyn turned around toward the womanly voice. A thin woman with a tight grey bodysuit and high heel shoes walked in their direction. Her dyed red hair was down by her hind legs as if she'd never gotten a haircut before. The smile she displayed was warm and friendly.

"Hey, girl," the woman said to Crystal when she walked up to them.

As Crystal talked with the exotic dancer, Jocelyn noticed a familiar woman who she worked with from time to time. Jocelyn smiled and walked up to the lady. Although the woman was much older than she or Crystal, she still looked well kept like she took excellent care of herself. Jewelry from necklaces to earrings to the exquisite wrist and arm bracelets bedecked her.

She recalled the woman at work almost catching her with Buck inside a guestroom months ago. Her two supervisors embraced as Jocelyn gazed at them.

"Hi, Pearl," Crystal addressed the woman. "Funny to see you here this early."

"Girl, I had nothing to do after work so I came here," Pearl said, her eyes looking from Crystal to Jocelyn. "You're never here this early either."

"Pearl, you know Jocelyn from work, right?

"Of course, I know the loveliest lady who works with us," Pearl said to Crystal as she smiled happily at Jocelyn. "Hi, Jocelyn."

"Hola! Como Estas!" Jocelyn spoke to Pearl. "How are you doing?"

The two of them followed Pearl to a table closest to where another exotic dancer was dancing on stage. When they all took a seat, an attractive server came up to them and took their orders. Jocelyn and Crystal engaged in conversation as Pearl got up from the table. Jocelyn watched as Pearl walked up to the girl on stage. Pearl reached into her bra for several folded dollar bills and put each one neatly under the dancer's G-string.

Crystal looked at Jocelyn and Pearl. "Pearl, I don't think you should tip strippers in front of a subordinate. It's inappropriate and unprofessional."

Pearl smiled and giggled. "So, what if it is?" she told Crystal. "We are not at work right now. Plus, we're all grown women! Jocelyn, as enchanting as she is, isn't a child."

"I take it you like that stripper?" Crystal asked Pearl.

"She's fine as hell," Pearl said to Crystal when she came back to the table. "Girl, I've been trying to get that one to come home with me for weeks."

"That's Tonya," Crystal said. "I think she only likes men."

So, Pearl was a lesbian, Jocelyn guessed. Just as Crystal was. And from the looks of it, they both frequented go-go bars like this one. That explained why Pearl had caressed her face inside the employee lounge that day.

Jocelyn studied the room, seeing the red and neon green lights blinking, illuminating the club. To the side near the walls, there were a group of women sitting on a long white suede sofa chatting and laughing. At the bar, three bartenders were working where two female customers sat in front of them sharing a passionate kiss. There was Gaelic writing on both restroom doors. Two femmes were playing a game of pool on a large crimson pool table ten yards away from the bar on the left.

"I have the method of melting her down," Pearl was saying to Crystal. "She likes men now. It won't always be the case."

Jocelyn regarded Pearl. When she first observed her, Jocelyn thought Pearl looked average and took wonderful care of herself because she appeared two or perhaps three decades older than she and Crystal. But upon a second glance, Pearl was a lovely woman. Her eyebrows arched. Make-up faded that had been applied to her face probably hours ago. But regardless, Pearl appeared as far different now from the professional and hardworking woman from work.

Pearl looked in Jocelyn's direction. "You like what you see?" she asked Jocelyn.

Jocelyn smiled. "Excuse me?" she begged.

"I can see you watching me hard from out of the corner of my eye," Pearl said with a straight face. "Do you like what you see?"

Rather than retort, Jocelyn stayed silent. Her focus shifted to the dancer Tonya on stage. She wasn't sure if Pearl was giving her a reason to talk to her or if she didn't like Jocelyn looking at her, so she felt it was best not to reply just in case Pearl got the wrong idea.

When the bartender came back with their drinks, Pearl looked in Jocelyn's direction as Jocelyn and Crystal lifted their glasses. They each drank their liquor while Tonya stepped off of the stage. When Jocelyn saw Pearl ogling her, she looked away.

"Are you Puerto Rican?" Pearl asked Jocelyn, the older woman's eyes meticulously studying her.

Jocelyn's eyes met Pearl's. "Yes," she answered, smiling, eyeing from Crystal to Pearl, and remembering her listening to her problems with Lorenzo at work. "How did you know?"

"Your face and your eyes," Pearl said with a sparkle in her eyes. "You look like someone who I once knew. When we are at work, I gaze at you inside the cafeteria and wonder what Latin country you were from. I see I guessed right."

"My parents were both born in Puerto Rico and moved to New York during the early 1960s. I was born in New York though."

"Brooklyn?"

"Spanish Harlem," Jocelyn said to her.

Pearl picked up her glass and sipped her drink. She turned to Crystal and smiled. Tonya was there smiling at all of them. When Pearl saw the young woman, she stood up straight.

"How is everyone?" Tonya asked.

Tonya had huge breasts, a tiny waist, and a firm, round backside. As Pearl regarded the young woman, Tonya waved at her.

"We're all fine," Crystal answered her with a smile.

"I wanted to stop by your table to thank you for the dollar bills," Tonya said to Pearl.

Pearl smiled. "Well, I couldn't help myself, seeing as though you are irresistible and talented," she said to the young dancer.

Tonya smiled. "Thank you," she offered.

"Tell me something," Pearl said. "Am I the only woman who finds you attractive?"

Tonya shook her head. "I get compliments from both sexes," she said.

"How old are you, dear?"

"Twenty-five," the stripper answered.

"Have you ever been curious to know what a night would be like with someone like me?"

Jocelyn and Crystal looked at Pearl as their eyebrows rose and placed a hand over their mouths. Pearl was old enough to be this girl's grandmother. Pearl was just exuberant and untamed even if she didn't mind robbing the cradle. Tonya stood there in front of them smiling.

"It's crossed my mind before, honestly," the girl admitted.

"Well, give it more action than thought," Pearl told Tonya.

"I appreciate that but I have to go backstage," Tonya told them.

"Before you leave, I want to give you something."

Pearl reached inside her pocketbook and pulled out two twenty-dollar bills. "There you go," Pearl said to the young dancer.

The young woman blew them all a kiss and walked off. Crystal gazed at Pearl and laughed as Jocelyn sipped her drink.

"You really like her, don't you?" Crystal asked.

"I like them all!" Pearl declared.

Several female dancers performed on stage before they left *Lounge Electra*. As Crystal walked ahead of them, Jocelyn hung back a little and walked next to Pearl on the way to the truck. When they all reached the vehicle, they all got inside it.

"I'm going to take Jocelyn home and head to Long Island," Crystal said to Pearl.

"That's where you live?" Jocelyn asked, feeling buzzed from the three cocktails she enjoyed.

"Yes," Crystal answered gleefully. "I live on Long Island in Bethpage."

"I had a fun time," Pearl said to them. "Jocelyn, it was nice hanging out with you."

Jocelyn felt Pearl's hand touch her shoulder. Pearl leaned up from the backseat and kissed Crystal on the cheek. A split-second later Jocelyn felt Pearl's wet lips on her cheek.

"I didn't know you liked girls," Jocelyn said to Pearl, eyeing the older woman. "I thought you were married."

"Married?" Pearl asked, a smile touching her lips. "I used to be! My last man broke my heart, something terrible! I had to get counseling because I had trouble moving on! My psychiatrist, Gretchen O'Connell, was a godsend! She charmed me and would kiss me tenderly during our sessions. She was the first woman I ever got involved with!"

Jocelyn looked at Pearl as the older woman gazed back at her wild-eyed. "For real?" she asked her boss.

Crystal nodded. "Yes, she did," she answered.

"How long did it last?" Jocelyn asked curiously.

Pearl closed her eyes and rubbed her hands together. "I was in a relationship with Gretchen for eight years," she answered gladly. "This was many, many years ago. She had to move back to Ireland to take care of her mother. But I still hear from her twice a year. If it weren't for a no-good man, I don't think I would have met Gretchen. I don't think I would have been a lesbian either. Every once in a while, life throws us some nice curveballs!"

"So, the man who broke your heart was the last man you were with romantically?" Jocelyn asked Pearl.

"Men are such pencil dicks!" Pearl said loudly. "Yes, he was my last one forever and ever. Fuck men!"

"I see," Jocelyn said.

"Jocelyn, let's hang tough," Pearl suggested. "Just you and me. We work together but don't really know each other well. What do you say?"

Jocelyn's heart raced as she shivered. Pearl seemed to be quite wild, but somewhat fun.

"I'm going to go with Pearl," Jocelyn decided and opened the passenger side door. "Crystal, it was fun. I'll see you later."

"Okay," Crystal said, combing her fingers through her hair. "I'll see you tomorrow at work."

Both Jocelyn and Pearl exited Crystal's Ford Explorer. They all said their last goodbyes, and Crystal sped away as her truck disappeared down the street. Pearl took Jocelyn by the hand and led her down the street to where her car was parked. When they got to Pearl's vehicle, Jocelyn saw the older woman had an unmarked police car.

"Where are we going?" Jocelyn asked. "Your place or mine?"

"Where do you live exactly?" Pearl asked.

"Forest Hills, Queens. What about you?"

"I live in Washington Heights."

"Let's go to my place because it's closer."

Pearl shook her head. "I'd rather we go to my place," she said as they got into the car.

Pearl lived on Wadsworth Street in Washington Heights in the farthest northern Manhattan neighborhood. Jocelyn's buzz had worn off just a little on the journey from Queens to uptown. Now she sat on the edge of Pearl's king-sized bed as she waited for Pearl to come into the bedroom. Pearl had stepped into the shower after they got there. As Jocelyn waited, she smiled and looked towards the window.

When Pearl entered the bedroom, she had a red towel wrapped around her thin body. Her hair had been rolled up and placed inside another towel of the same color. When she sat on the bed, she looked directly at Jocelyn.

Jocelyn returned Pearl's gaze. Usually, she never went to a stranger's home. But Pearl was really no stranger.

"How old are you?" Jocelyn asked Pearl.

Pearl remained quiet for a moment. "Does my age truly matter?" she asked Jocelyn.

Jocelyn shook her head. "It doesn't at all," she said. "I'm intrigued by your comeliness. You're a very gorgeous woman. I know you're older. I just wanted to know your age."

"Thank you for the compliment," Pearl said with a slight smile. "If you really want to know, I'll tell you. I'm sixty-seven."

"Sixty-seven?"

Pearl was slightly more than twice Jocelyn's age just like she'd suspected. One could tell she wasn't a young woman, but her beauty was very evident. Jocelyn only hoped she would still be that attractive by the time she reached Pearl's age.

The woman is simply ageless, Jocelyn thought.

Pearl climbed into the bed and crawled over to where Jocelyn sat. As Jocelyn watched her, her heart raced just a small bit. When Pearl got to where Jocelyn was, she placed a gentle hand on her shoulder. Pearl sat up on her knees behind Jocelyn and pulled the tee-shirt she had on over her head. As Jocelyn's arms exited the short sleeves, she smiled up at the other woman.

Pearl tossed Jocelyn's t-shirt across the room and leaned down to place her chin on her shoulder. Pearl placed both of her fingers under Jocelyn's bra straps and stretched the straps upward and let them down. When Jocelyn felt comfortable enough, she leaned back into Pearl's body. Pearl embraced Jocelyn from behind and caressed her stomach.

As the magnificent feel of Pearl's touch aroused her, Jocelyn's pulse rate increased as she closed her eyes and bit her bottom lip.

Pearl reached towards the headboard for a royal blue jewelry box. She opened it, reached inside it, and took a hold of something. She looked at Jocelyn with a smile and extended her hand.

"I want you to have these," Pearl said to Jocelyn.

Jocelyn leaned over as Pearl handed her two exquisite emerald earrings. "They're exquisite," she told Pearl delightfully. "Thank you, Pearl."

"You're welcome," Pearl said to her. "My last pencil dick boyfriend gave me those a few months before he broke up with me. I never wore them. You can take them to a pawn shop and get money for them if you want. They're worth $2,300.00 or more. You can probably get $1,800.00 for them at the very least."

Jocelyn smiled brightly. "That's very kind of you," she said to Pearl. "I appreciate this a great deal. I'm going to keep them. Thank you again."

"How are things with your husband?" Pearl asked, scratching the side of her face. "I remember you telling me inside the employee lounge one time you and he were having problems."

Jocelyn shook her head and smiled to herself as she peeped at Pearl. "We're divorced now," she told Pearl, nodding her head. "I don't have to deal with him frustrating me anymore."

"Young lady, I'm sorry to hear about the stoppage of your marriage," Pearl told her with a long face. "Perhaps it's for the best."

"All of my family left New York just when I met my husband," said Jocelyn, forcing a smile to her face. "I would have gone with them but he and I fell in love and had children. I haven't seen my parents and siblings since. I miss them so much."

Pearl lifted her voice. "You should visit them!" she suggested. "I'm sure they miss you."

"And I miss them," Jocelyn said. "My parents haven't met my daughters."

"You're living in New York City. They're living elsewhere. You need to catch a flight with your daughters and stop by to see them. I'm sure your mom and dad would be thrilled."

Pearl crawled over to where Jocelyn was and sat right next to her. Jocelyn looked at her. Both women shared a friendly smile and Pearl placed her arm around Jocelyn and pulled her close. With two rapid kisses on her face from the older woman, Jocelyn stared dreamily at Pearl and paid close attention to the other woman's calm, yet serious facial expression.

"What do you want to do?" Pearl asked.

"I want you to kiss me again," Jocelyn quickly suggested, reaching over to touch the towel wrapped neatly around Pearl's body.

Pearl smiled and shook her head. "No," she said much to Jocelyn's chagrin. "But I'll tell you what I will do."

Jocelyn looked away from Pearl, smirking. Pearl got up and knelt down in front of Jocelyn. She unzipped Jocelyn's pants and loosened her belt. When Jocelyn saw what Pearl was doing, she stood up and pulled her pants down. Next, she stepped out of her Nike sneakers and removed her pants. When she sat back down, she gazed directly at Pearl. Pearl reached for Jocelyn's panties and pulled them from off of her until she had on nothing but her bra.

Jocelyn's eyebrows arose when Pearl leaned forward and placed a gentle hand on her thigh. She massaged her all the way down to her knee. She wasn't sure why the woman did it but it made Jocelyn smile. The smile turned into a chuckle as Pearl's lips sweetly found Jocelyn's cheek. As she watched the older woman, Jocelyn took deep breaths as she felt her adrenaline rush through her.

"Your face is so soft and tender," Pearl said to Jocelyn.

So are your kisses, Jocelyn thought to herself. *I thought you wouldn't kiss me anymore.*

Pearl placed her hand on Jocelyn's stomach. As Jocelyn grabbed a hold of Pearl's hand to stop her, she eyed the older woman curiously. Jocelyn removed her hand as Pearl looked at her. The older woman's face was emotionless but there was something peaceful in Pearl's eyes that made Jocelyn feel like she could trust her.

Pearl said, "But for now, go take a shower. When you're done, I'll give you a soothing massage that will put you right to sleep."

Jocelyn got up from off of the bed and hurried to the bathroom.

Fourteen

Chapter 14

"You don't have to look pretty to do this, I assure you," Lorenzo grumbled to Eboni.

Holding her pocket mirror, she smiled, trying to suppress a laugh as she glanced at him from beside her. He sat back in the rear seat, his face plain, looking at her calmly as Eboni applied her make-up.

A chuckle escaped Eboni's gleeful countenance as she eyed away from him. She turned and looked left out of the window, seeing the minor roads, surfaces of dirt, grass, and trees becoming smaller as the *Falcon Warrior* airplane ascended further and further into the sky. As the aircraft soared through the clouds, she returned her gaze to Lorenzo.

As she fidgeted, her heartbeat, and breathing quickened. Eboni looked at her beautiful polished fingernails, thinking of chewing at them. She closed her eyes and put three of her fingers into her mouth as anxiety slammed into her stomach. As she finished putting on her lipstick and eyeliner, she could feel her palms sweat.

Lorenzo was motionless and still as a glass of water sitting on a kitchen counter for days. He appeared relaxed and so at peace. She gazed at him from the brown Timberland boots he wore on his feet to the white jumpsuit which covered his legs and body. Her eyes fixed on the black skullcap on his head.

"We're approaching 15,900 feet," the female pilot said from the cockpit. "We're a little above maximum altitude. I can't take her any higher. I'm going to put her on autopilot so you guys can make your descent."

Eboni placed her make-up kit and her small mirror inside an extra pocket in her blue jeans. This was it. A part of her didn't want to go through with this. But she'd told Lorenzo she wanted to skydive with him. Looking at the nonchalant visage on Lorenzo's face caused her to pump her fist, her racing heart slowing down.

Eboni thought back to her reoccurring dream of being robbed. She hadn't experienced the dream for months. The threat of being mugged had triggered her perilous dream. She experienced being overpowered when she first dreamt about the incident. After taking minor lessons in martial arts from Lorenzo, it had triggered some sort of confidence in her. When the dream came to her again, she faced it head-on. She'd faced it head-on and won. Therefore, those dreaded sensations never returned when she slept.

If she could overcome that, she could jump out of this aircraft and still live. She knew she could do it.

Lorenzo turned to face her. She saw him smile at her. She smiled back at him as he touched her hand.

"I can see your fear," Lorenzo said, looking into her eyes. "Eboni, there's no need to be afraid of anything. I'm here with you and I don't plan on dying just yet."

As Eboni peered deeper into Lorenzo's eyes, she saw a profound intensity that equaled the strength of fifty men. His assurance and unwavering confidence allowed her to cast away her fears and doubts. His wink at her hinted at untamed invincibility that effortlessly took on all of life.

The pilot walked to the back of the plane to where they sat with a parachute pack. As she fit the straps properly over his shoulders, Eboni reached in her back pocket for her pink goggles. After the lady pilot placed the parachute pack on him and Eboni, she hastened back to the cockpit. She came back with a large backpack with multiple belt sized straps. She fastened Eboni to Lorenzo quickly and handed Lorenzo a pair of clear goggles. Smiling, the pilot opened the entrance door on the side of the plane and lifted it up.

Eboni felt the turbulence hit her in the face. She instantly grimaced and rubbed her hands together as she closed her eyes. She kissed Lorenzo on the cheek as he pulled his goggles down over his eyes.

"You guys ready?" the lady pilot asked them, standing back as she brushed her fingers through her long, blonde hair.

"I can't be any more ready," Lorenzo said phlegmatically.

This is it, Eboni told herself, shaking as her heart raced wildly again. Lorenzo reached back and grabbed her hand.

"You ready, baby?" Lorenzo asked her.

"Yes," Eboni answered, and took the deepest breath she ever took in her life.

Lorenzo jumped out of the plane as Eboni held onto him. She could hear a violent roaring of strong wind penetrating inside her ears. She saw Lorenzo press a button on his pack.

They shot up into the sky about close to twenty feet. After Eboni looked up and saw the red and green parachute spread out like a vulture's wings, she smiled.

To her, this did not differ from flying inside a plane and gazing down to a town from the way above. The only difference was she wasn't inside an airplane.

They unhurriedly descended to the earth below in a paced, steady decline. As they did, Eboni's smile turned brighter. They journeyed through the illimitable foggy clouds, Eboni feeling her heart racing again.

"How are you feeling?" Lorenzo asked her.

"This is not as bad as I thought it would be," she said to him as she looked down on Orange, New Jersey.

From the unbounded aerial view, a bar-headed goose would ascend, Eboni saw what appeared to be wider warehouses, grass fields, and dirt roads coming into view. She touched Lorenzo's shoulder and kissed him on the cheek again. She saw him smile as he looked behind him. As he puckered his lips at her, she smiled. She kissed him soft-heartedly and felt her heart beating normal again.

Eboni caught sight of two beautiful owls flying past them. She caught sight of a yellow-headed blackbird flying overhead in the same direction.

"Sometimes I wish I was a bird," Eboni said, the smile still on her face.

The fierce wind still blew. Eboni gazed up and saw the airplane turning around and heading back into the direction of the Skydiving academy.

About six minutes later, they saw a grassy area in front of what appeared to be a dark wooded area just to the east. Eboni looked downward, seeing a large rectangular bed of bright sunflowers and lavender perennials they barely glided over. Lorenzo stretched out his legs as they came in for a landing. Their feet hit the earth as they came to a halt on a hill full of grass and bushes. The parachute folded when it hit the turf just ahead of them.

"That was fun!" Eboni said, looking up at Lorenzo as he unfastened the straps to his parachute pack. "I might want to do that again."

"Enjoyed yourself, did you?" he asked her, removing his goggles from his face.

"What an exhilarating experience!" she said happily.

Lorenzo spread his arms and peeked down at her hands resting in front of his body. Her arms clutched around him.

"You're still holding onto me," Lorenzo informed Eboni.

The smile on her face vanished. She placed her chin on the back of his shoulder and kissed him on the cheek once more. "I just don't want this experience to be over, my love," she said to him.

Fifteen

Chapter 15

As Eboni walked inside the psychiatrist's office, she scratched her fingernails against the back of her hand. For the past 130 days since she booked her appointment with Dr. Ruiz, she had waited for this day. But even for weeks past her appointment date, Dr. Ruiz was still unavailable. So, she had to settle on another surgeon and schedule another appointment. When Eboni took a seat in front of the psychiatrist's desk, she looked the woman in the eye. Dressing conservatively in a long navy-blue skirt, loafers, and a grey blouse, she appeared every bit of a female schoolteacher from the 1950s. Her hair was pinned up in a bun. She had almost no make-up on.

The professional sitting at the desk across from her was motionless and straight-faced as she kept her eyes on Eboni. Eboni carefully gazed at the woman with a bright smile. The woman grinned at her and looked away momentarily. Their eyes locked in a staredown before the woman's grin disappeared.

She had already told Lorenzo and Stuart that she would not get booty implants or get injected with silicone. Eboni thought she'd decided but uncertainty remained.

"Hello, Eboni," the psychiatrist spoke.

Dealing with the never-ending stress of managing a restaurant, living with diabetes, missing her parents who she thought she hated, and worrying about Coco and Thorne got to her sometimes. It made her depressed... and she needed someone other than Lorenzo to talk to.

"Good afternoon, Dr. Schneider," Eboni spoke back.

"What's going on in your life, Eboni?" the other woman asked, lines appearing on her forehead. Short thin lines could be seen on the ends of her bifocals as if they were cracking. She wore a thin green sweater with a matching scarf draped around her shoulders. The doctor's brunette hair was neat and shiny. And her face.... to Eboni Dr. Schneider held a prestigious resemblance to Grace Kelly.

Eboni thought fondly of Lorenzo. "I'm in an intense, loving relationship with the most wonderful young man," she shared right away.

Dr. Schneider nodded as she remained straight-faced. "How long have you been with this man?" she asked.

"A little over six months. We live together. He has two daughters who live with us too on the weekends."

"You've never mentioned this relationship to me before. What is your relationship with these two daughters?"

"I'm like their stepmother when they're around," Eboni answered gladly. "One of them loves me very much. I love her too. The other one doesn't love me as much yet, but I'm confident she will."

"How do you feel about the man in your life?" Dr. Schneider asked, cracking a smile.

"Lorenzo," Eboni said the name, closing her eyes as a source of warm energy flowed through her. "I'm deeply in love with him."

"How does he feel about you?"

"He's deeply in love with me too. I have a strong feeling he's going to ask me to marry him soon."

Dr. Schneider nodded as she showed a tiny smile. "That's very positive," she said, peering at Eboni. "What about your love life with him?"

"We've been intimate only once," Eboni said, eyeing the ceiling.

Dr. Schneider showed a brighter smile before it vanished. "So, there's a ton of romance?" she asked curiously.

"There's a lot of deep caring," Eboni answered. "Lorenzo has supported me in every way. He's stood up to his own father in defending me. He's quite a real man. I'm learning Taekwondo, Brazilian Jiujitsu, and Kyokushin from him. We shower together. He washes my hair and gives me pedicures. Whenever we eat, we feed one another. We do so many things together."

Dr. Schneider's eyes widened as she showed the largest smile Eboni had ever seen from her. "All of that sounds so wonderful," she said to Eboni. "It truly sounds like a blissful love affair!"

For a moment the room was silent as Dr. Schneider regarded her. Eboni showed a smile and peeped away for a moment. When Eboni eyed Dr. Schneider again, the doctor stood up from out of her seat, placed her hands behind her back, and viewed Eboni. Dr. Schneider placed her hands in front of her and sat back down behind her desk.

"Why are you truly here, Eboni?" Dr. Schneider questioned.

"I've been quite unhappy with my body," Eboni expressed softly.

Dr. Schneider nodded. "Unhappy how?" she asked.

"I don't like my ass," Eboni revealed to her. "It's not ---."

Dr. Schneider cut Eboni off. "Phat enough?" she asked.

Eboni smiled. How did Dr. Schneider know of this slang term to describe a woman with a well-sized butt? Eboni eyed her curiously.

"I have three daughters. Two of them have silicone injections," Dr. Schneider told Eboni.

Eboni opened her mouth to talk, but closed it. Eboni's eyebrows rose as she eyed Dr. Schneider bewilderedly. It was a mostly urban word that served as an abbreviation for pretty hot and tempting, and it almost always referred to a woman's caboose.

But Dr. Schneider continued as her face instantly became long. "With awful results," she kept on sadly.

Eboni shivered and swallowed. "What happened?" she asked.

Dr. Schneider nodded again. "My daughter Joan is suffering from complications of pulmonary embolism," the woman said most melancholy. "My youngest daughter Claire was a stripper for years and had silicone injected into her rear end. Now she's having breathing problems."

Eboni jolted backward in the chair as she peeked away from Dr. Schneider. She gazed disbelievingly back at the psychiatrist.

"They are both in standard health," Dr. Schneider went on. "Joan went through the proper channels and got hers done using implants that broke whereas Claire ventured into the black market and had hers done. Both turned out pathetically bad. My advice to you is *don't* do it."

Dr. Schneider tapped the top of her desk with her finger as her emotionless state returned. She glimpsed away from Eboni. She placed her hands together and looked Eboni straight in the eye. It was by far the most serious inspection Dr. Schneider had given her.

Dr. Schneider got up from out of her chair and walked around to the front of her desk where Eboni was sitting, revealing a maroon skirt and brown flats. She sat in the chair next to Eboni and smiled as she glanced at her. She reached for both of Eboni's hands and gazed straight into Eboni's eyes. As Eboni beheld her, it appeared Dr. Schneider was looking into the depths of her soul. Eboni swallowed and allowed herself to relax as Dr. Schneider's grip on her hands became firmer.

"I'll listen to your advice," Eboni said. "I won't go through with it."

Dr. Schneider's lightened gaze hit Eboni. "Alright," she said as she got up.

Dr. Schneider walked behind her desk, stood, and eyed Eboni with a half-smile on her face. She placed both of her hands on the back of her chair as her smile vanished.

Eboni peered towards the ceiling again as she thought about Lorenzo. Thoughts of martial arts and warm feelings constricted her as she focused on him. "Dr. Schneider," she said as she stood up, her eyes now fixed on the psychiatrist once more. "I have to get home to Lorenzo."

The two women smiled at each other. Eboni took in the sight of Dr. Schneider as if she would see her for the last time. Taking a shallow breath, Eboni turned away and headed for the door. She thought about turning around to take one last peek at the doctor. This will be the last time I ever see her, Eboni decided. She reached for the door handle and turned it. She pulled the large brown mahogany door open, stepped outside it, and closed the door behind her.

****

As she smiled, Eboni walked into her apartment building singing songs by Michael Jackson. She jumped up and down as she entered the lobby. She caught sight of the doorman eyeing her. She blew him a kiss and her smile got brighter. Eboni caught the elevator and got off on the fourth floor. She walked straight down the hall until she reached her apartment. Once she opened the door, she found Lorenzo sitting on the floor in the living room with his eyes closed.

As soon as she walked up to him, he seemed to feel her near him as his eyes opened. Lorenzo stood up quickly and greeted Eboni with a warm kiss on the lips before grabbing a hold of her hand. She was eager to tell him about her good news, but before she could he guided her to the bedroom door.

"I have a giant surprise for you," Lorenzo said to her. "Close your eyes."

When Eboni closed her eyes, she heard their bedroom door open. She felt his hand cover her eyes as he turned the light on inside the bedroom. Still holding onto his other hand, he guided her as she took twelve paces. He stopped and removed his hands from over her face.

"Open your eyes," Lorenzo said to her.

When Eboni opened her eyes, she visioned towards the bed and spotted a Siamese kitten and a white pit bull puppy with brindle markings snuggled up together by a pillow. Eboni's chin dropped to the floor. She placed a hand over her mouth as she jumped up and down. A smile appeared on her face as she stepped into the direction of the bed. Once she got there, she sat on the edge of the bed and rubbed the coats of both pets before picking them up.

"They're a present for you," Lorenzo said to her. "But that's not all."

Lorenzo walked up to her and knelt down to one knee. He reached into the pocket of the sweatpants he had on and retrieved a small box. When he opened the tiny box, Eboni saw the sparkling, precious stone on a diamond ring. Her eyes widened as she knew what Lorenzo was trying to say to her.

"Eboni Law, will you marry me?" he asked her softly.

Eboni's eyes widened as she fixed her sight on the elegant ring. Her eyes watered and tears fell down her face as the smile she wore only moments before grew even larger. Her eyes met Lorenzo's as she gazed from him to the ring three times. She walked in his direction and regarded him as her eyes sparkled.

Remembrance of seeing him for the first time outside *The Camelot* when he beat up the punk who tried to rob her flashed before her. The recollection of her spending time with his children and lying on top of him and kissing him in the pouring rain one night after he'd given her a crash course in self-defense came to her. Eboni's heart raced as she looked from the ring to Lorenzo three more times.

"Yes, Lorenzo Royal!" she answered him, fanning her smiling face with her hand in order to cool off and settle down. "I would love more than anything to be your wife."

Lorenzo removed the ring from out of the box and slid it onto Eboni's ring finger. Holding both pets in her hands, she jumped up and down again and embraced him warmly.

They shared a passionate kiss as his arms fastened around her. His lips tasted like chocolate-covered strawberries. There was an inferno raging inside her. It softened her innermost portion to its core. If she died in his embrace here and now Eboni knew she would live eternally. This was the first time in her life her heart had grown so silken and intensely blistering.

They sat next to each other on the edge of the bed. Eboni handed Lorenzo the puppy as she kept the kitten in her possession.

"I have news, Lorenzo," Eboni said as she stroked the head of the little kitten. "I'm not having the butt injections done. I was still confused about it. I thought ultimately I didn't need it."

Lorenzo's heartwarming smile found her. "I've told you all along you shouldn't," he said to her.

Eboni smiled as she shook her head. "I know," she told him, remembering having the same conversation with Stuart.

Eboni handed the kitten to Lorenzo and stood up. She walked over to the closet and undressed. She undid the bun in her hair and allowed her long kinky hair to fall down her back. She reached for a pair of jeans and quickly put them on. Seeing they were skin-tight, she knew they brought out the sexy shape of her legs. She grabbed a red short-sleeved top from off of a coat hanger and put it on. Next, Eboni kicked off her loafers and grabbed a pair of opened-toe high heel shoes, and stooped down in order to put them on her feet.

Eboni walked to the mirror in front of her dresser. She had gone from a conservative 1950s school teacher look to a modern-day appearance that was provocative. She placed her hands on her hips and turned around to eye Lorenzo. She could tell by the way he watched her she appeared striking.

"Well?" she asked him.

"You're sexy as hell," he complimented. "I love you in those jeans."

Eboni smiled. "Thank you, Lorenzo," she said. "Where should we go?"

"I'm not sure. Let's go somewhere loud."

****

Chelsea's Arena was one of the most popular clubs in New York City. Eboni hadn't been there in over two years, but she felt it was the best place to celebrate her engagement with Lorenzo. They stood in a long line. It extended from 24th Street to around the corner on 7th Avenue before Lorenzo and Eboni finally made it inside.

Eboni automatically got into a dancing mood when the disc jockey played Prince and Neyo back-to-back. Lorenzo gently took Eboni by the hand and led her through a crowd of humanity across the top floor to the bar on the far end, seeing the sizeable crowd, Lorenzo took her down the stairs to the bar on the lower level. When they got there, Eboni noticed the darkroom where countless people were dancing to the sounds of Rihanna.

Lorenzo went to the front of the bar and ordered Eboni an apple martini and ginger ale and bourbon. He paid for their drinks and tipped the bartender. Lorenzo took Eboni by the hand and led her to a table on the other side of the crowded room. When he sat down, Lorenzo playfully pulled Eboni down onto his lap. She peeped out at the boys and girls dancing as she sipped her drink.

When the DJ went old school and played a Jermaine Jackson classic, Eboni got up out of Lorenzo's lap and pulled him up. She went to where the men's restroom entrance was and danced. While the song was halfway over, Eboni felt perspiration on her face. As she boogied, Lorenzo moved freakishly with her.

They both finished their first round of drinks after the song was over. When Lorenzo ordered them both ginger ale and bourbon with an apple martini again, Eboni paid for it. When they found their table this time Eboni sat down and pulled Lorenzo into her lap. At first, Eboni noticed he appeared uncomfortable, but when he placed his arm around her and began sipping his drink, he didn't seem to mind.

"What are we going to name the puppy and the kitten?" she asked Lorenzo.

"I'm not sure," he said as he shrugged his shoulders. "I was hoping you would name them."

"I'll name the kitten and you name the puppy," Eboni suggested. "I'll name the kitten Tabatha. I saw it was a girl. The puppy is a boy, isn't it?"

Lorenzo nodded as he sipped his ginger ale and bourbon. "Yes," he answered her. "Let me think for a moment." Lorenzo sipped his drink and regarded her. "Raleigh."

Eboni watched him. "Raleigh?" she questioned.

"I'll name the puppy Raleigh. Raleigh is a city in North Carolina."

"Tabatha and Raleigh," Eboni said more to herself than to Lorenzo.

Lorenzo finished his second drink and got up. As she laid back and sipped on her tasty apple martini, she watched as her fiancée walked back to the bar. When he returned, she saw he had two Blue Moon. He sat down in the seat across from her and drank his beer.

A Don Omar song rocked the crowd. Eboni smiled and got up. She peeked back at Lorenzo as she made her way next to the bar. She danced in an artful, stylish way to the music. As she danced, she sang the lyrics of the song as she smiled back at her future husband. She sipped her apple martini until she finished and sat the empty glass on the bar.

As she continued dancing, she noticed many people were admiring her. Eboni smiled as she became oblivious to their watchful eyes. Soon, Lorenzo was there dancing with her. As she moved artfully from left to right, she pulled her shirt over her head and tossed it in her vacant chair in front of their table. She saw the jovial expression on Lorenzo's face as she danced in nothing but her tight jeans and bra. She knew she was totally irresistible to him.

Lorenzo winked at her as she took a few sips of his beer. When the song was over, she bowed as she received whistles and handclaps from the fanatics who witnessed her elegant style of dance. As Eboni made her way to her seat, the DJ turned the Don Omar track to a Marilyn Manson classic.

She felt a strange sensation on her booty. Eboni eyed behind as she felt Lorenzo fondling her ass. She took a seat in her chair and put her shirt back on as Lorenzo sat in front of her and continued to sip his beer. Eboni turned right and saw a pretty blonde-haired woman sporting nothing but a sky-blue swimsuit underneath a fur coat with a drink in one hand and a pair of high heel shoes in the other walking up to their table barefooted.

"Hello," the woman spoke to them.

Lorenzo gazed up at her. "Hi," he said to her.

"I saw what you just did," the woman said as her eyes commended Eboni. "That was truly uninhibited. I'm into couples and was wondering if you guys would be interested in a threesome with me."

Eboni smiled as Lorenzo studied her. "I haven't been with a woman since I came out of my mother," she said to the lady.

Lorenzo peered at her. "No," he told the woman. "We appreciate the offer, but my wife and I are totally monogamous."

"Well, thanks anyway," the young woman said. "Have a good night."

The woman walked off and disappeared into the crowd of people. Eboni eyed Lorenzo for a moment. A lot of married or engaged men would have welcomed the alluring young woman into their bedroom. Either Lorenzo was about Eboni only, or threesomes just didn't suit him. It was probably both.

When Lorenzo finished drinking his beer, he leaned back in the chair and placed his hand on his stomach. His eyes stared directly at her. Usually, when he examined her in that way, it meant he wanted to kiss her or hold her. But as she considered him more carefully, she knew the way he watched her could have meant something else.

"Are you hungry?" Eboni asked him. "You want to go out and get some dinner?"

Lorenzo smiled. "How did you know?" he asked her.

****

When they went inside, they had to wait nearly thirty minutes for a table. Eboni saw servers walking frenzied from the kitchen to the tables with trays of delicious food to serve their customers. Finally, the host seats them near the front of the restaurant.

After waiting nearly another half hour for their food to be served, Eboni and Lorenzo ate. She had gotten the crabmeat with vegetables and a glass of red wine. Lorenzo decided on two plates of mussels with broccoli and a glass of white wine. As they sat and ate, Eboni stared into Lorenzo's plate.

"How is your food, darling?" Eboni asked as she gazed at the exquisite candlelight in front of them.

"It's pretty good," Lorenzo answered her, lifting a fork full of food. Eboni watched as his fork aimed straight for her lips. She opened her mouth and took in the food. "I've been wondering about something. How is Stuart doing?"

"The last time I saw or spoke with Stuart was the day I met your father," Eboni answered as she chewed. "Stuart is on extended leave."

They agreed to delicious seafood and journeyed to *Doc's Seafood*, a dynamically popular seafood restaurant known for its delicious lobster, crabs, shrimp, and mussels on the Upper East Side.

Lorenzo finished his first plate of mussels rather fast. Eboni watched as he sipped his wine before he started on his second plate. She stabbed into the crabmeat on her dish and took a few sips of her wine, and watched him ogle her. As she ate her food, she saw him looking at her rather straight-faced.

"What?" she asked with a smile.

"Are you ready to intensify your martial arts lessons?" he asked her as he watched her bring her fork full of vegetables and crabmeat to his mouth.

"Yes," she told him.

"Are you ready for me to push you?" Lorenzo asked as she fed him.

Eboni nodded. She had to admit the night he started teaching her in the Bronx and again at Riverside Side Park had been introductory lessons. But the day she visited his dojo for the first time and saw him doing Chi, and observed all of those pictures and trophies throughout the hallways, her heart had become even more intrigued. Her friend Rahima Zubair had told her she had gone to Lorenzo's martial arts school with two friends every day for a fifteen-day period and learned some pretty simple, but effective ways of fighting and self-defense.

"Yes, I want that," Eboni told him. "Did you ever teach your ex-wife martial arts?"

Lorenzo smiled. "I knew you were going to ask me that eventually," he said to her, setting his eyes on her as she eyed into his handsome face. "No. I never taught her martial arts. Jocelyn simply didn't wish to learn any of it. In the time I was married to her, she never once came to my school."

"Have you taught any of it to Joy and Lori?" she asked, returning his smile, placing a hand on her wineglass.

"I've shown both of them some things, but I never taught them anything on a primary level. I started them both off in Wing Chun."

"I'm very grateful to learn from you, sensei," said Eboni, regarding the gorgeous diamond ring on her finger.

"You're welcome," he answered her. "Taekwondo for offense, Judo for tossing people, jujitsu for submission holds, and Kyokushin to mix it up."

"Imagine an innocuous sweetheart like me using kung fu on someone," Eboni said. "You have a black belt in all of those disciplines?"

"Yes, and three more in Moo Duk Kwan, Sambo, and Krav Maga," Lorenzo told her. "I started out in Wing Chun and Shaolin kung fu as a teenager and learned the basics."

"Have you ever competed in a martial arts tournament?" Eboni asked.

"I used to before I became an instructor," Lorenzo said. "When Master Kimlau Li trained me, I came in second place in my first tournament. I was in my late teens then. I entered thirty-three tournaments the next eight years afterward, and I won twenty-four of them. Before my training finished, Master Kimlau Li told me I would be a much better teacher than he was to me and my best students were going to become better instructors than I am."

"Have you and this Master Kimlau Li ever tested wills against each other?"

"Him and me?" he asked her.

Eboni nodded as she ate the last of her crabmeat and vegetables. "Yes," she said.

"I could never defeat Sensei Kimlau Li," Lorenzo said to her. "He was too good. I came close a few times."

"Has any of your students ever defeated you?"

Lorenzo nodded. "No," he said to her. "I had one student I

trained for six years. He was very good. He actually defeated Master Kim-lau Li in the dojo. But he could never defeat me."

Eboni cocked an eyebrow. "Strange," she said. "You can't defeat your teacher, but you had a student who could, and you could beat your student."

"Most of the time it's all in the style of fighting or how one fights," Lorenzo said. "It's the style and the way one uses it that carries him or her to victory over their opponent."

****

As they sat in the backseat of another New York City cab, Lorenzo fell asleep. His head hit Eboni's shoulder. Eboni yawned as her head nodded. Her eyes kept opening and closing. She stayed awake for the journey as they headed to the Upper West Side. She put her arm around Lorenzo and gently positioned his head on her shoulder.

She kissed his forehead. Eboni kissed Lorenzo's head softer a second time. As she reflected on this auspicious day which had been the greatest day of her life, Eboni smiled.

Eboni held Lorenzo closer to her. She kissed his forehead for the third time. Eboni placed the back of her hand in front of her face and peered towards the elegant diamond ring Lorenzo had placed on her finger hours ago. After years of settling on immature and insincere husbands of other women or men who never had the testicular fortitude to commit to her, Eboni had finally found the one.

As they got closer to home, the cab driver came up on Broadway. As soon as he turned on West End Avenue, Eboni saw they were at 88th Street. Eboni kissed Lorenzo's forehead for the fourth time. She cradled his head and laid back in the backseat. Lorenzo's head fell onto her breasts. She smiled and cradled his head against her bosom and stroked the side of Lorenzo's head.

As the cab driver pulled up in front of her apartment building, Eboni reached for her purse. She took her lovely sparkling black fingernails and gently scratched against Lorenzo's forehead as he snored ever so slightly.

Eboni kissed Lorenzo's forehead for the fifth time.

Sixteen

Chapter 16

"*Push!*"

Jocelyn pushed. And pushed. And pushed harder. This was her first childbirth in five years. Back then when Joy and Lori were born, she remembered their entry into the world had been easier than this. With this third child, the exercise was indeed a little more difficult.

"*Push!*"

While shopping for silverware in Corona, Queens yesterday after work with Crystal, Jocelyn had gone into labor. The EMTs were called by a store clerk and an ambulance had arrived and speedily taken her to the Queens Hospital Center in Jamaica. And here Jocelyn was a day later giving birth to her third daughter or perhaps her first son.

"*Push!*" *the nurse demanded for the third time.*

Through the pain and anguish, Jocelyn pushed and pushed. And pushed. Her ears heard the crying sounds of a precious newborn. The strain she had shown on her face for the past fifteen minutes turned into joyous relief as the nurse cut the umbilical cord.

"*The baby is six pounds, two ounces,*" *a man said from beside the nurse moments later.*

Jocelyn lay back comfortably in the bed and watched as the nurse walked towards her with her baby covered in a white receiving blanket. Jocelyn took a deep breath as the baby howled. When the nurse presented the newborn to her, Jocelyn smiled.

"It's a girl," the nurse said to her.

Pearl and Buck stood at the foot of Jocelyn's bed. Upon hearing the news about the child, Buck had been working on a construction site in New Rochelle in Westchester County when Jocelyn had called him and told him about her water breaking. Pearl had been waiting in the emergency room since she got a text from Jocelyn stating she was in labor.

"What did you name her?" Pearl asked Jocelyn.

"Victoria Cortez," Jocelyn told Pearl as she held her daughter.

"Victoria is a pretty name," Buck said.

"How are you feeling?" Pearl asked her, touching her shoulder.

"Completely exhausted," Jocelyn said, rolling her eyes and breathing deeply. "Thanks for being here and waiting it out."

"Jocelyn, I wouldn't be anywhere else," Pearl said, her Diane Sawyer-like face appearing beautiful as she smiled. "I would wait with you until the end of the world."

Jocelyn smiled. "Thanks, Pearl," she said.

"How soon until you're discharged from the hospital?"

"The nurse told me they would discharge sometime me this evening," Jocelyn said to her.

Pearl smiled and walked around to Jocelyn's bedside. She squatted down and kissed Jocelyn on the cheek.

"I'll leave you two alone," Buck said in a pleasing tone.

"Buck, don't leave just yet," Jocelyn said to him, blinking her eyes as a buoyant expression appeared on her face. "You want to hold her?"

Buck walked towards the side of Jocelyn's bed on the right. He took the baby from her and held her. Buck kissed Victoria and gave her back to Jocelyn. Jocelyn gazed at him questioningly. She had wanted Buck to hold their daughter longer. But for whatever reason he didn't.

"I have to head back to Westchester County," Buck said, forcing a smile to his face. "I told my boss I wouldn't be away long."

"Okay," Jocelyn said.

Buck waved goodbye to Jocelyn and Victoria and left out of the room as Pearl kept a watchful eye on her. Pearl folded her arms and kissed Jocelyn tenderly on the cheek.

"I'm going to head out too," Pearl said to her. "I'll be back to pick you and the baby up this evening. Just text or call me to tell me when."

Pearl rubbed the side of Jocelyn's face with her thumb as she smiled. She gave Victoria a small peck on her little face, slung her old heavy MCM handbag over her shoulder, and walked out of the room.

A nurse pushed Jocelyn's wheelchair through the double doors leading to the hospital's exit from the emergency room as Jocelyn carried Victoria in her arms. Pearl texted her to let her know she is in traffic on 78th Avenue but would be there to pick her up shortly. Taking a deep breath, there was nothing to do but peer into the parking lot as she waited on her friend.

When Pearl's unmarked police car drove up, Jocelyn pointed. The nurse pushed her wheelchair outside onto the sidewalk. From there Jocelyn got up and walked with Victoria in her arms to the curb to Pearl's car. She opened the passenger side door and got into the seat. She turned to gaze at Pearl as her friend pulled off.

"Just take us home," Jocelyn said, her face and voice weary.

"Where is home?" Pearl asked, appearing beautiful with strands of hair covering her left eye.

"One Ascan Avenue in Forest Hills," Jocelyn told her friend.

Pearl drove down Queens Boulevard on her way through Kew Gardens. She turned off Queens Boulevard and got on Union Turnpike. From there they entered the Forest Hills Gardens neighborhood. They came upon Ascan Avenue rather quickly. When Jocelyn directed Pearl where to park her automobile, it was slightly up the street but yet a stone's throw away from Jocelyn's apartment.

"Thanks," Jocelyn said to Pearl as she reached for the door handle.

"Are you going to invite me in?" Pearl asked, her voice raspy and her face highlighted by a deep pink lipstick and fading blue blush on her *eyes and cheekbones. "After all, I've never been to your place before. And besides, while you recuperate from childbirth, you'll need someone to watch after you."*

Jocelyn smiled. "That's very kind of you," she said to Pearl. "I could definitely use your help."

But abruptly and out of nowhere, Pearl's face altered and became unrecognizable as she ripped Jocelyn's newborn away from her. The steering wheel morphed into some sort of black steel straightjacket that jumped into Jocelyn's lap and bound itself around her. Through blurred vision, Jocelyn somehow saw Pearl- or whoever it was who had been driving laughing at her like a broken clown. But when her vision cleared Jocelyn saw a familiar face look back at her with a haunting smile. She saw as Eboni kissed her baby on the head. Despite the woman's pretty smile, Jocelyn couldn't mistake the avowed evil in Eboni's sickly red eyes.

"Give me my baby, you bitch!" Jocelyn screamed as she helplessly kicked her feet.

Jocelyn stared horridly into the piercing serpentine eyes of the other woman as Eboni smiled at her.

"No," Eboni's strange automated voice told her. "Victoria is mine! She's mine and Lorenzo's."

Eboni's pupils disappeared as her eyes glowed maroon inside her head. The scary smile disappeared while her visage remained sinister. A dust devil- or some kind of whirlwind had Jocelyn spinning high above the Seven Seas beach in her father's hometown of Fajardo.

Jocelyn heard Eboni's echoing laugh as the violently swirling wind turned into a corybantic tornado and quickly swallowed her up. She desperately turned in all directions trying to locate Victoria and Eboni. They were nowhere to be found as she whirled up into the sky and thrown into what seemed to be several directions....

Jocelyn's eyes opened as she lifted herself up on the sofa. She fell forward and landed on her forehead as she puffed. She eyed down and saw a pair of ghastly feet inside a pair of flip-flops. As she glanced up, she saw a pair of cellulitis-filled legs, wide hips, and a body with a pair of sagging breasts concealed in a white bra and underwear. When she looked further up and saw Pearl's face peering down at her, Jocelyn placed her hand over her heart and took a deep breath.

"Thank God," Jocelyn said to herself.

"Jocelyn, are you alright?" Pearl asked as she stooped down next to her.

"It was a delightful dream, and it turned terrible at the end," Jocelyn said to her friend.

"What?" Pearl asked.

"I dreamed I had a baby, and my ex-husband's fiancée took her from me."

Pearl frowned. "I hope you're over him," she said as she stood up.

"I am over him," Jocelyn assured her. "Where are Joy and Lori?"

"They are outside playing and making friends with the kids in the neighborhood," Pearl said, extending a hand to Jocelyn. "Are you hungry? I can order something."

"I am a bit starved," Jocelyn told her as Pearl grabbed Jocelyn's extended hand and helped her up. "But there's food here. You care to cook for me?"

"I would love to," Pearl said to her with a smile. "Sit down on the sofa and relax."

"There are a couple of frozen lamb chops in the freezer," Jocelyn told her. "Just fix me that along with some red beans. You can cook yourself something if you like."

"I'll have what you're having," Pearl said on her way to the kitchen.

Pearl placed a pair of lamb chops in the oven and prepared the other food they were going to have with them.

"You have a marvelous place here," Pearl said to Jocelyn.

Jocelyn knew Pearl was referring to the broken mirrors skillfully pasted onto the walls. Along with the Greco-Roman art displayed throughout the apartment, Jocelyn knew her home had a very artistic and sort of cultural feel to it. The Forest Hills Gardens was one of the most prominent neighborhoods in Queens. She had been fortunate to receive a good deal on an apartment.

From where she stood, Jocelyn saw Pearl beaming at her from the kitchen. There was a look of seriousness, pain, and a hint of jocundity. Pearl turned away from her and gazed down at the beans cooking inside the skillet. She turned around and looked in Jocelyn's direction.

"Do you like me, Jocelyn?" Pearl asked her.

Jocelyn smiled. "Of course, I like you," she answered.

"I like you too. Do you want a relationship with me?"

"I thought we were in one already."

"I know how painful a split from a husband can be," Pearl said, eyeing Jocelyn in a convivial way. "As a former wife, you don't get over something like that for a while. You mentioned a moment ago you had a dream about your former husband's fiancée. Maybe your subconscious mind is telling you you're not over him yet. Why would you dream about his fiancée if you weren't completely over him?"

"Pearl, I'm not sure. I have dreams of my mother and father all the time. I also dream about my sisters Consuela, Barbara, and Doris. Every once in a while, I dream about my two brothers Jose and Hector. My family left New York and went back to Puerto Rico over six years ago three months before I married Lorenzo. I don't know why I dreamed about Lorenzo's fiancée. It was just a dream."

"Okay, Jocelyn."

"Do you have children?"

"I had two sons early in my first marriage."

"Where are they now?"

"My oldest son Jeffery lives in Montreal with his wife," Pearl answered her. "My other son Paul lives on Staten Island with his girlfriend."

"Do they have children?"

"I have four grandchildren," Pearl said. "Both of my sons each have two sons of their own."

Pearl walked over to the sofa and sat next to Jocelyn. As Jocelyn gazed at her, she could tell Pearl had a few war stories about the men she had been with.

"Jeffery and Paul's father never came home from Vietnam," Pearl told Jocelyn. "I married a cheating bastard a few years later. Years later I found a man I was in a relationship with for four years. He left me and broke my heart. I remarried and a week into my wedlock with him, I came home and found him dead of a heroin overdose."

"Who was the man who broke your heart so bad you had to see a psychiatrist?" Jocelyn asked.

"Tim! He was a jackass and a pencil dick! He was possessive and insecure. Things got crazy with him. But I loved him despite him being a jackass and a pencil dick!"

"And he was the last man you were with?" Jocelyn asked.

"Yes!" Pearl said, sounding like an asp's hiss.

It was obvious to Jocelyn Pearl had been scorned or just simply let down by men. She probably had carried so much baggage and had so many hang-ups based on her history of being involved with the wrong men. Those experiences probably were the reason she had turned to women in order to rest her heart.

"How long have you been involved with the same sex?" Jocelyn asked.

"You mean how long have I been a lesbian?" Pearl asked. "Since my mid-thirties."

"Have any guys ever shown interest?"

Pearl nodded her head. "Yes," she answered. "Even in the thirty years I've been a lesbian, I've come across some really nice guys. Guys who didn't want only one thing from me at all but just wanted to take me out to a movie or to dinner. Or guys who needed my advice on dealing with the crazy bitches they were married to or in relationships with. But I gave up on men a long time ago."

Jocelyn clearly understood. Men had smashed Pearl's heart so many times. There wasn't enough of her heart left to give to a man. And to think even if Pearl had gotten over those long-ago experiences, it had probably taken a very long time to put those negative experiences with men behind her.

"Paul and Jeffrey's father would be the only man I would want if I wanted a man," said Pearl, her voice quiet as she folded her arms.

Jocelyn scooted closer to Pearl. She rested her head on the other woman's shoulder and placed her hand in her lap. Pearl placed her chin on top of Jocelyn's head and put her arm around her. Pearl held Jocelyn close. Jocelyn felt Pearl's lips on her forehead. Jocelyn lifted her head up and stared into Pearl's eyes. Their noses rubbed, and Jocelyn closed her eyes and allowed her lips to find Pearl's.

It was a warm, ice-melting kiss. To her, it was the same as kissing Lorenzo so many times. Yet it was far different. Yes, the same but different. Unlike Lorenzo, Pearl's lips felt much softer. The kiss itself was tender and sweet. It felt like eating some kind of sweet fruit. It felt so good Jocelyn begged another. Their lips touched tenderly. Only this time their tongues tasted each other. To Jocelyn Pearl's tongue tasted saccharine. As they kissed more feverishly, Jocelyn placed her arms firmly around Pearl in a warm embrace.

Pearl detached her lips from Jocelyn's. "What are we doing?" she asked Jocelyn.

"I'm not sure," Jocelyn said. "But whatever we were doing, I think we should stop."

Pearl shook her head. "I wholeheartedly agree," she said. "I should check on the food."

Jocelyn watched as Pearl got up and rushed into the kitchen. She walked to the window and eyed down onto Ascan Avenue as she thought back to what she and Pearl were just doing.

Ten minutes later Pearl came back into the living room. She rejoined Jocelyn on the couch and the two women studied each other. Jocelyn turned away from Pearl. Jocelyn breathed deeply as she hungered for yet another kiss.

"You're mad with me, aren't you?" Pearl asked, her voice serene and her face plain.

"I'm not mad," Jocelyn said, her eyes darting from the sight of Pearl to the broken mirrors on the wall. "I just wish we could have continued with what we were doing. I was enjoying it."

"I was too," Pearl said.

"Why didn't we continue? We shouldn't have stopped."

"Jocelyn, you're not a lesbian. You're a heterosexual woman."

"So? A heterosexual woman and a lesbian can't kiss each other?"

Pearl smiled. "Of course, they can," she answered. "Just in case it was your first time, I didn't want you to go too far."

"Whether I have or I haven't, I don't see where it matters."

"It matters a lot, Jocelyn. I don't want to rush you into something. This is unfamiliar territory for you. Being with another woman isn't the same thing as being involved with a man. It's better if we take our time. If we are going to do this, we should take it real slow."

Jocelyn smirked. "Fine," she said and smiled.

****

Fifteen minutes later Pearl got up from off of the couch. She went into the kitchen to check on the food again and came back to the living room. As she smiled at her friend, Jocelyn thought back to their kiss a second time. Why couldn't she stop thinking about it? Perhaps Pearl was right. Perhaps it was better if they didn't behave so impulsively.

"The food is ready," Pearl said forty minutes later. "Just give me a moment while I fix our plates."

Within six minutes Pearl had placed the lamb chops with a pile of beans on two separate plates and took them into the dining room. There she had placed the plates of food on a long dining room table with a beautifully crystallized chandelier hanging above the center.

She walked into the dining room as she heard her stomach growl. She salivated at the sight of the juicy meat on a plate at the head of the table with a bunch of beans next to it. Jocelyn stretched for a second and sauntered to the head of the table.

Pearl sat down first. Jocelyn took her seat and regarded Pearl. Pearl's eyes found Jocelyn's. Jocelyn took her mind completely off of any possibility of intimacy and tried to concentrate on the lamb chop she couldn't wait to bite into.

"Are you going to say grace?" Jocelyn asked.

The two ladies bowed their heads and gave thanks for their food. Jocelyn thought back to the day she had told Pearl about her problems with Lorenzo inside the employee lounge while on break. She remembered Pearl playfully eyeing at her lips. At the time she didn't know of Pearl's sexual orientation. But as her hand washed over both of her breasts, Jocelyn did the same thing. Jocelyn stared intensely at Pearl's lips as the much older woman formed her lips into a smooching kiss and blew into her smoking spicy food in order to cool it off. Pearl's lips were full and pretty. The fading two-tune lipstick she'd applied hours ago made her lips irresistible. Jocelyn found herself not only fond of Pearl, but she was also growing attracted to her.

Pearl picked up her fork and dipped it into her plate without saying a word. Jocelyn watched as Pearl started on her beans first. She took a steak knife and cut her lamb chop into pieces and devoured them.

"We Italians know how to cook, don't we?" Pearl asked Jocelyn.

"Yes, y'all do," Jocelyn answered her with a smile before she bit into her lamb chop. "So, do us Puerto Ricans. This lamb is delicious."

They talked a little while they ate. Pearl finished her meal first. Jocelyn took her time eating hers. By the time she finished eating Jocelyn had suppressed four yawns. As Jocelyn got to her feet, Pearl was clearing the table of the dishes they had used.

Jocelyn yawned twice and watched Pearl. Pearl walked closer to her as Jocelyn felt her eyes become instantly exhausted. She yawned again as her eyes were half-closed.

"You look extremely tired," Pearl said.

"I am tired," Jocelyn said.

"You need to get some sleep," Pearl suggested.

"What about Lori and Joy?"

Pearl smiled. "When it gets too dark outside, I'll go get them," she told Jocelyn. "I'll also fix them something good for their dinner."

Jocelyn recalled when Joy and Lori were babies. When she and Lorenzo first brought both of them home from the hospital one cried continuously during the day and the other had cried endlessly at night. She and Lorenzo couldn't get a decent night's sleep for weeks. If Jocelyn could sleep for even a few hours, it would suit her just fine but she hoped not to revisit her twisted nightmare.

Jocelyn walked in the direction of her bedroom. When she went inside, she allowed herself to peer down at her full-sized futon. When she stopped just outside her door Pearl walked by her and entered.

"I'm a little tired myself," Pearl said, her eyes studying the room from its vaulted ceilings to the multiple paintings of Mark Anthony and Cleopatra adorned on all four walls along with a large Puerto Rican flag pinned to the ceiling above the bed. Furniture, a tall lamp, and a fancy dresser made of plywood stood by the window on the other side of the room "This is a pleasant bedroom, Jocelyn."

"Thanks."

Pearl's hand touched her shoulder. "Jocelyn, I want you to know something," she said in a voice above a whisper.

Jocelyn's sleepy eyes peered at Pearl, sneaking a peek at her lips once more before looking into her eyes. "Yes?"

"I haven't taken a vacation in five years," Pearl said to her, her hand rubbing Jocelyn's shoulder. "My last vacation was to Montreal when Paul and I went to visit Jeffery. I asked Crystal to inform human resources I wanted to denote the vacation time I've accumulated in the past five years to you."

Jocelyn's eyes widened. "To me?" she asked Pearl, the slumber leaving her a bit.

Pearl nodded as she pressed her lips together. "Yes," she retorted.

"Why?" Jocelyn asked, rubbing her right eye as she stifled another yawn.

"I want you to take a flight to Puerto Rico to see your family," Pearl said to her, a friendly smile forming on her face. "I know how much it means to you."

Jocelyn nodded. "You would do that for me?" she asked.

"I'd do anything for you," Pearl said, removing her hand from Jocelyn's shoulder and bringing it down to her side.

Ten heartbeats went by as the two women stared at one another. Jocelyn took a deep breath as she looked away for a moment. Her eyes soon located Pearl's face again.

"That's so generous of you," Jocelyn averred, her eyes moistening.

"Human resources should let Crystal know something in a day or two," Pearl told her. "Neither Crystal nor I expect them to say no. Whatever vacation time you're eligible for, I will confer my time to the total."

"Just a week," Jocelyn told her, the clear saline fluid vamoosing from her eyes.

Pearl's smile was like a ray of bright light when she touched Jocelyn's shoulder again. "I have five weeks' time for vacation," she said, reaching her other hand to Jocelyn's face and wiping away her tears. "So, that's six entire weeks you get to stay in Puerto Rico with your family."

"With pay," Jocelyn said to Pearl.

"Yes."

Jocelyn kissed Pearl's tempting top lip and squeezed the older woman tightly in her arms. "Thank you," she said, feeling Pearl hug her closely as well.

"You're welcome, Jocelyn," Pearl said to her.

"Thank you again," Jocelyn said as they both broke from their warm embrace.

"I should go outside and bring your kids in now," Pearl suggested.

Thinking of the time when she had slept in Pearl's bed, Jocelyn crawled in her comfortable futon and her head quickly hit the pillow. She felt a tender kiss on the cheek from her friend kneeling down above her. Smiling, Jocelyn reached for the lamp on the left of her and turned it off. There in the darkness, Jocelyn closed her eyes. Before Jocelyn knew it, she had fallen asleep.

Seventeen

Chapter 17

"By the power invested in me, I pronounce you husband and wife," the dark-robed lady pastor said to Lorenzo and Eboni. "Lorenzo, you may kiss your bride."

Lorenzo gazed at Eboni and took in the prestigious sight of her. Eboni's hair was down past her shoulders. She wore a white sleeveless wedding dress along with a gorgeous sparkling pearl necklace. Her make-up was splendid- a touch of eyeliner with blue eyeshadow. Her cheeks had just a touch of pink blush and her lips were a marvelous decorated red.

Lorenzo kissed his bride. He kissed her more passionately than he ever had before in the time they had known one another. This would be the only first time he would ever get to kiss his bride. As he kissed her, Eboni hugged him tightly. Lorenzo made sure he hugged her as well. Their lips for a moment were like four very close friends who loved one another. They were like four very close friends who had been sweethearts for years.

Their souls were aflame as they kissed. It was a powerful expression of their love. When the kiss was over people in the audience inside The Manhattan Ballroom at The Ritz-Carlton Hotel applauded them. Eboni kissed Lorenzo's lips one more time before they turned towards the crowd of spectators.

Lorenzo could see Battery Park through a window near the entrance besides Ellis Island and The Statue of Liberty in the distance.

Eboni had invited nearly over two hundred people she knew. Her good friend Rahima Zubair was sitting in the second row with her husband. A group of women who Eboni had known for years sat in the same row with them.

Joy and Lori had been sitting in the front row with Jocelyn, and a woman named Pearl. Although Lorenzo was oblivious to it, he knew his ex-wife was in some kind of intimate relationship with the older woman. Was his ex-wife now a lesbian? He really wasn't sure. He would have to ask her about it when he had the chance.

If Daddy Vincent were still alive Lorenzo knew he would have traveled to New York City just to be here. As Lorenzo gazed towards the horde, there stood a man with a clean-shaven face and graying hair clad in a three-piece black pinstripe suit with a matching bowtie approaching him and his bride.

"You have a little of my lipstick on your lips," Eboni said to Lorenzo as she wiped some of it off with her thumb.

As the man got nearer to them, he saw it was Xavier. Lorenzo remained calm as he put his arm around Eboni's shoulders. Xavier stared at them, smiled, and approached Eboni and Lorenzo as their eyes fixed on him.

"Congratulations to you, Lorenzo," Xavier said as he smiled. "And you too Mrs. Royal. I am happy for both of you."

"We thank you," Eboni said to Xavier as she smiled back at him. "Thank you kindly."

Xavier's smile shone as he saluted them. He turned and walked away. Lorenzo watched Xavier until his focus shifted to his daughters smiling and waving to him.

Lorenzo and Eboni both held hands and together they walked out of the ballroom as everyone continued to applaud.

****

Lorenzo stuffed Eboni's mouth with a giant piece of wedding cake as the waters of the Hudson River crawled past. Eboni greedily devoured the cake as she giggled, seeing her husband's eyes squinting towards the bright sun in the cloudy blue sky. She saw him displaying a warm grin on his handsome face as he turned to view her.

While they stood on the edge of the deck in front of a table with plenty of cake and tequila inside a gigantic punchbowl, an older couple approached them from the other side of *The New Amsterdam Cruiser.* Lorenzo saw his father walking arm in arm with a woman he had not seen in years. Despite her wearing eyeglasses and sporting an aqua dress with a big handbag draped across her small shoulders, she hadn't aged a day. Her short, thick wavy hair and adolescent face made her appear just as young as Lorenzo was. He cracked a smile as his parents approached him and his wife.

"Simone!" Lorenzo said the woman's name as a number by Usher played from the other side of the ship.

"Lorenzo, my boy," the woman said to him as she reached for him.

Lorenzo hugged Simone and regarded his bride. "Mother, this is Eboni," he said to her.

As his parents admired the striking woman clad in the white wedding dress, Eboni reached for Simone's hand.

"It's very nice to meet you, Eboni," Simone said to Eboni. "I've heard a lot about you."

"From who?" Lorenzo asked.

"From your father."

"My father talks about my wife to you?" Lorenzo questioned. "Anything he says about her better be positive."

"I told your mother about how your wife is a restaurant owner and a college graduate," Xavier explained.

"You're exquisite, Eboni," Simone said, lines appearing in her forehead. "I'm sure you've been told that a million times."

Lorenzo watched as his wife showed his mother a humble smile.

He turned and saw Jocelyn with her arm around Lori and Joy as they approached him. The woman he had seen Jocelyn with at his wedding ceremony brought up the rear.

"I'm back for good, Lorenzo," Simone said, removing her eyeglasses, and eyeballing him and his lovely bride. "We have a lot of catching up to do."

"Indeed, mother," Lorenzo said with a nod. "You're going to have to tell me all about what's been going on with the family in North Carolina."

Lorenzo waved to his parents as they walked off, disappearing into a crowd of people standing around talking and drinking glasses of champagne. Before he and his wife could turn and walk away, he saw Jocelyn, and this woman named Pearl that Joy and Lori had told him so much about getting closer to him. As both of his girls ran up to him, Lorenzo noticed their matching perms.

Lorenzo stooped down and gave his daughters both a hug and a kiss. He gazed up at Jocelyn, and the older woman with her.

"Congratulations, Lorenzo," Jocelyn said to him, holding two glasses of champagne. "I'm thrilled for you."

"Thank you," Lorenzo said to her, studying his ex-wife's open-mouthed smile before eyeing the direction of the senior woman. "Who's your friend?"

Jocelyn turned, looked at the woman behind her, and turned her gaze on Lorenzo. "This is Pearl," she told Lorenzo. "Pearl and I are together."

"You mean the two of you are a couple?" Eboni asked Jocelyn.

"Yes, we are," Pearl answered, stepping in.

"Congratulations to you as well, Jocelyn," Lorenzo said to her.

"Are you enjoying yourselves?" Eboni asked.

"This is a wonderful reception!" Pearl said with excitement. "The food is delicious and everyone is so friendly. Lorenzo, tell your brother Silas to stop trying to kiss me."

Silas appeared almost from out of nowhere, smiling and staring down at Pearl and Jocelyn. His bald head glistened from the sunlight. He was dressed in a sharp three-piece navy-blue suit, black shirt, and a white necktie. He had Pearl's lipstick smeared on one side of his mouth as if he tried to steal a kiss from her. Lorenzo glimpsed at the bottle of Johnnie Walker Silas held with both hands. Silas blew kisses at Pearl and leaped into the air. With a twinkle in his eyes, Silas scratched his hairy eyebrows, appearing not much different from Xavier.

"Lorenzo, congratulations to you and Ebenezer!" Silas slurred to him, his face happy and his deep dark eyes unfocused.

"It's Eboni," Eboni corrected him.

Silas saluted them, put the half-empty bottle of scotch to his head, and stumbled away smiling. Lorenzo watched as Silas walked hastily towards the direction of Simone and Xavier.

Jocelyn and Pearl smiled at Eboni and Lorenzo. Pearl placed her arm around Jocelyn, and the two ladies walked towards the front of the ship. As Lorenzo watched Joy and Lori follow them, a thought entered his mind. He extended his hand to his wife. Eboni held his hand in hers. Lorenzo climbed up the side of the ship and gazed out at the river. He turned and peered down at Eboni. He rubbed her knuckles, kissed the back of her hand, and pulled her up with him.

"Lorenzo, what are you doing?" she inquired with a joyous smile.

"Matrimony is a leap of faith," Lorenzo said to her as he regarded her seriously.

Lorenzo now stood on the railing. Eboni stood next to him. He saw her smiling down at the waters of the Hudson. She stooped down slightly, removed both of her white high heel shoes, and tossed them on the deck behind her. Eboni smiled broadly as she closed her eyes. When she opened them again, she eyed him.

"Faith, confidence, love, and commitment," Eboni said to him. "I'm ready. What about your family? They'll wonder about us."

"Eboni, let them wonder."

Eboni laughed as she looked at him. "Let's do it," she insisted.

They jumped off the railing and dipped fifteen feet below into the water. As they fluttered their legs and sculled their arms to stay afloat, Eboni pulled Lorenzo to her. As *the New Amsterdam Cruiser* headed into the direction of the George Washington Bridge, the newlyweds watched it go, sharing a gleeful laugh.

Eboni kissed Lorenzo's lips as she held his face in her hands.

Eighteen

Chapter 18

Eboni gazed out of a window watching a clan of bobwhites soar through the sky. Her arms folded, and she felt more like herself but she bit her lip and grimaced in order to deal with the unbearable stimulus of agony. The anesthesia had completely worn off. Lorenzo had taken Lori and Joy back to New York so their mother would have them on the weekend. But Lorenzo would come back for Eboni to take her back to her home by sunset.

"Hi, Eboni," a familiar voice said from behind her.

Eboni turned around and saw Dr. Schneider smiling at her. Eboni returned the smile and put her back to the window. Dr. Schneider was dressed conservatively in a pantsuit. Something about her seemed different from how she had been before in the many times Eboni had visited her.

"Hello, Dr. Schneider," Eboni spoke. "What brings you all the way to Trenton, New Jersey?"

"I'm just following up," Dr. Schneider said, showing an exceptional smile. "Have you had the surgery?"

But Eboni knew fully well Dr. Schneider was her psychiatrist. She had no link to the doctors here. Why was she following up? What was she doing here? Eboni knew she must be dreaming.

"I did," Eboni told her. "I had it yesterday."

"How do you feel?"

"Happy and proud," Eboni said to her, her face radiant and happy. "I'm in so much pain though."

"Wonderful," Dr. Schneider said. "How long until you're discharged from the hospital?"

"A few hours," Eboni said. "I'm waiting for my husband to come back and get me."

Dr. Schneider's eyes widened. "You got married already?" she asked.

"I got married in lower Manhattan just a few weeks ago," Eboni told her.

"His name is Lorenzo, right?"

"Yes," Eboni answered.

"The last time you were at my office during our last session, you told me you had a feeling he would propose marriage to you."

"It was sooner than I thought it would be. Lorenzo proposed to me when I got home that day."

"I'm so happy for you, Eboni," Dr. Schneider said to Eboni, her smile friendly. "Congratulations."

"Thank you, Dr. Schneider. "We're going to Japan for our honeymoon. I can hardly wait to go."

"Japan?" Dr. Schneider asked.

"Yes," Eboni said.

"Should be nice."

"I'm sure it will be."

"I've been to Tokyo one time many years ago," Dr. Schneider said, placing her hands inside her pockets and peering up to the ceiling as if remembering. "I went on an educational trip there with my class when I was a young student attending Brigham Young University. We visited Osaka as well."

"Yes," Eboni said. "Lorenzo and I will go visit a few friends of his *that are noblemen. He wants me to fine-tune my sword fighting. My husband is very ambitious."*

"Tell me a little about him."

Eboni smiled and thought fondly of her husband. "Lorenzo is a martial arts instructor with seven black belts," she told Dr. Schneider. "He's divorced. He's a father. He teaches all forms of martial arts. He fights for those who can't fight for themselves."

"He sounds rather adventurous," Dr. Schneider said.

"Life with him has been an adventure," Eboni said.

Dr. Schneider smiled. "Has he taught you any?" she asked Eboni.

"I'm in pursuit of my black belts in Jiujitsu, Judo, and Taekwondo," Eboni said to Dr. Schneider. "Lorenzo has taught me so much. I'm scratching the surface in Kyokushin, Wing Chun, and Shaolin Kung Fu."

For a moment there was silence. Eboni turned back around and saw the bobwhites still flying through the sky. Or maybe those were a different type of bird than before. She walked closer to the window and placed her hand on the glass. With her left pinky finger, she wrote Lorenzo's name in cursive letters. She felt a gentle hand on her shoulder. Eboni turned to see Dr. Schneider gazing at her.

"Are you hungry?" Dr. Schneider asked.

"Are you?" Eboni asked. "We can go to the cafeteria and get something to eat."

Smiling, Eboni walked slowly to the elevator on the other side of the lobby. Dr. Schneider followed her. When it came, both of them got on it. As the elevator descended, Eboni eyed Dr. Schneider.

"I'm very thrilled for you, Eboni," Dr. Schneider professed.

Eboni smiled again. "Thank you, Dr. Schneider," she said, placing her hands into the pockets of her bathrobe....

"Wake up, Eboni!" a little girl's voice was saying. "You're talking in your sleep!"

Eboni felt herself rocking from side to side. When she opened her eyes, she saw Joy and Lori shaking her. Her heart raced as she gazed across the room to a bunch of scattered newspapers spread out all over her leather sectional. She quickly smiled as she stood to her feet. She glanced over to the calendar posted on the wall next to the kitchen entryway.

Lori and Joy each grabbed her hand. Eboni smiled and walked towards the window behind the sofa. They all peered down at the traffic jam on the corner of 88th and West End Avenue. Eboni knelt down and gave both of the girls a hug. She kissed them both at the same time the door to the apartment opened.

"Hey!" Lorenzo said, wearing a red karate gi and black belt with a matching red headband as he walked in.

"Lorenzo!" Eboni said, smiling at the sight of his abrupt presence, seeing a small manila envelope in his hand.

Lorenzo closed the door behind him and scooped his daughters up in his arms when they ran up to him. "Eboni," he said. "You have a worrisome look on your face."

"Lorenzo, I just had the most peculiar dream!" she exclaimed.

"About what?"

"About having butt injections," she told him and laughed. "It was so surreal."

"Eboni, does this mean you still want the surgery?" he asked as Joy grabbed onto his leg.

"I doubt it."

"You're not having second thoughts?"

Eboni smiled as she shook her head. "That ship has sailed, my love," she said to him. "But in my dream, I alluded to our honeymoon."

"You did?" he asked, handing her the manila envelope.

Eboni nodded. "Yes, I did," she said to him, opening up the envelope and pulling out a piece of paper. It was a receipt from the property manager for payment of rent for *The Camelot*. Her husband not only helped her pay the rent in order to keep her business afloat, but he had also gone to the property manager personally to pay them. She couldn't love him any more than she did right now. "We talked about where we would travel to and you know what I said?"

Lorenzo folded his arms before his eyebrows rose. His head nodded at her while his hands spread out.

Eboni smiled at him and walked over to the sectional. She took a seat on the dispersed newspapers and crossed her legs. "Japan," she answered, smiling as she studied him.

"Japan?" he asked with a chuckle.

"Yes," Eboni answered him.

Lorenzo put his hands in his pockets. "In this dream of yours?" he asked her.

"Yes," Eboni Law-Royal said jovially. " But truthfully, I want us to go to Egypt."

Lorenzo picked Joy up. He walked over to the sofa and Eboni heard the crinkle of the newspaper as he sat down next to her. His girls both climbed into his lap. "Egypt sounds really nice," he told her. "I'll call my travel agent first thing in the morning."

"Perfect!" Eboni said and kissed his cheek.

Nineteen

Chapter 19

"Boom," Eboni said into the March cool as she showed Stuart her wedding ring, holding a leash attached to Raleigh's collar as her puppy sat between her boots.

Stuart's eyebrows arose. "Is that what I think it is?" he asked her, stroking Tabatha's hairy head as he smiled.

"It is," Eboni said to him, her eyes staring right at him.

"Bruce Lee married you?" he asked her.

"We got married just months ago," Eboni told him.

"Eboni, I'm so happy for you. Congratulations!"

The two friends placed their arms around one another's shoulders and pulled each other close.

"Thank you," Eboni said, seeing him grinning as her eyes sparkled. "Guess what else?"

Stuart glanced at her and shrugged. "What?" he inquired.

"I decided *not* to get the operation," Eboni said with a smile as her eyes circled the greenery of Central Park. "I struggled with the decision. If you recall, I had already told you I would not do it. I changed my mind. But I came back to my original decision."

"No?" he asked as he stood up from the bench as a group of teenagers walked by them.

Eboni nodded. "No," she told him. "I love myself just the way I am."

"And you should! Girl, you don't need a big phony ass to be happy."

"I'll be heading to Egypt for my honeymoon next month," she told him and let out a delayed chuckle.

Stuart embraced her. "I'm so happy for you, old friend," he said to her.

"I sent you an invitation for my wedding, Stuart. Lorenzo and I didn't see you there."

Stuart's hand touched his face. "Eboni, I had to stay home and take care of my boyfriend all that weekend because he had the flu," he said sorrowfully. "I couldn't come to your wedding. But you know under normal circumstances I would've been there."

"I know you would have," Eboni told him, putting her hood to her black coat over her head as the brisk wind blew towards them.

"I'm sorry I left New York without letting you know," he said sorrowfully. "My dad needed me in Louisville. I stayed there longer than I thought I would have. I just got back here two days ago."

"My sister-in-law Olivia had the wedding recorded," Eboni said into the brisk air. "I'll make a copy and give it to you so you can watch it."

"I would love to," Stuart said, removing his arm from around her as he cocked an eyebrow. He looked down at Tabatha clawing at his pants leg as she purred. "Eboni, I'm thrilled for you and your new life. May God bless you always."

Stuart removed a blue leather glove he was wearing and placed it into the pocket of his brown leather jacket. Eboni felt his hand on hers. Their eyes stared towards the grass area at a group of teenagers playing kickball.

"Thank you, Stuart," Eboni said as she thought of her husband. "Thank you very much. Lorenzo and I appreciate it."

****

"Jocelyn, there you are!" Crystal said when she walked inside room 406.

Jocelyn looked over her shoulder, seeing her exotic boss step towards her with a pleasant smile on her face. She saw the Emo-styled hair Crystal had been sporting lately had been cut down to a light brown Mohawk with intriguing tiger-striped markings. Through Crystal's frown, she displayed a heartwarming smile.

"Hi, Crystal," Jocelyn said, placing a pillow down at the head of the bed.

"I'm just coming from HR," Crystal said, her face happy. "They've officially granted you to have Pearl's five weeks' vacation time. Pearl already spoke to them on your behalf. Human Resources stated you've already put in for a week, so this extra five weeks will be in addition. Your vacation starts the first business day of next week."

Jocelyn's smile lit up the room. "I appreciate you coming to me and telling me, Crystal," she said, taking a seat on the bed.

Crystal placed a hand on her hip and walked towards her. "I've known Pearl for over ten years," she said, gazing at Jocelyn. "I've never known her to be the generous type. She has to like you to do something this open-handed."

Jocelyn nodded. "We're friends," she said to her.

"Will it develop into something more?" Crystal asked curiously.

"It seems like it's going in that direction," Jocelyn answered joyfully. "But we're still learning about each other. Pearl is very nice to my kids. We only kiss about once or twice a week now. Pearl and I are taking this very slow."

Crystal smiled as she placed her other hand on her hip. "You should," she vocalized, as she backed away towards the door. "Her age doesn't bother you?"

Jocelyn shook her head. "Ms. Bianchi is like an older friend," she said to Crystal. "She's a year older than my mother, but I don't see her as a parent. I see her as sophisticated, sultry, and beautiful. She's never treated me like a child. She's charming, friendly, and odd. I like her. Pearl is one of as kind."

Crystal turned and headed towards the door. "If I don't see you again before you take your vacation, have a relaxing time. Enjoy your vacation and I'll see you when you report back."

"Thank you," Jocelyn said with a bright smile and watched Crystal place her hands into the pockets of her long skirt as she walked out of the room.

****

"It's so nice to be in New York City again," Coco said, giggling and sliding her fingers through her dyed green hair as she looked over at Eboni.

Eboni folded her arms and eyed across the table at her younger sister. Coco still had that exuberant presence. She was always smiling, always feeling happy. She never got down, never allowed the negative to downcast her spirits. Perhaps Coco had inherited this from their mother Lucinda.

Eboni before today hadn't seen Coco in over fifteen years. "I'm so glad you're here," she said, peering over Coco's shoulder, seeing the sea of humanity walking down both sides of 42nd Street through the window by the entrance.

"So, you're married now?" Coco asked Eboni, her eyes wide as she displayed a happy face.

Eboni nodded, glancing at the open buttoned shirt Coco wore with a black t-shirt underneath. When Eboni had greeted her at Penn Station earlier, she was surprised to see her younger sister wearing a black short leather skirt and high heel shoes. She looked far too appealing. Coco never thought of herself as beautiful or even pretty. But to Eboni she was. Coco once thought she wanted breast augmentation, but settled on remaining flat-chested. She had always been meticulous with the ladies she let in her life. Coco had once dated a girl for five years before getting serious with her.

Eboni wore faded light blue tight jeans, a pair of black Reebok sneakers, and a grey Russell Athletic sweatshirt. Her beautiful fingernails were polished a splendid purple, and she wore very little make-up. She wore her hair shoulder length.

"Yes," Eboni said, lifting her glass of Private Stock. "I'm happily married now."

"Mom and Dad talk about you sometimes," Coco said, sliding fingers through her hair again. "They miss you."

Eboni's bottom lip twisted. "Do they?" she asked, bringing her hands down onto the table.

She peeked at all the people inside the BBQs restaurant, hearing countless conversations as she awaited Coco's reply.

"They do," Coco told her.

"I wonder about mom and daddy sometimes," Eboni said, a pleased smile appearing on her face. "I wonder how many times they've thought about me since my falling out with them."

"Eboni, reach out to them," Coco said, dropping her fork into her bowl of chicken salad.

"I might in time," Eboni smiled uncomfortably.

"I'm seeing someone new," Coco said, changing the subject.

Coco's fatuous smile made Eboni grin. Her sister fanned her face with her hand, and her merry visage even glowed.

"Is she a femme or a butch this time?" Eboni asked, eyeing past Coco's shoulder again to 42nd Street.

"She's a femme," Coco answered. "Our modeling agency in Toronto discovered her. She admitted to once being into drugs and porn, but she's changed and started going to school. She says she never finished up her senior year at LSU when she lived in Baton Rouge. She's a model and an accountant."

Eboni chewed inside her cheek. "Does this young lady have a name?" she asked, folding her arms again.

"Valerie Wright," Coco said, smiling.

"I'd like to meet her someday," Eboni said.

"You will," said Coco.

Eboni watched Coco for a pair of heartbeats and stood up from the table. "I'll be back," she said.

Eboni turned from her sister and walked towards the women's restroom. She turned back to the front of the restaurant to Coco grinning as she sipped her cola through a straw. Smiling, Eboni pushed open the lady's restroom door and saw three women yelling at a young girl.

"I want my money, you little thieving bitch!" one woman was saying when Eboni stepped inside the restroom.

The girl turned in Eboni's direction. Eboni noticed a fresh scar above the girl's eye, a dark bruise above her left cheekbone, and tears in her eyes. Eboni didn't know what the girl was mixed up in, but it couldn't be good.

"Time to pay up," a second woman included, holding a Karambit knife, which was one of the deadliest blades in the world. "Did you think you would get away with this? Time to pay the piper!"

"We want our money back or the K-2 and cocaine you stole," the third woman said.

Eboni's eyes shifted to the girl standing by the bathroom sink shivering as she cried. The girl couldn't have been over 14 years old. She was black, wearing a long brown weave, pink lipstick, and a jean jacket with matching pants. The young girl nodded in defeat and pulled a plastic bag containing what appeared to be marijuana or K-2 from her pants pocket and placed it on the floor.

"The other bag!" the first woman shouted.

The girl wiped her tears, reached into a jacket pocket, and pulled a bag of what appeared to be heroin or cocaine. She knelt down and placed it on the floor next to the other bag.

Eboni took her eyes from off of the scene and walked towards a nearby bathroom stall. But just before she could open the revolving barrier leading to the toilet, she heard a most frightening scream.

"Ayhghhahhh!" the young girl hollered.

Eboni eyed over her shoulder, seeing the second woman place her hands around the girl's throat as the woman with the knife placed the tip of its blade to the girl's face.

Eboni's voice lifted, cocking an eyebrow. "Stop!" she said, turning around and facing the four individuals. "She gave you what you wanted! There's no need to hurt her!"

"The hell if it ain't," the first woman said with a burning fire in her eyes.

Eboni became enlightened as she had recollections of the dream, she'd had the night before Lorenzo's and his ex-wife's court date. "Stop this!" she shouted to the women.

Eboni stepped slowly into their path, seeing all three women eyeing her menacingly. The girl slithered out from under their grasp and ran behind Eboni. A smile played around Eboni's lips as thoughts drifted back to Lorenzo liberating her from being robbed the night they met. Now this child needed her help just as much as she had needed Lorenzo's then.

"Reach down, pick up your drugs, and leave this girl alone," Eboni challenged them with a mischievous, yet confident smile.

One woman laughed as another smiled. The woman armed with the knife frowned. Eboni watched them carefully as she remained calm.

"You must want to die in her place," the woman with the knife threatened.

Eboni smiled and motioned the women towards her. "Foolish words from a fool," she dared them.

One woman charged Eboni. Eboni stood calmly, leaped up, and extended a nasty foot perfectly to the woman's chin. As the woman stumbled back, the other two came to her aid. But with a kick to a thigh and a spinning heel kick to the face, one woman was instantly knocked out cold while the other one was barely standing, hopping on one leg. The woman who first charged Eboni got up and charged at Eboni again.

The woman's sternum ran right into Eboni's lifted knee and she crumpled over her, the wheezing air leaving the woman's lungs. Eboni grabbed her by the shoulder, folded the troublemaker's arm behind her back, and flipped her towards the wall on the other side of the restroom. The woman's face collided with the wall before she fell to the floor.

The woman hopping on one leg glanced into Eboni's direction, wincing in pain, seeing Eboni watching her smiling with her right fist turned upright resting by her hip and her left forearm extended above her head with her left fist closed. The woman quickly looked towards the door and limped as she hurried from out of the restroom.

Seeing both of the remaining troublemakers down on the floor defeated, Eboni walked inside a nearby restroom stall. As she stood near the toilet, she heard the squeaking stall door open behind her. Eboni turned over her shoulder at the girl watching her. A sort of thankful smile came to the girl's lips as she gazed at Eboni.

"How did you learn to fight like that?" the young female asked.

After using the toilet Eboni made her way to the sink. She cleaned her hands and turned in the direction of the girl.

"A very special man taught me how to fight," Eboni answered minutes later with a prideful smile.

"Thank you so much," the callow girl expressed with a smile, her eyes on the two women lying on the bathroom floor now struggling to pick themselves up.

Eboni nodded and placed a firm hand on the girl's shoulder. "Stay out of trouble, honey," she noted in a friendly tone. "It was an honor to come to your defense. Go in peace and have a nice day."

Eboni regarded the girl with a bow and left from out of the restroom. As she stepped towards the table, Eboni saw Coco's plate was now empty and her kid sister was finishing up her cola. Eboni sat down and grabbed her glass of Private Stock as her eyes found Coco's delightful and amused facial expression beaming at her.

"So, when am I going to meet this Lorenzo and visit your restaurant you always talk about?" Coco asked Eboni.

"Probably as soon as today," Eboni retorted, lifting her glass.

****

Pearl waited inside LaGuardia Airport, holding Joy's and Lori's hands as Jocelyn walked away from a nearby newsstand with three newspapers. She held a cup of decaffeinated coffee in her other hand. Her plane would start boarding its passengers in less than two minutes. Smiling to herself,

Jocelyn thought of Lorenzo. She'd called him yesterday to tell him she was flying to Puerto Rico with the girls and had left a message for him to call her. He still hadn't called her back. She thought it fortuitous that after they divorced, the two of them had found older people to continue their lives with. Wherever he was, she hoped he and Eboni were okay.

"I want to thank you again," Jocelyn said to Pearl when she walked upon her and the girls.

Pearl eyed Jocelyn with a straight face "There's no need to thank me, darling," the older woman said, letting go of the twins' hands and putting her hands into the pockets of her purple sweater. "Your happiness gives me happiness."

"Continental Airlines Flight 49 from New York City to Fajardo, Puerto Rico will board in less than two minutes," the announcement came over the airport's interior intercom.

Pearl's hand reached for Jocelyn's. Jocelyn felt the older woman rub her knuckles as they stared deeply into each other's eyes. Jocelyn came closer to Pearl, kissed her fondly on her soft cheek, and took Lori and Joy each by the hand.

"I have to get going," Jocelyn said to Pearl. "We'll see you when we get back."

"Have a pleasant trip," Pearl said to her with a lovely smile. "And tell Mr. and Mrs. Cortez that I said hi."

Lori looked back and waved to Pearl as the three of them walked away. Jocelyn walked into a narrow corridor. It led to an entrance behind a curtain. She showed her ticket to the flight stewardess before going through a large entrance. She immediately saw an aisle and rows of four seats from the front to the rear.

"We're on the airplane now," Jocelyn told her children.

Jocelyn selected a seat near the window on the right side. Since her kids were both toddlers, they shared a seat. Jocelyn strapped her daughters into their seatbelt. Her head turned, seeing the night sky through the window and five airplanes close by. When she turned back around to look at her girls, she saw Joy was sitting back comfortably with her eyes closed while Lori eyed straight ahead towards people boarding the airplane.

Fifteen minutes passed. Jocelyn saw only sixteen other people were catching the nightly flight onboard with her and her daughters. The airplane began to roll forward. As it began to head towards the runway and accumulate speed, a declaration came from the cockpit.

"Good evening, passengers," a woman's gruff, breathy voice said over the loudspeaker. "I'm Captain Marisol Benitez. You are aboard Continental Airlines Flight 49 from New York, New York to Fajardo, Puerto Rico. The estimated distance is 1,624 miles. The estimated time for travel is three hours. Enjoy your flight."

Jocelyn smiled as the airplane took off from the runway. As the airplane ascended into the dark sky, her eyes caught the wondrous sight of the moon and stars high in the distance. Her hand reached over a sleeping Joy and touched Lori's.

"Mami, papi, here I come!" Jocelyn said enthusiastically.

Twenty

Chapter 20

Eboni chased Lorenzo through the forest, half dry leaves from withered branches descending on them freely. He tripped over his own two feet and fell sideways onto the dirty earth. Lorenzo scrambled to his feet and attempted to run on, but Eboni tackled him from behind, causing both of them to collapse to the ground.

Lorenzo gazed down at her with a smile. "I didn't know you could run that fast," he said, peering into her eyes shown through the beige veil she wore.

Her smile was invisible to him, but he knew it was there. He could tell by the beaming twinkle in her eyes Eboni was smiling.

"Neither could I!" Eboni exclaimed as she gazed up at him, catching her breath. "Being on the verge of fifty-two years old, I didn't know I could still run that fast either!"

Eboni got to a knee and stood up. She peeked down at him and extended her right hand. He reached out his own hand, and they both smiled as she pulled him to his feet. He gazed at the tall trees surrounding them and closed his eyes. Eboni stepped to him and plucked two leaves from off the top of his head.

Lorenzo walked over to the nearest tree and leaned with his back to it. Eboni walked up to Lorenzo and laced her fingers around his shoulders. This time a leaf fell on her, and Lorenzo swiped it off of her. They gazed into each other's eyes. It seemed time never moved whenever Lorenzo observed her.

"You do know I love you, don't you?" Eboni asked him and removed her veil and matching headdress which had been hiding her beauty from him all day.

Lorenzo blew kisses at her, admiring the shorter hairstyle she now wore. Her hair had been dyed auburn with red streaks just days ago and cut to the neck just before they had left the United States and landed on Ghana soil before heading to the Arab Republic.

His eyes found her. A smile turned into a full, grinning giggle. "I love you more," he said to Eboni.

"Do you know why I love you?"

"Why do you love me?" Lorenzo asked her.

"I love your ability to fight, your tender and courageous heart, your strong convictions, your wholehearted support, and not to mention that beautiful body of yours," Eboni relinquished, a lighthearted smile on her face. "I love you deeply because you've made me strong, far stronger than I had been before. It takes someone strong to make someone strong."

Lorenzo placed his hands behind his back as Eboni rubbed the side of his face with her thumb. "That means the world to me and more," he told her.

"And, I love you just because," Eboni said in addition.

"I love you because you exemplify what a woman is," Lorenzo said, and smacked Eboni on her ass and ran.

"Hey!" Eboni shouted and ran after him.

They had only been in Egypt for two days so far, and they didn't know when they would head back to America. Neither one of them thought about going back. They were going to enjoy themselves as much as possible while they were here. Lorenzo had recalled when he took Jocelyn on their honeymoon. They had gone to Polynesia and stayed at a beautiful resort.

As Eboni would have it, they would end up going to someplace farther. They stayed at the luxurious Four Seasons Hotel Cairo Nile Plaza, where there was a lovely view of the Nile River atop their hotel room from its balcony. Just after their plane had landed in the ancient city of Akhenaton, Eboni and Lorenzo rode inside a jeep 370 miles to Cairo.

Lorenzo eyed behind him, seeing Eboni was in pursuit of him again. He ran to the edge of the forest and stared down a steep, grassy hill. He turned his head, only to see Eboni charging at him. She collided roughly into him, and as they held onto one another, Lorenzo and Eboni fell and tumbled down the hill. Eboni screamed as if she were on a rollercoaster. When it was all over, they both shared an endless laugh.

Lorenzo peered up past her shoulder to the top of the mountainous hill as she lay on top of him. Abruptly, his face was in front of hers. Smiling, Lorenzo blew her kisses as the tip of his finger ran across her lips.

"Why do you like doing that?" Eboni asked him.

"Doing what?" Lorenzo asked his wife.

"Flirting with me," she answered him as he secured an arm around her.

"I can't help it," Lorenzo said to her. "Maybe it's because you're so ravishing."

Eboni rested her head on his chest. "I am?" she asked him.

Lorenzo kissed her forehead. "Indeed, you are," he answered her.

Lorenzo took in the sight of her. Everything about her was beautiful. Her gorgeous face, lovely hair, enchanting lips, and alluring eyes made his heart melt in his chest every time he gazed at her. Her style and grace are what he always loved about Eboni the most.

"I'm in the mood for a demonstration," Eboni happily said to him as she smiled back.

Lorenzo's eyebrows arose. "Demonstration?" he asked as his smile disappeared.

Eboni got up and helped Lorenzo to his feet again. She stood right in front of him and squatted low to the ground with one leg bent and her foot planted, both of her fists down by her hips. Lorenzo nodded and stood with one of his legs in front of the other, with his left forearm crossed in front of his eyes and right fist pinned firmly to his ribcage.

Eboni leaped up and threw a flying fist towards Lorenzo's left shoulder. But he instinctively turned sideways to avoid the blow. She attempted four rapid kicks to Lorenzo's right hip, but his reflexes were too sharp for her onslaught.

Lorenzo quickly swung a blow to the side of her head, but Eboni blocked it intuitively with her forearm and threw a crisp punch to Lorenzo's chest that was intercepted. She attempted a sidekick to Lorenzo's abdomen, but he blocked it effortlessly. Lorenzo smiled, seeing his wife stand on one leg while lifting the knee of her other leg up to her chin as she raised both of her hands above her head and made them into claws.

"Tiger Crane," Lorenzo said, with a straight face, nodding his head. "I see you've learned your basic self-defense rather fast. You can rival some MMA fighters I've trained."

"I credit you with teaching me so well," Eboni said as she still held her knee to her chin until she placed her foot firmly on the ground and put her hands on her hips.

It was just one more thing to love about Eboni. Unlike Jocelyn, she wanted to be a part of something he loved doing.

But as he stared at her, he smiled. He put his arm around her and together they climbed the hill and walked through the forest the way they came. Before long, they paid for a carriage to take them to the marketplace so they could shop on Cairo's streets. They found merchants, young and old, male and female, selling jewelry, fruit, vegetables, and clothing such as scarves, and even expensive leopard skin.

As the couple held hands, they walked by several mosques and Islamic schools in the area. Many people watched them strangely. As Lorenzo noticed several women and men regarding them, he noticed they couldn't keep their eyes off of them. When he saw his wife had examined the people watching, she eyed Lorenzo.

"Why are they looking at us?" Eboni asked Lorenzo.

"In the Arab world, they don't express affection openly the way we do," Lorenzo conveyed sharply. "Let them look."

Once they made it back to the hotel and took a shower, they headed back out. Lorenzo dressed conservatively in a DNKY buttoned shirt opened at the collar and a pair of black slacks, while Eboni wore a grey blouse and a long black skirt. She had also put on her favorite pair of high heel shoes.

They rode a camel to the shore of the Nile River and tied it to a pole. Once there, they saw countless people getting on small boats. Eboni glanced towards the vessels for a minute and peeked at Lorenzo. Lorenzo stepped to the left and went towards a yacht docked at the shore.

The sight of the vessel was grand and sleek with a bit of finesse and flash styled in chrome on its exterior. Eboni followed him up a wooden ramp and boarded the elegant craft. They made it to the front of the yacht and saw a rather skinny old man standing at the wheel wearing a shirt and tie with a black turban on his head. He also had insignia over the shoulders of his shirt. Eboni walked ahead of him and tapped the man on the shoulder. When the man turned around and saw them, he displayed a friendly smile.

"Bonjour!" Eboni said to him as she grinned back at the man.

But the man said something back to her in an unfamiliar language. Eboni eyed Lorenzo, and he walked to stand beside her.

"What language is that?" Eboni asked him.

"The official language here is Arabic," Lorenzo said, returning her gaze. The man repeated something in Arabic to them. Eboni and Lorenzo remained silent as they looked at him, bewilderedly. The man smiled at them for a moment and started speaking to them in several languages. When Lorenzo reached into his pocket and showed the man the American flag on his United States passport, the man gazed at him and smiled.

The skinny man rubbed his hands together and held a tight smile. "Why didn't just say you spoke English?" the man said to them. "Most Americans do."

"What can you tell us about this river?" Eboni asked, staring out at the Nile.

"It flows from south to north from Uganda," the man said. "It's over 4,100 miles long and is the longest river in the entire world. We'll be heading up south, maybe to Tanzania before turning around and heading back."

"How come no one is boarding your ship but us?" Eboni asked the man.

"A lot of the tourists like to get on the boats for voyage because it's a slower ride," the man answered her.

"You have a name, sir?" Lorenzo asked him.

"I am Captain Al-Nasser," the man said to them.

"It's nice to meet you, Captain," Eboni said to him.

"Likewise," Captain-Al-Nasser told Lorenzo and Eboni. "You both are newlyweds, aren't you?"

Eboni smiled as she and Lorenzo regarded each other before returning their gazes on the inquisitive captain.

"How can you tell?" Lorenzo asked.

"Yes, we are," Eboni told him.

"I can tell," he told Lorenzo and Eboni. "Congratulations on your courtship."

"Thank you," Eboni and Lorenzo responded.

Lorenzo turned around and eyed a row of double seats on both sides of the vessel. He took Eboni by the hand and led her to the front seat on the left. He sat down in it and pulled her gently onto his lap. She put her arm around him as he rested a hand on her thigh.

"We should be back tomorrow morning," Captain Al-Nasser said to them before starting the engine. "Now we head towards the edge of Eritrea. Once there, we will turn around and head back. There will be a beautiful crescent in the sky tonight marking the new month. Enjoy your ride aboard *The Silver Bullet*."

Soon the ship was moving along the waters of the river. As Lorenzo regarded the colossal ancient structures surrounding the beautiful city close by, he smiled to himself. As he did, Eboni kissed his forehead. Her nose rubbed his. Lastly, she kissed his lips. Lorenzo put his arm around Eboni and held her close to him as they journeyed the River Nile.

****

The next morning at sunrise, Eboni and Lorenzo made it back to the Arab Republic's capital city. They rode a camel to the Great Pyramid. As Lorenzo gazed up at the magnificent edifice, he smiled. It had always been a goal in life for him to climb to the highest stone of this pyramid. He didn't know whether it was illegal to do it, but there was only one way to find out. But in the 4,500 years this impressive structure had been here, he knew there had been at least one soul who climbed to the very top.

"Wait for me," Lorenzo said to Eboni as he peeked at both pyramids on each side of this one.

"Are you really going to climb all the way up this thing?" she asked him.

"That's my intention," Lorenzo responded, as he touched the nearest limestone brick.

"If you're going to climb it, I am too!" Eboni voiced eagerly.

Lorenzo smiled at her and reached for her hand as he climbed the first giant limestone block. Daddy Vincent had told Lorenzo and his siblings when they were younger stories about people trying to climb up the Egyptian pyramids and falling hundreds of feet down to their deaths. But Lorenzo would not allow stories, if they were true, to put doubt in his mind about accomplishing such a feat.

On their way up, he and his wife saw an entrance. He knew this opening probably led to the Pharaoh's burial chamber. It once buried the king, responsible for the construction of the structure, of the fourth dynastic period. They had moved his mummy to another location.

Halfway up, Lorenzo and Eboni tired. Their breathing was hard as they both bent over with their hands resting on their knees while they tried to catch their breaths. They rested for a moment and pressed forward. Thirty-six minutes later, they saw the very top of the building in sight. Smiling, Lorenzo kept climbing as Eboni clung to his arm for support. He noticed the dirt and a bit of grime on his shirt, but he brushed the crud off and continued with their journey while Eboni's outfit remained spotless.

Ten more minutes had gone by. Lorenzo smiled, as the very top of the pyramid was right before his eyes.

"I see it!" Eboni said as she perspired.

"I see it also!" Lorenzo said as he smiled.

They caught their breaths one more time and pressed onward. As soon as Eboni and Lorenzo reached the top limestone block, they spotted a hot-air balloon ascending overhead.

Lorenzo climbed atop the remaining block as he pulled his wife up with him. As soon as he got there, Eboni struggled as she made it to the very top with him. They both stood to their full heights and gazed farther down on Cairo.

"We made it!" Eboni said to him.

"Indeed, we did!" Lorenzo said happily.

"My goodness!" Eboni exclaimed, pointing a finger four hundred and eighty feet below. "Look at the beautiful city from way up here!"

The hot-air balloon floated further away as Lorenzo and Eboni laughed. He didn't know how many people beside him and his wife had accomplished this goal, but he was grateful they could do it.

She glanced at Lorenzo, seeing his head raised with his eyes set on the white clouds above. She knew although ending a promising marriage had crushed him; it overjoyed him he had her. Her husband had two wonderful daughters who were growing stronger each day, a franchise of martial arts schools, a bodyguard service, supportive parents, and he was grateful for being able to breathe God's fresh air every moment of every day. For some people that wasn't enough, but Eboni knew that was more than enough for Lorenzo. What more could a man ask for?

Eboni reflected on her courtship, her blossoming romance, and the glorious journey from the moment she met Lorenzo. She never in her wildest dreams thought her life would end up the way it did. From the moment he rescued her outside her restaurant, she not only bonded with him in the following days, but she had learned so much from him. She learned confidence, mastery of fighting, and courage. She had conquered all of her fears and overcame all of her doubts. She loved Lorenzo for his humility, his toughness, and his support. And she loved him just because. She glanced at the beautiful diamond ring on her finger and smiled.

Lorenzo and Eboni shared another blissful kiss and looked earthbound towards the marvelous city of Cairo.

The End

M.J. Grayson is the debut author of the critically acclaimed novel The Courtship Of Eboni Law. The story explores how a couple's eventual incompatibility led to a passionate love affair for one woman and placed another lady on a path to rediscover herself. M.J. Grayson is a martial artist, author, and Washington, D.C. native.